THE ART OF VIOLENCE

THE ART OF VIOLENCE

S. J. ROZAN

PEGASUS CRIME

NEW YORK LONDON

THE ART OF VIOLENCE

Pegasus Crime is an imprint of
Pegasus Books, Ltd.
148 W 37th Street, 13th Floor
New York, NY 10018

First Pegasus Books edition December 2020

Interior design by Sabrina Plomitallo-González, Pegasus Books

Library of Congress Cataloging-in-Publication Data is available.

ISBN: 978-1-64313-531-1

10 9 8 7 6 5 4 3 2 1

Printed in the United States of America
Distributed by Simon & Schuster
www.pegasusbooks.com

for
Grace Edwards and Phil Martin
two of the finest

THE ART OF VIOLENCE

Shifting colors on a monster billboard bled through the April evening mist, showed me a shadow in the alley.

My heart sped up but I didn't, just walked past, to my door. Maybe I had time to unlock the door and slip inside, but if I did that, whatever this was might happen again sometime when I wasn't ready.

I unzipped my jacket, reached inside, just a guy looking for his keys. Uneven footsteps came up the block, pseudo-soft like a stage whisper. If he went on past, that would be that. But I didn't think he would and he didn't. He stopped behind me.

I spun around, arm out, gun level. "Hold it there."

"Whoa! Whoa, man, put that down." The shadow stumbled back, reaching for the sky like a desperado in a bad western. In his right hand was a silver automatic, small but enough to do damage. "I just need to talk to you."

"Then what's the gun for?"

"To make you listen."

The words were slurred but the voice was familiar. I said, "Step into the light."

"It's Sam." The shadow lurched forward. "Sam Tabor."

And it was. Skinny and pale; jittery hands; eyes that looked everywhere but into yours. Six years since I'd seen him, and I couldn't say he'd changed.

My adrenaline blast faded. "Give me the gun."

"The . . ." He peered at the automatic as though it were news to him. "It's not mine."

"I won't hurt it."

With a shrug he gave it over. He grinned crookedly and asked, "Surprised to see me?"

"At my door with a gun, yes. In general, no. I knew you were out."

"Everybody does, huh? Everybody knows all about Sam Tabor. I need to talk to you. Let's get a drink." He ticked his head at the Budweiser sign in Shorty's window.

"I don't drink with ex-cons waving guns at me."

"Shit." He slumped against the wall, wiped a hand down his face. "I fucked this up, didn't I?"

"Depends what you were trying to accomplish."

"I need your help."

"Then yeah, you did. The gun . . . ?"

"Because you'd say no. If you knew what I wanted."

"And then you were going to shoot me?"

He shook his head, back and forth, back and forth, the exaggeration of alcohol. "I said. To make you listen. So you'd see I'm serious."

I had to concede he'd made that point. Pocketing his gun, holstering mine, I said, "No drink." I unlocked my door and held it open for him. "Coffee."

Upstairs, I pointed Sam to an armchair, boiled water, and put coffee through while he sank against the cushions. He didn't move at all, except for his hands, fingers drumming in ever-changing rhythms, and his eyes. His gaze wandered the room randomly, the way you drive when you're so lost all ways are equally likely, and equally unpromising.

I wondered how long this bender had been going on and when he'd last eaten. A few nights ago Lydia had brought over a box of Chinese almond cookies; I put them on a plate.

"You take anything in your coffee?" I asked.

"Scotch."

I gave him the cookies, and his coffee black. I took mine to the couch the same way. He held the mug in both hands and sipped slowly, resigned to this medicine he'd been taking most of his life for his chronic condition—drinking. Between sips, he said, "At least you're not telling me how good I look."

"You look like hell."

"But my public loves it! The tortured artist."

"I saw the *Art Now* cover."

"You weren't impressed? Come on, that was a Tony Oakhurst photo. You didn't think I looked like a mad genius?"

"You looked like twelve miles of bad road. But better than you do now."

He nodded earnestly, got into the rhythm of it, shook his head to stop himself. "You see? You see? That's why I'm here. You never lied to me. And you're not afraid of me."

"Why would I be? Now that I have your gun in my pocket."

"Not the gun, I don't mean the gun. It's not even loaded. Because of how I am. But you always treated me like a regular person. I liked it when you came to meetings."

"I don't recall any of those meetings did much good, in the end."

Abruptly, Sam met my eyes. As always on the rare occasions when he did that, his were unnervingly clear and sharp. "Yeah, well, you see," he said, "the trouble with the insanity defense you guys were pushing is, it makes people think you're insane. Then they send you to the bin. You forget I've been to the bin before, all on my own. I didn't need anyone to slip anything into my drink and I didn't need to kill anyone to get there the first time."

"I didn't forget. But that was twenty-five years ago. You were young, you'd had a breakdown, you were drinking."

"I'm still drinking."

"The point is, before you killed Amy Evans, you'd never been violent. Never, until the night those girls gave you PCP."

"No, the point is, I stabbed Amy seven billion times!"

"When you were high on a drug you didn't know you'd taken."

"Eleven other people drank that punch. None of them killed anyone."

"Two were hospitalized with hallucinations."

"For fuck's sake! They didn't *kill* anyone. A jury might have bought the idea I was temporarily out of my mind, but the point, like you say, the *point* is, I really *am* out of my mind. The thing about temporary insanity is, it's temporary. They let you out when you get sane. Which I will never be, never, never, Smith, never!"

Six years ago, Sam's defense attorney, Susan Tulis; Sam's younger brother, Peter; and I, tag-teaming, had all lost this argument with Sam. Sam, as he said, might have been out of his mind, but the court declared him sane enough to participate in his own defense. His participation amounted to pushing everyone's advice aside and taking a plea deal. He got fifteen-to-life and was sent upstate. The image of skinny, confused Sam in Greenhaven never sat well with me, and over the years I dropped him a couple of notes, which he didn't answer, and I called Peter a couple of times, to be told Sam was doing "as well as could be expected." I didn't expect, myself, that that was very well.

Then, about a year ago, I picked up a leaflet at a Chelsea art gallery and learned there was a campaign to get him out. A thrilling genius of an outsider artist, a man with a unique, electrifying vision, had been discovered behind prison walls by a therapist, who, unable to contain his excitement, had sent slides of the man's work—without the man's knowledge—to a friend at a gallery. There on the leaflet was the work, and there was the artist. It was the same skinny, confused Sam.

The gallerist friend showed the slides to a critic, the critic wrote a piece in an art magazine, and a whole lot of people got excited as hell.

They visited the prison; they wrote about the painter and the paintings. The campaign hit the culture pages soon after I saw the pamphlet, with strategically planted curator interviews, photos of the work, and artists' and critics' comments.

I wasn't part of the Free Sam Tabor crusade; the art world VIPs orchestrating it didn't need me. Or Susan Tulis, or even, really, Peter Tabor. The Free Sam Tabor Committee hired a hotshot celebrity attorney. They told Peter what letters to write, what petitions to sign, and when to appear at the parole board. Sometimes Peter's wife and partner, Leslie, went with him; most of the time he showed up without her, but even at those hearings, he was never alone. Peter was an architect with a solid reputation, regularly published and never lacking for work, but he was definitely B-list in the Free Sam Tabor crowd.

"I saw your show," I said to Sam.

"What?" His focus had drifted.

"Your show. It got good reviews."

"It got great reviews." A strange bitterness edged his words. "You really went?"

"I was curious. The whole time I was working on your case I never knew you painted."

He pointed across the room. "Until now, I never knew you played the piano."

"It's nobody's business."

"That's what I used to say. Now it's everybody's. Ain't life grand? You weren't at the opening."

"I don't do openings."

"I should try that. I'll just tell them I don't do openings. You think they'd let me stay home if I said that?" His hopeless tone made it clear he knew the answer. "So, tell me. Did you like my work?"

"Is that why you came here with a gun? For a review?"

"You know good art. I didn't know that before, but I can see. Those are Santlofers. That's an Ellen Eagle."

"You're not serious."

"You didn't answer me."

I lit a cigarette, shook out the match. "All right. No, I don't like it. I'm impressed by your skill, your craft, especially someone self-taught. But I can't separate out the content."

"Come on, that's my unique daring, my horrifying genius." He lifted a lecturing finger. "'Only at first glance does Tabor's work resemble the nostalgic folk-based traditions of much outsider art. His true and dazzling gift is to subvert and interrogate that maudlin aesthetic, forcing us to acknowledge the ghastly basis of our banal quotidian existence.' *Art Now* said so. 'Quotidian.' I had to look it up."

"Well, I'm sure they're right." I drank more coffee, waited, but whatever he'd come for, he wasn't ready yet. "As long as you're waving guns around," I said, "I want a free question."

"Seems fair."

"What I saw: is that the kind of work you did before you went upstate? Or did the content change in prison?"

"That's a goddamn indirect question, isn't it? What you mean is, Did you always paint such pretty violence, Mr. Tabor, or did that only start after you butchered that blond girl?"

I said nothing.

"Christ, Smith, before I went upstate, I was a waiter! I painted in a basement in Queens and no one except my brother ever saw my shit. God, I wish it was still like that!"

"What you painted," I said evenly, when he was done. "Was it what you paint now?"

"You never give up. I remember that, too. It's supposed to be one of the good things about you, like not lying. Yes. Yes! All right, yes, it was. It's all

I've ever painted. Over and over. Always." The agitation of his hands and voice began to spread to the rest of him. With an obvious effort he pulled himself back under control. "But you're not saying all that blood and destruction creeps you out? Big, gun-carrying macho man like you?"

I put my coffee down. "All right, Sam. You got your review. You want more coffee, or are you ready to leave now?"

"That's not why I came."

"Oh, no shit?"

He seemed not to hear my sarcasm. "I knew you wouldn't like my work. I just asked to make sure you still wouldn't lie to me." He picked up his mug, wrapped his hands around it, but didn't drink. "There's a serial killer in New York. Did you see it on the news?"

"No."

"Fox had it, and the *Post*. The rest will pick it up any minute now. A woman last week, and one six months ago."

"Two? Who says it's a serial killer?"

"Why, that's not enough? You want more? Half a dozen? Ten? Would that make you happy?"

Without heat, I said, "They're careful with that term. Whatever the news says, the cops won't call it a serial killer at two, even if they're sure those two were the same guy."

"There might be three soon. Is that good enough?"

"I think that's the technical threshold, yes. Why are we talking about this?"

"Because it's me."

2

I got up, poured myself more coffee, filled Sam's cup, too. This time I put milk and sugar in his. I handed it to him; he took a sip and said, "Yecch. What is this shit?"

"Ballast."

I took a cookie from the plate by his elbow; maybe that would encourage him to eat. As I sat, he said, "Aren't you going to tell me I'm not the serial killer type?"

"I don't know that."

"I guess in some weird way that's a compliment."

"It's not. Why did you come here, Sam? Anyone else, I might think he was trying to impress me, but not you."

"I'm not the type?" A sly smile.

"I hope you didn't come for help leaving town, laying low, something like that. If you killed those women, you know I'm going to have to turn you in."

"Good luck."

"I have the guns," I reminded him.

"You won't need them but they won't help. I already tried it."

"Tried what?"

"Turning myself in. The detective told me to get lost. She said I wasn't the type. Actually, what she said was, I'd better get my ass the hell out of her squad room, because she didn't need another nutcase trying to claim the credit so he could join the serial killer club."

"What made her think you were a nutcase?"

"First of all, I am a nutcase."

"Sam."

"Okay, okay. Because I couldn't give her any details. I don't remember either one." His words were steady, but his hands were trembling.

"So what makes you think you did them?"

"I don't remember killing Amy, either."

"That's your logic? You must have done them because you don't remember them, just like you don't remember the one you actually did? What's your plan, to confess to every crime in New York you don't remember?"

"Goddamn it!" He jumped up, started pacing. "That wiseass shit from you, I remember that, too. Fuck, Smith, I came here for help!" As he strode the room, his hands made meaningless gestures, waving things away, reaching for things not there.

"Sam? Tell me what you want."

He stopped all movement, stood completely still. "Prove it," he said. "Prove it's me."

Another pot of coffee, a lot of theorizing from Sam, a lot of questions from me, and this was as far as we'd gotten: both the women the *Post* described as victims of a serial killer were blondes, like Amy Evans, and had been stabbed to death, which was how Sam had killed Amy Evans. Sam drank, and his drinking led to blackouts.

"But I'm a high-functioning alcoholic," he said in the jargon of recovery, a road he'd gone down so many times he'd put ruts in it. "I could've been drunk as a skunk and pulled off something like this, easy. Like before."

I don't know how high-functioning you can call a wasted waiter painting in a basement, but I didn't argue that point. "When you killed Amy Evans, you weren't drunk," I said. "You were high on PCP you didn't know you'd taken. And if by 'pull it off' you mean do it and not get caught, you didn't pull it off. You just sat there crying and waiting for the cops."

"Big scary killer, huh?"

"That's my point."

"I guess I must have learned."

Sam's logic, because it was never reasonable, was never refutable. He didn't look at me, or at anything but the floor. His right-hand fingers massaged his left-hand fingers.

"Sam, I don't buy it."

"You still think I'm not the type?"

"I don't know what the type is. I just don't think it's you. Everything you know about these murders you read in the paper. You don't remember anything about either one, and you say there's no physical evidence, no blood, nothing. What's to say you were anywhere but in your own bed all night, either time?"

"Not my bed, the first time. That night I was still at Peter and Leslie's."

"Even better. You think you could have snuck out, killed someone, and snuck back in, the day after you got out of prison, and they wouldn't have noticed?"

"But there it is. The timing. You want facts? That's a fact."

The timing was Sam's strongest, and to me his only, interesting evidence against himself. The first killing had happened the day after he'd gotten out, and the second last week, the day after his one-man show opened.

"You see? Big events," he insisted. "Times like that, I get stressed, I drink more. All my life."

"Even in prison?"

"Did you take a stupid pill? We were swimming in moonshine inside. We used to bottle it for the COs so they wouldn't 'find' the still."

"So you think—"

"I *think* I get stressed, I get drunk, I kill women. Is that so hard to understand?"

"No, to believe. But say I did believe you. What do you want me to do about it? Babysit you so you don't do it again?"

"Follow me around for the rest of my life? That's idiotic."

"I'm glad you think so, because I wasn't planning on it."

"It wouldn't work anyway. I could give you the slip. I could fire you. I could wait months, until we were both sure I wouldn't do it again. I read a book that said some serial killers can go for years between murders."

"I read one that said silver bullets kill vampires."

"Goddamn it, Smith! *Do not laugh at me!*"

"Sit down, Sam. I'm sorry. I'm not laughing. But monsters are monsters. Scary stories. If you'd read a different book, you wouldn't have come to me, you'd have gone to an exorcist."

"In the monster stories I read when I was a kid, the scary part was the monster getting you. Not being the monster."

"The scary part is whatever scares you. If you want my two-bit analysis, this all has to do with your guilt about the past and your fear of the future."

"Thank you, Dr. Fucking Freud! No, I don't want your two-bit bullshit."

"Then what do you want?"

"I told you. I want you to investigate. Find evidence. Prove it's me."

"Why?"

The crimson anger faded from his face. "Don't you get it?"

"No. Tell me."

He waited a long time before he spoke again. When he did, his voice was low and muffled, a directionless echo across a great distance.

"If you bring the cops something real, they'll arrest me."

"And that would be good?"

"Of course it would." Now his words were almost too soft to hear. "If I'm inside, I can't kill anyone else. Smith? I don't want to kill anyone else." He sat folded tight, arms wrapping his chest. "And soon," he whispered. "You have to do it soon."

"Why soon?"

"They stuck me in a group show at the Whitney. At the last minute. Aren't I lucky? It opens tomorrow." Abruptly, he boomed, "Stress, stress, stress! That stress train is coming, it's speeding down the track! Chugga chugga chugga *blam*!"

"You think you'll kill someone? The day after?"

His voice dropped back to normal. "My, you catch on quick."

"If you're really worried, there are ways to get locked up without being arrested. You could commit yourself."

"Oh, I don't think so. If you think I'm going back to the bin, *you're* crazy! The one I went to, it was a nice private bin, gardens and everything. Eight months. It made me the man I am today. Drugs, restraints, bright lights, other lunatics screaming all night. No. Never again."

"But prison? Sam, if you are this killer and I prove it, they'll put you back in for the rest of your life."

He smiled. "You know how I survived inside? Scrawny little white guy like me? I did drawings of the other cons. And the COs, sometimes. They'd give them to their girlfriends or their kids. A lifer told me his wife had a picture of him a guy in Central Park did but mine was better. He meant it as high praise and I took it that way. So they all looked after me. Isn't that a joke? My whole life I never showed anyone my work, like I was afraid of something, and the first time I let people see it, it's gangbangers and killers. And they love it."

"Those drawings must be valuable now."

"I know, right? That's even funnier. All those hard men's baby mamas with signed Sam Tabors. Cracks me up. I can handle prison, Smith. But not the bin."

He was trembling all over. I got up, got the coffee, poured him what was left.

"Shit," he said. "Don't you have any scotch around here?"

I said nothing.

"What, no lecture? 'Sam, you need to stop drinking, you're a fucking alkie drunk no-good boozehound'?"

"I thought we agreed I wasn't babysitting."

"Peter still lectures me. He's still trying to make me a responsible adult. Don't tell him I came here, okay? He's not paying you for this. I am. I'm Sam Tabor now, you know. I'm rich." Sam paused. "Oh, shit."

"What?"

"I think I asked him for your address."

"You think?"

"No, I did. But don't tell him why. I don't want him to know about this until . . ." He threw back some coffee, made a face. "When we were kids, I did stupid things all the time. Not Peter. I was older, but he was smarter. He knew painting the couch was a bad idea, even if Mom and Dad hated the upholstery. They'd beat the crap out of me, and Peter would beg them to stop. They would, because he was so adorable, crying like that. Later, everyone would yell and scream. Dad would yell at Mom how I couldn't help it, it was just how I was, and Mom would yell back that I had to learn. And Peter would scream at me. It was all . . .

"See, they all, even Dad, thought I did stupid stuff on purpose. That I knew it was stupid and did it anyway. But it wasn't like that. I just . . . I just . . . There are so many things I don't *get*, Smith. Does that make sense?"

"Sam," I said, "I'm not arguing that you're not crazy. I just don't think you're a serial killer."

He lifted his coffee again, this time sipping it slowly, savoring it like the fine liqueur he no doubt wished it were. Gently, he put the mug down on the table. "Fine," he said, his voice tired. "Then prove that."

3

I sat for a long time after Sam left, just looking at my own walls, the drawings and photographs there. Finally I went to the piano. I was working on a Schubert Impromptu and I'd been having trouble with the fingering. I tried a few things, but I couldn't get anything to work. I gave it up and went to bed.

What felt like ten minutes later, the phone blasted me out of a deep sleep. I fumbled for it, croaked, "Smith."

"Smith, it's Peter Tabor. I'm sorry to call so early."

"Peter?" A current surged through me. "Is Sam all right?"

"As far as I know," Peter said. "Do you have a few minutes?"

"What the hell time is it?" I moved the blind aside. A streak of light sliced the floor.

"Seven thirty. I have an eight o'clock meeting. I wanted to talk to you before my day got started."

We were already talking long before my day usually did. I slumped back against the pillow, reached for my cigarettes. "Okay," I said. "Go."

"It's about Sam, of course." Peter paused. "Did he go see you last night?"

"Yes."

"Did he try to hire you?"

"You'll have to ask him." I lit up, felt that first flash of nicotine.

"You may be misunderstanding me. I'm not asking why, just if."

"And if?"

"Did you agree?"

"Peter, I'm sorry, but that's between me and Sam."

A breath, while Peter collected his thoughts. "Smith, listen to me. Whatever he wants—please, remember he's *crazy*. He may be out and walking around, his paintings may be selling for a fortune, but that doesn't mean he knows whether he's in Kansas or Oz."

"That didn't come up."

"You can imagine the pressure he's been under. He's not handling it well."

"It would be hard for anyone to handle."

"He's . . . On and off, he's been delusional. Nothing enormous, nothing dangerous. Actually, nothing so different from the way he's always been. But I'm sure whatever he told you sounded strange, bizarre . . ."

"You're fishing. I'm not biting."

"No, no, I'm not. I'm not asking what he wanted. It's just, no matter how bizarre it sounded, I'm hoping you agreed to do it."

"You are?"

"Yes. If you turned him down, I'd like you to reconsider. If you don't feel he offered you enough money, tell me what you need."

He was right, I'd misunderstood. "Why?"

Peter paused. "This is the first time in Sam's life he's ever had a chance. The first time he's somebody. Lemuria Gallery, Sherron Konecki, these are major players. Other galleries wanted him, too, do you understand? For any artist to have a New York gallery is a big deal. To be courted when you're new instead of going from one gallery to another on your knees, that's just about unheard of. But Lemuria! Sherron gave him the whole gallery, both levels—"

"I saw the show."

"You did?" Peter stopped, sounding as surprised as Sam had.

"I was curious."

"I—What did you think?"

I gave him my review, the same one I'd given Sam.

"Well, a lot of people agree with you," Peter said. "The paintings are unnerving. But a lot of people also do *not* agree with you, including the art world establishment. The critics, the collectors, they think Sam Tabor's the greatest thing since sliced bread. He got reviews in the *Times* and the *Journal*. He had the *Art Now* cover. He's important."

I thought of Sam, hunched over, saying, *I painted in a basement in Queens . . . I wish it was still like that.*

"But lately," Peter said, "lately he's been getting more agitated. It happened just before he got out, just before his show opened, and now again, leading up to the Whitney. It's partly my fault. We've been really busy in the office, and Leslie keeps pushing me to focus here and not on Sam. But still, I should have seen it coming. I should've backed those people off. The press, Sherron, the collectors. That gonzo photographer who wants to live in Sam's pocket."

"Tony Oakhurst?"

"What a jerk."

I didn't know Oakhurst, so I couldn't pass judgment on the man, but his work was oddly similar to Sam's: striking surfaces with an underlayer of violence and threat. I wondered if Peter saw the resemblance.

"But we owe them," Peter said. "They got Sam out. So I let them come around. Up to the prison, over to the house when he got out, now to his studio. By the time I realized what was happening, it was too late."

"Too late how?"

"I've seen Sam in stress situations all his life. He cooks up delusions to distract himself. And he revs up his drinking. But those things don't always keep the demons under the bed. The Whitney opening is tonight, and Sam's right on the edge. He's got this idea you can help him. Help him do what, I don't know. Stop the Martians from beaming him up or something. Whatever it is, I'd like you to do it. Or pretend you're doing it. To keep him from capsizing. Do it very, very quietly so it doesn't get around that Sam Tabor's afraid of the Martians, but do it."

"You think these important art people don't already know Sam's crazy?"

"Of course they do. It's part of his attraction. That he's a convicted killer, that he was discovered in prison. They see the violence in the work, they think it's also in him, and they adore it. 'Oh, yes, darling, you must meet him, I get the shivers when he looks at me.'" Peter's voice had gone up and nasal, mimicking a vapid patron of the arts, and pretty well, too. "'We bought one of his newest, we hung it where the Koons used to be.'" Himself again: "But it's a haunted house in a theme park. You can let it scare you because it's not real. It's under control. But Sam isn't. He needs to be at the Whitney tonight, maybe not in a suit and tie, but with his pants on. And sober enough to stand. If he thinks you hunting the Martians will help, then please, do it?"

"All right," I said.

"You will?" Peter almost audibly stumbled, like a man pushing on an open door. "That's great. I appreciate that. Thank you. I'll send you a check, will that be okay? Or you could come by."

"No, this was Sam's idea. I'm sure, these days, he's good for it."

"He is," said Peter. "But if he writes you a check from the National Bank of Oz, let me know."

I hung up, made coffee, poured a cup, and thumbed the speed dial on my phone.

"You have to be kidding me," Lydia answered, before I said anything. "You're still up from last night, right?"

"Wrong. A potential client woke me from a sound sleep and offered me a lot of money. If you'd spent the night, you'd know that."

"And you'd be explaining yourself to my mother right now. Besides, except for the money, that doesn't sound like a client you'll be happy to have."

"I didn't take it. You free for lunch?"

"Why? You want to give me the client because our clocks are in synch?"

"It's more complicated than that."

"Good, because that would be dopey."

"You're undervaluing a good night's sleep. Anyway, I may need you, or I may not."

"I thought you always needed me."

"For the case."

"That's better."

"I'll know by midday. Either way, you'll get lunch out of it."

"Can I pick the restaurant?"

"Keep in mind I didn't take the money."

"The Fatty Crab. Hudson Street. Haute Malaysian."

"I've heard of it. I don't think I'm cool enough."

"No, but I am."

I made two other calls, then headed out. By now, it was half past eight. Traffic choked the streets, and pedestrians wove complex patterns on the sidewalks. All traces of last night's mist had burned away under the April sun. The slanting whiteness of the light, the thin freshness of the day, dazzled me.

Lydia's suggested any number of times that I consider changing my ways, getting up earlier, taking this in more often. She thinks it's laziness and old habit that keep me from it. But she's wrong. This unsullied light, this bright vision, they're beautiful, but they're false. They paint over the truth. They promise something they can't deliver. It's not until the day gets older, wearier, that it stops making the effort to lie.

4

The 19th Precinct is a modern building behind an old façade. I remember when they built it. They tore off the roof, razed the interior, left the brick fronts of the police station and the firehouse next to it standing like movie sets propped by steel beams. Then they started to build. The old openings were fitted with new doors and windows and given new rooms to open on, designed for uses the old rooms couldn't have envisioned or fulfilled. Everything behind the stage-set fronts is new, but from outside it looks like nothing's changed.

The desk sergeant grunted me upstairs. Twisting corridors took me to the squad room, where half a dozen detectives sat behind scarred desks. Only one of the appraising stares leveled at me as I walked in came from a woman. I headed in her direction.

"Smith?" she asked. When I nodded she said, "Grimaldi. Go on, sit down."

Detective Angela Grimaldi looked a little younger than I, probably midthirties. Her brown hair was blond-streaked and wild, the kind of tight curls a lot of women cut short; she wore it shoulder-length, with a comb stuck in one side to persuade it to mind its manners. Her shirtsleeves were rolled up over smooth, muscular forearms.

I sat. The other stares dropped back to paperwork, coffee, and keyboards, but no question every cop in that room knew where I was every minute.

"Thanks for seeing me," I said.

"Yeah, well, what I'm thinking, I talk to you, you keep that whack job away from me." Grimaldi's chair creaked and bounced as she leaned back, crossing her legs.

"You mean Sam."

"Freaking lunatic," she said cheerfully. "I got too much to do, I don't need him. Creepy, the way he sits all squeezed in like that, won't look you in the eye."

"He's afraid he killed those women."

"Afraid." Grimaldi snorted. "Hoping, you mean. So, what can I do for you?"

"I'd like whatever you can give me on those two homicides. The one here, and the one on the West Side."

"What makes you think I got anything on the West Side one?"

"I know it's too soon for the NYPD to call this a serial killer. But the papers did, which means the cases have a family resemblance. You and whoever caught the one across town would have shared information by now. One of you would be the lead. If it weren't you, you'd have sent me across town when I called to see the other guy."

She tilted her head, maybe reappraising me. "Okay, it's true. No task force yet or anything like that, and officially the department's still telling the *Post* they're full of shit. Mason over at the two-oh is working his like just another homicide. Which it might be, except it's a cold case by now, almost six months. I'm working mine that way, too. But I'm the clearinghouse. In case another one turns up. There's a whole protocol for this serial killer shit, you know."

"I didn't know, but I'm not surprised."

"I spent time at Quantico two years ago. Did the FBI serial killer course."

"Is it like *Silence of the Lambs*?"

"Quantico? It's a pit. Roommates, reveille—I wanted that, I'd've stayed in the army."

"Sounds like you didn't enjoy it."

"You kidding? I loved it. Put in for the advanced course next summer. But I'll tell you this for free: your guy, Tabor, he don't fit the profile."

"Why not?"

"Don't get me wrong. I'd love to nail him for this. Not a cop in New York wouldn't. Lots of crying in the beer when he got sprung."

"He spent five years upstate."

"And it should've been life. No new evidence, no one saying he didn't kill that girl, but suddenly the guy's Picasso, he can't rot behind bars like normal mutts. Gimme a freaking break! And you seen the shit he paints? Kind of pretty, like what my folks have over the couch, until you look close. You seen it?"

"Yes."

"So you know. But there you go. I just lock 'em up. People with juice want 'em out walking the streets, what can I do?"

"I'm not sure Sam wouldn't agree with you."

"I told you he was a whack job."

"He is. But then why do you say he doesn't fit the profile?"

"Before I answer that, what exactly are you supposed to be doing here? You said you were working for him, you didn't say doing what."

"He thinks he killed those women. He wants me to prove it, or disprove it."

"Why?"

"Don't you think a guy would want to know whether he did something like that?"

"I'm just saying. Not a lot of people, they can't get arrested, they hire private talent to prove they're good for it."

"He's afraid he'll do it again. If it is him, he wants to be stopped."

"You're shitting me."

"No."

"He wants his ass locked up, you mean? Tell him to jaywalk. Spit on the sidewalk. Carry a gun."

I didn't mention the gun Sam had been carrying last night. "Detective, he wants to *know*."

"What a crock." She shook her head. The comb in her hair loosened, threatening a cascade. "So," she said, jabbing it tight again. "You and me, are we at cross purposes here? I'm trying to find who killed my vic. I got no one I like for it right now, but I know I don't like your client. You don't like your client for it either, but he does. I got to tell you, this is a new one on me. Am I going to be tripping over you? You going to confuse my witnesses, contaminate my evidence?"

"I'll try to keep out of your way. I won't go to the witnesses unless I have to."

"What means 'have to'?"

"I'm hoping to be able to prove it couldn't have been Sam. If I had the facts, the timelines, all that, I might be able to eliminate him without talking to anyone."

Grimaldi nodded. "Well, I already talked to people. So did Mason. No one puts Tabor anywhere near either crime scene. No evidence he ever laid eyes on either vic."

"You did? I thought you thought he was a whack job."

"I do. But being as it's him, I had to at least think about it. Even called Ike Cavanaugh, detective from the Amy Evans case, to ask what he thought. He, by the way, almost jumped through the phone and punched my face for sending Tabor away."

"He thinks it's him?"

"Wants it to be. So does his captain. And in case you're wondering, so does *my* captain. The whole NYPD and Sam Tabor, everyone wants the same thing, and here's Grimaldi saying, hold your horses. Like I'm that little Dutch kid with his finger in the dike. Ain't that a kick?"

She didn't seem too upset about her lonely position, so I let it go. "What makes you so sure it's not?" I asked.

A uniformed cop walked by, dropped some papers on an empty desk. He didn't give me a glance. That was someone who'd never make detective.

Grimaldi, on the other hand, kept her eyes on him until he was gone. "Like I told you, Tabor don't fit the profile." She turned to me. "There's two kinds of serial killers. Quantico calls them 'organized' and 'disorganized.' You know about this?"

"No, tell me."

"The organized ones are the charming, handsome ones, the ones everyone says afterward, 'Oh my God, I had no idea, he was just the nicest guy.' The others are the drooling lunatic head cases. The ones people say, 'I always knew something was off about him.' If Tabor was one, that would be his category. But what makes us think maybe these two killings are related is, they're organized. The vics looked alike: short-haired, skinny little blondes in their late twenties."

"The woman Sam killed looked something like that."

"That's true. But these were both drinking in hot bars, bars with a scene. The killer either picked them up there, or followed them when they left. Your guy, no way a bouncer would've let him in one of those places. And they were stabbed a couple times, not a couple dozen, like he did Adams. And both outdoors, in the park, not in a basement. With a different kind of knife than he used."

"The same knife in both?"

"Can't tell, which is one of the reasons we haven't called it yet. But the same kind. And this guy, it looks like he took trophies. They do that sometimes, to remember by. Your guy didn't do that with Adams."

"What kind of trophies?"

Grimaldi wagged a finger at me. "Nuh-uh, sorry. We're holding that back, to ask each of the loonies that confesses. Before you ask, of course I tried it on your guy. He has no idea. See what I'm getting at? The things that make these two like each other make them different than the one Tabor did."

"Sam was in prison for five years. And he lives in his own head. Isn't it possible he changed? Hardened?"

"I thought you didn't think it was him."

"I don't. But I can't help but wonder."

"What you're asking is, could a disorganized killer get organized? I never heard of that. It happens the other way. The organized ones crack up near the end. A lot of them, that's how they get caught. People talk about them getting careless, but it's not careless. They want to keep it together like at the beginning, but they just can't."

"Still, wouldn't it be worthwhile to search Sam's place? You wouldn't need a warrant. He'd let you in."

She frowned. "What are you talking about? Of course I did."

"You did? He didn't tell me that."

"Jerk. He was wasted, so he probably doesn't remember."

"He said you threw him out."

"I told him he was a fucking lunatic and I wanted him out of my squad room. Then I drove him home. All the way to goddamn Greenpoint. He was drunk as a lord. Fell asleep on the way. Woke up when we got there, giggled, told me to come on in, have a look around. Goddamn right I was going to have a look around, what did he think, I was an Uber? Head case fell down on the couch and started snoring. You know there's nothing on the walls, almost no furniture? Mattress on the floor, couch, chair, table. And one of those paintings, tacked on the wall. Up close and personal, that stuff is still revolting."

"I wish he'd told me you did that."

"Look, the guy's a convicted killer. I swear to God, he's blowing smoke out of his ass, but I had to look."

"And you didn't find anything?"

"Of course not. If your boy wants the world to think he's a serial killer, he's going to have to try harder than that. Jesus, you have any idea how many confessions we have since the *Post* came out? Fourteen. Not including the one who said it wasn't him, it was his twin brother. Jerkoff doesn't have a twin brother. Three of them are ex-cons, one with a homicide sheet. Mason and I looked at all of them. They're all full of shit, and we knew it, but we gotta look."

"Are you planning to check out Sam's studio?"

She nodded reluctantly. "Sometime this afternoon. Waste of time and taxpayer dollars."

"What about forensic evidence?"

"What, at Tabor's place? You got the budget to send a forensic team where there's no probable-cause reason for them to go, I'm sure my captain will be happy to hear it. Otherwise, I say your guy's a fruitcake and he can go to hell." She sat back and crossed her arms.

"All right," I said. "I hope we're both right about Sam. And I hope you find the real killer fast. But can I have the information I came for?"

"Yeah, okay." Grimaldi pushed to her feet. "I still think he should just jaywalk." She picked up a file folder. "Let me go xerox some of this, whatever's okay for you to have. I can't give you the autopsy reports, but there's some stuff. Just remember, I wouldn't even be giving you anything"—a stern look—"except you're going to keep that freak out of my face from now on, right? Oh, oh, check it out."

I twisted to face the door. Filling it was a big-bellied, mustached man with an NYPD twenty-year pin in his lapel.

"Hey, Ike," Grimaldi said evenly. "You didn't say you were coming."

"Yeah, but I'm here. This him?"

I stood as he crossed the room. "Bill Smith." I offered my hand. To Grimaldi, I said, "Am I? Him?"

"Yeah," she said. "This is Ike Cavanaugh, from Queens North Homicide. He worked the Amy Evans killing."

"We never met, but I remember your name," I told Cavanaugh.

"And I remember yours." He stared at my hand until I dropped it.

"I told you I called Ike when Tabor came in," said Grimaldi. "I also called him this morning, when you called me. Seeing as I'm the clearinghouse, you know. He thinks I'm wrong."

"Damn right, I do," Cavanaugh said. "That fucking sicko says he's a serial killer, why argue? Grimaldi here, she's got women's intuition." He laid a heavy and sarcastic emphasis on the words. "Plus they sent her to Quantico with the Feebs, so now she knows everything about serial killers. Only thing, she don't know shit about Sam weird-as-fuck Tabor. She didn't see what he did to Amy Evans. Sixteen years working Homicide, that was one of the worst I ever saw. And now he says he killed two other girls? Fine, lock his ass back up. He never should've got out."

"There's no evidence he did those other two," I said.

"There might be, if someone was looking for it. Instead of sniffing the air or feeling the vibes or whatever horseshit."

Grimaldi stiffened. Cavanaugh eyed her. The squad room quieted as the two detectives took each other's measure, like dogs deciding whether to get into it or just piss and move on.

Cavanaugh turned back to me. I guessed that meant Grimaldi had won that round. "When those arty snoots started that committee about 'Tabor's a great artist, he has to get out so he can paint us more paintings,' it burned my butt. I sent money to the *Don't* Free Sam Tabor Committee. You probably didn't hear about that. It wasn't big shots like on the other side. Just Amy Evans's family, her friends and neighbors. Entire neighborhood signs petitions against that sicko, some bleeding-heart judge lets him out anyway. I guess regular people don't count anymore."

"You came all the way in from Queens when you heard I was coming here," I said. "Why?"

"You were the PI helped that bastard get off the first time."

"Off? He was sentenced to fifteen-to-life."

"He shoulda got life plus ninety-nine. Then he couldn't of been out after five. Grimaldi here"—Cavanaugh jerked his thumb at the other detective—"yesterday she calls to tell me he wants to turn himself in but she won't take him up. Today she calls to say he hired you. So I guess he changed his mind. Fucking little worm wants to squirm off this hook, too. So I came to say this in person, so nobody makes a mistake: there's a deep, deep pile of shit waiting for anyone who gets him off again."

I met his stare. Then I turned to Grimaldi. "You were going to xerox something for me?"

"Yeah," she said. Her cheeks were flaming but her voice was cold. "But Ike? It might interest you to know, Tabor didn't hire Smith to prove he didn't do it. He hired him to prove he did. Now, move. You're in my way."

5

I called Sam from the street when I left the 19th. I got voice mail and left a message, wondering if he was sitting huddled over himself in his empty-walled apartment, listening to his cell phone ring. Or if he wasn't there at all but in his Manhattan studio, brushes in hand, lost to everything else.

I found a diner, had a cup of coffee, and read the police reports on the murdered women. I didn't learn anything Grimaldi hadn't told me, except some background facts: where they'd lived, their next of kin. Where they were from. What they'd done for a living. Who they *were*, before their metamorphosis into crime victims, public property, chapters in their killer's story.

Annika Hausman and Tiffany Traynor, hip young women with favored careers. Tiffany a photo stylist, Annika in the M&A department at Chase. Both bar-and-club types, knew what to wear, where to go, and, according to their friends, what type of man to go home with. That either would have let Sam Tabor so much as buy her a Stoli struck me as dubious, the way it had Grimaldi, as did the idea of Sam getting past the velvet rope in the first place. I supposed it was possible he'd spotted them, waited somewhere, and followed them, but if he'd been so drunk he didn't remember, he would have been drunk enough to shake off. Unless Annika and Tiffany were even more smashed. Not out of the question, but not likely, either.

Unless Sam *wasn't* drunk, he was in some kind of fugue state, and in that state, more—Grimaldi's word—organized than anyone thought possible.

Maybe Sam, out of his mind, made a habit of this. Maybe he lurked outside clubs and followed women all the time. Maybe he'd tried to bundle women off into the park before, and Tiffany and Annika were the only ones who'd gone. Because after a stress trigger event, he was—what? More determined? Better at it?

Or maybe he'd been successful before, just not in a way that matched these. Other places, other weapons. I called Grimaldi.

"How's your buddy Cavanaugh?"

"Jerk. But it's good you called, because I want to say something. Cavanaugh's a shoe-leather, by-the-book guy. He starts with a theory and looks for evidence. You learn that at the academy. That's fine, but me, I see things and put them together in different ways until they click. Cavanaugh thinks what he does is police work and what I do is some women's intuition bullshit. I generally don't give a shit, but I want to make sure you know if I say it's your boy in the end, or I say it isn't, it's based on evidence, not sniffing the fucking air."

I almost laughed. "Detective, I have a female partner. If I ever accused her of using 'women's intuition' instead of doing actual investigative work, she'd shoot me."

"Good for her. And something else. Cavanaugh's an asshole, but this thing he has about Tabor, any cop might have it. Some cases eat at your gut, you know? Maybe you don't know."

"I do. It's not so different, what I do. Sam's unfinished business for me, too."

"Yeah, well, speaking of business, I'm kind of working here. You call for a reason?"

"I was wondering: You have other unsolved homicides in the time since Sam got out?"

"Not like these."

"No, like anything."

"Why? What are you thinking?"

"That what we're seeing as the pattern might be too narrow." I gave her a thumbnail of my theory.

"Fugue state? They talked about that at Quantico. But that's close to MPD. Multiple personality disorder. Last I heard, Tabor doesn't have that."

"No. But whoever killed these women might."

"Hey. If you're trying to help me out, investigate my case for me, you can stop right there. I don't need you screwing in it, and I don't need you telling me how to do my job."

"Sorry. I didn't mean to do that."

"And here I thought you were mostly trying to find Tabor an alibi."

"I was just reading through these files, though, and I couldn't help wondering."

Grimaldi was quiet, and then she sighed. "Yeah, well, it's actually not a bad idea. I'll check it out. And yeah, since you thought it up, I'll let you know."

I thanked the detective, paid for my coffee, and headed downtown to see what you ate in a restaurant where the cuisine was haute Malaysian.

⎯

From way down the block, I could see Lydia lounging at a sidewalk table. I stopped, for just a second, to look at her in the warm spring sunshine. She wore a green sweater and a black leather jacket and looked terrific, but then, to me she always did. I started forward again. She looked up through big round sunglasses that she didn't take off when I kissed her.

Things between us had changed since we went to Mississippi a few months earlier, but in some ways they were still the same. The kiss was warm, soft, and—as usual, unless we're in bed—too short. Lydia wasn't into public display. And, as before, she set the rules.

"You can have the shady side," she offered when I stepped back. "Since your eyes are probably still in shock from seeing the morning."

"No, it's the dazzlement of you." I settled in and picked up the menu. "What do we eat here?"

"Everything's good. But if you order the quail egg shooters, I'm leaving."

We chose watermelon pickle with crispy pork, and grilled skate on a banana leaf, both to share. Lydia already had a half-drained Pellegrino. I ordered a Singha lager.

"So, who's this client who dares call you before nine A.M.? In fact before eight A.M.?" Lydia asked. "My hat's off to him."

"I told you, I didn't take the money."

"And yet, you said you might need me. So, something's up."

"It's those astounding powers of deduction that are, um, so astounding. I didn't take it because I already had a client."

"That you got even earlier in the morning? No way."

"No, late last night. You remember Sam Tabor?"

She pondered over her drink. "He's that painter. He murdered someone years ago but he got parole last fall. It was a big deal. He's supposed to be a major genius. You worked on the original case, right? Do I have the right guy?"

"That's him. He's been out six months."

"He's in trouble again?"

"Not exactly." While we waited for our lunch, I told Lydia what Sam feared, and what he wanted.

"Wow," she said. "Is he really nuts, do you think?"

"Yes. But not that way."

She raised skeptical eyebrows.

I said, "Sam's weird. I don't know exactly what's wrong with him, but apparently it always has been. He's had a raft of different diagnoses—OCD, AD/HD, Asperger's. In his early twenties he had a breakdown and committed himself. He doesn't look you in the eye, his timing's off when he talks. He drifts into his own world and has to keep on pulling himself back. And he drinks. The word a lot of people use is 'creepy.'"

"Does he hear voices? See black helicopters?"

"No. And he doesn't get messages through the fillings in his teeth."

The waiter interrupted this cheerful discussion with plates of pork and fish and bowls of coconut rice. Lydia rattled around in the jar of chopsticks on the table until she made two matching pairs.

"He really did kill someone that first time, though, didn't he?" She handed me a set.

"But do you remember the whole story?"

"No, except you thought he got a raw deal."

"I didn't think he should have gone to prison. I know how this sounds, but it wasn't his fault. He was drugged."

"Someone drugged him and made him kill someone?"

"Might as well have. Sam was a waiter, working at a diner. He was good at his job, careful with the orders. But the people he worked with kept their distance. He didn't have friends there."

"Because he was creepy?"

I nodded. "Then one night, two waitresses invited him to a party."

"Now I remember! There was something in the punch."

"PCP. The girls had gotten hold of some and wanted to try it out."

"They did a science experiment on their friends?"

"And on themselves. Two people besides Sam had psychotic breaks. They were hospitalized with hallucinations, paranoia. Sam took Amy Evans down to the basement, screwed her, and killed her."

"Didn't anyone see him? No one stopped him? How did he get her to go down there?"

"He doesn't remember any of it, and neither do most of the others. The one witness who was relatively straight—the punch was gone by the time she got to the party, so she'd had a beer but that's all—she says Amy was high as a kite and went with Sam, cuddling and laughing the whole time. Then she—the witness—heard screams from the basement. She started down the steps and saw Sam stabbing Amy over and over. She ran back up, bolted the basement door, and called the cops."

A terrier sniffed my knee while its oblivious owner at the next table gossiped with her lunch date. I slipped the dog some pork.

"One of the things I was hired to do back then," I said, "was to reconstruct the party, find witnesses willing to swear Sam didn't know what was in the punch."

"Did you?"

"Yes, including the girls who'd put it there. But the case never went to trial because the defense would have been temporary insanity and Sam was afraid he'd end up in a mental hospital. The DA offered a plea bargain and he took it."

"He preferred prison to a hospital?"

"That's what he said then, and he said it again last night."

"That by itself might be enough to prove he's nuts."

"I'm not so sure. Prison's not a bad place for a guy like Sam. Not a lot of choices, lots of rules and boundaries. Sam's confused a lot."

"A guy like that, though—wasn't he afraid?"

"Not as afraid as he was of the hospital. And it turns out that in Greenhaven they appreciate great art." I told her about Sam's portraits of the other cons. "What's interesting is that outside, he hadn't ever let anyone but his brother see his work. In prison, he felt safe enough to do the portraits, and then to paint. That's how he was discovered."

"So, now he's free and sitting in your living room, telling you he's a serial killer. Is there a chance it could be true?"

"There's a chance," I said. "One way or another, we need to find out."

The sidewalk began to fill with people waiting for a table. I gave Lydia the part of the project I thought she would carry off better than I could:

talking to relatives and friends of the victims. She'd try to get an idea of the women's lives, of their movements on the nights they were killed, to see if Sam popped up anywhere.

"Keep your eye out for a cop named Ike Cavanaugh," I said. "You may find him shadowing you."

"Pro or con?"

"Once he meets you, he'll probably find you as irresistible as everyone else does. With me, definitely con."

"You've alienated yet another of New York's Finest?" She sighed. "What is he, the cop on one of these killings?"

"Not these two. Amy Evans. He's holding a grudge." I told her about Cavanaugh and Grimaldi. "She told him to back off, but he seems pretty determined to prove it's Sam. You might run into him."

"Sounds like he doesn't much care for Detective Grimaldi, either."

"You, on the other hand, will love her. She's nearly as tough as you are."

"Me? I'm a marshmallow."

I couldn't see a way to win on that one, so I stuck to business. As the waiter put down the check, I handed Lydia a copy of Grimaldi's file. "While you do this, I'm going to go from the other direction. Try to establish Sam's movements, see if I can find an alibi even he'll have to believe."

"Bill?" Lydia finished a last cup of tea. "Is he really a great painter?"

"He may be."

"But you don't like his paintings. I can tell from the way you said that. Why?"

Maybe I should get a column in *Art Now* if I was going to keep doing reviews. "Like Sam, they're hard to be with," I said. "They may be great, but you want to get away."

"So what makes them great if people don't want to stand there and look at them?"

"They seem to reach deep into you. Everyone has a strong reaction, even if it's disgust."

I tucked cash in with the bill and we stood to leave. Before we'd gone three steps, our table was pounced on by waiting foodies.

"Can you describe them? The paintings?" Lydia asked as we walked.

"I'm not sure I'll do them justice, but: Your first impression is, very pretty. Landscapes, or seascapes, or cottages with gardens and picket fences. Winter twilight on a frozen pond. The kind of paintings you'd see at a sidewalk art fair. Nice colors, good composition, artistically lightweight. They give you that twinge of nostalgia for a life you never lived. You know what I mean?"

"I think I do."

"So, you move in, you stand there, trying to spend a little time with that warm feeling. Then, as you look more closely, it dawns on you that all these serene images and lovely colors are made up of tiny scenes of horrendous, graphic violence. Blood, bombs, people in chains, being beaten, killed. Pain, rage, fear, despair—they're everywhere. Those images dissolve when you're standing back, like the dots in a newspaper photo. But they're what all that prettiness is made of.

"When I went to see his show, I watched people lean close to a picture and then almost jump back. But once you've seen it, you can't un-see it. You feel sucker-punched. You feel—" I searched for the words. "You feel like you were caught in an enormous lie. Like you've been exposed for the hypocrite you are. It's an uncomfortable feeling."

"Uncomfortable? It sounds awful."

"It's hard to dismiss the power, though."

"But is that what art's about? Power, even if it's power to make you feel bad?"

"Good question. I don't know. But it's what the art world loves about Sam."

"If they love that he makes them feel bad, maybe there's something wrong with them."

"Maybe that's what they feel bad about. You know, if you want to see the paintings, you can go up to Lemuria. Or the *Violence* show at the Whitney opens tonight. He's got three pieces in that."

"The *Violence* show?"

"*The Art of Violence/The Violence of Art.*"

"Seriously? Paintings of blood and guts?"

"Not generally, except for Sam's. More conceptual. Though I hear there'll be a Colt revolver that used to belong to the czar of Russia, with onion domes carved on it, broken down into its component parts, each in a gilt frame."

"Oh, goody. But listen, Bill, tell me something else. You don't like the paintings. Do you like Sam?"

I took out a cigarette. "I feel like I owe him. And it seems to me someone has to look out for him. His folks used to do that, and now his brother, but this isn't something he wants his brother to know about."

"If I thought I was a serial killer, I wouldn't tell my brothers, either. You know, if he is, he'll have to go back to prison, no matter how great an artist he is."

I nodded. "He's counting on it."

We split at the subway, Lydia to head to the East Side, me uptown to Sam's studio. If he was there, I'd talk to him; if not, it wouldn't be a total loss, because I also needed to have a serious discussion with his gun dealer.

6

Before he'd gone to prison, Sam, as he'd said, had never shown anyone his work. From the time he was in middle school he was a classic outsider artist, painting in private with a drive bordering on obsession. He didn't study art and had nothing to do with the glittering art world across the river.

But that art world had gotten him out of prison and it had made him famous. He belonged to it now. Though from what he'd said, and from what I'd seen in his eyes and the slump of his shoulders, "belonged to" didn't mean "fit in with." It meant "was owned by."

On the phone too early in the morning, Peter Tabor had put it plainly: for the first time in Sam's life, in the eyes of the world, Sam was somebody. To Peter, that was clearly a good thing. Sam would have disagreed, I thought, but Sam hadn't been asked. And while Nobody could paint under fluorescent lights in a basement in Queens, Somebody couldn't. Sam's current studio was a huge room in a former warehouse on the West Side of Manhattan, leased by and close to his gallery, the rent coming out of the sale of his paintings. Other studios, most smaller than his, filled the rest of the six-story building. Sam's faced north for good light, had running water for his convenience, was near the freight elevator for the handy moving of large canvases.

And Sam's was next door to his gun dealer's.

At the building, I tried Sam's buzzer first. I gave it two attempts, the second try long and insistent. When I was met with silence, I called and again got voice mail. So I buzzed the studio next to Sam's.

"Who's there?" It was more of a demand than a question.

"Bill Smith. I'm here to see Sam Tabor."

Nothing. I was just about to try again when the door was buzzed open. I was impressed that a buzzer could be made to sound grudging.

Upstairs, I walked along paint-splattered vinyl and knocked on the steel door identified by a nameplate as Sam's. I didn't expect a response and I didn't get one. Down the hall I knocked at the next studio, and after a pause I heard an annoyed shout: "I'm coming!" Eventually the door was yanked open. An angular, glowering woman stared me down. She looked fortyish, and angry enough to live forever.

"Are you Ellissa Cromley?"

A moment, and then a curled lip. "Why, who should I be?"

I had no suggestions. "Is Sam Tabor with you?"

She turned and walked back into the studio, leaving the door open. I guessed that was as close to an invitation as I was going to get. I followed through the overlaid smells of turpentine, dust, and stale coffee. A narrow path wandered among sawhorse tables, piles of art books, rolls of canvas, stacked boxes. Metal cans overflowed with brushes, milk crates with metal cans. In a corner, wood scraps; on a chair, sketchbooks. Taped-up drawings and torn-out magazine ads covered the walls. A pile of Free Sam Tabor leaflets fanned out under a table.

The path emerged into a clearing just big enough for a stained couch. Beyond it, by the windows, three easels held unfinished paintings.

Ellissa Cromley dropped onto the couch and retrieved a Brooklyn Lager from the paper-strewn table beside it. Already on the couch, his own beer in hand, was Sam.

"Hey," he said with an out-of-focus smile.

Cromley scowled at Sam. "You know this guy?"

Cromley wore a gauzy, gathered skirt, splashed with both flowers and paint, topped by a white, paint-smeared polo shirt. Paint streaked her arms, spotted her bare feet, and smudged her forehead behind long brown hair only partly contained by a clip.

"I need to talk to you," I said to Sam. There was no place in the room to sit except where the two of them were already sitting. I moved in closer. They both tilted their heads up at me. Well, if their necks started to hurt, maybe Cromley would clear off a crate and offer me a seat. I turned to her. "And to you."

"Me? I don't know you."

"Is this yours?" I held out the .22 I'd taken off Sam last night.

"Oh, that's him?" She turned to Sam, who nodded. After a pull on her beer she said to me, "He said you had it. I was going to come get it later."

"You think so? You know Sam's a felon on parole? Do you know what happens if he's caught with a gun?"

"He wasn't going to use it."

"He goes back upstate, no questions, no appeal. Sam, did you know that?"

Sam, fingers drumming on the couch arm, looked confused. He probably couldn't remember whether he knew it or not.

"He wasn't going to hurt you." Cromley smirked. "It wasn't loaded."

I put the gun back in my pocket. "The First Precinct will have it. You can pick it up there. It's a lot of paperwork, but they'll probably give it back to you in the end."

"You can't do that! It's mine! I have a license for it!"

"You don't have a license for Sam to have it. If he's arrested for carrying it, you'll be arrested for supplying it to him. I'm going to tell them I found it in the gutter. You can tell them whatever you want."

"Oh, screw you." Cromley settled back with a superior smile. "I do have another one, you know."

"I didn't know and I don't care, unless you give that one to Sam, too. Sam, I need to talk to you."

Uncomfortably, Sam said, "Okay." When I just stood there he said, "Oh, you mean, somewhere else? We don't have to do that. Ellissa knows all about it. Ellissa's my friend. She helps me."

"Really? She helps?" The look I gave Cromley wasn't any harder than the one she was giving me. "She knows why you came to see me? You told her?"

"Hey, yo, hello, I'm sitting right here," Cromley said.

"When Sherron first got me the studio"—Sam took a sip of beer—"right next door here, I didn't know . . . I wasn't used to it, being in a building like this, everybody here. So much light, so open. My dealer coming and going, other artists, collectors. I didn't know what to do."

"He was a mess," Cromley said fondly. "I looked after him. Showed him the ropes. Even though you signed with Sherron instead of coming with us." She gave Sam a playful poke and a smile that didn't include me.

"'Us'?" I asked.

Cromley looked at me and drank beer.

"Ellissa's part of a gallery." I guess Sam thought I deserved an answer, or maybe the daggers coming at me from Cromley's eyes made him think, like Leslie's and Peter's fights, of Mom and Dad. "She kind of runs it, actually. An artists' co-op. They all help each other. Like she helped me."

"We invited him."

"I wanted to. It sounded nice. But Peter told me to go with Sherron." Sam's tone was apologetic.

"Yeah, *Peter* thought Sam had bigger fish to fry. Like Sherron gives a shit about him. I helped him anyway." She poked Sam again, in the ribs. He grinned and squirmed. "And it's a good thing," she said, "because if I hadn't, you'd still be standing in the corner staring at those brand-new brushes Sherron bought like they were going to bite you. Or you'd be sitting in the hall because you couldn't remember the combination to your keypad."

Sam gave an embarrassed shrug and downed more beer.

"All right," I said. "Tell me: why did you say last night that Detective Grimaldi threw you out?"

"She did. She thought I was another nut just looking for attention. She said so."

"She drove you home. All the way to goddamn Greenpoint, and she searched your place. You didn't think that was worth mentioning?"

"Sam?" said Cromley. "Did she really do that, that detective?"

"I . . . yeah, I guess she did."

I said, "Are you claiming you don't remember?"

"What's the big deal if he doesn't?" Cromley demanded.

"No, I do," Sam said quickly. "Sort of. She was there. In the kitchen."

"She searched the whole place and she didn't find anything. Not a drop of blood, nothing. Why didn't you tell me?"

"Because what does it prove? Maybe I hid things. Maybe I threw them away."

"What things?"

"What I was wearing, my clothes, my shoes, I don't know."

"The knife," said Cromley, and she looked at me. "Some serial killers who use a knife throw it away or bury it and use a new one each time. The same type—maybe they even buy them by the dozen—but a new one for each victim. Oh, what, you thought you were the only one who knew anything about serial killers, big shot? I've read every book there is. I've heard John Douglas speak twice. You know who he is? He wrote *Mindhunter* and some other important books. You never heard of him?" She turned again to Sam, pointing her beer at me. "Are you sure he's the right guy to be doing this?"

"He's good," Sam said, though he sounded a little unsure.

Hey, yo, I'm standing right here. I said to Cromley, "You seem very up on this stuff. Is this since Sam decided he was one? Or you just have a thing about serial killers?"

"A 'thing'? What the hell is a 'thing'? I'm interested. So, sue me."

"Interested why?"

She gave me the look you'd give someone who was dripping wet and asking if it was raining. "Because the more you know, the less likely it is to happen to you."

"You mean, you think you'll recognize one if he comes down the street?" I stopped just short of telling her she was as crazy as Sam. "And what about Sam? He's sitting right next to you. What if he's right and he is one?"

"He is so wrong." She patted Sam's knee in a way that seemed neither companionable nor romantic, but proprietary. He gave a wavering smile, moved his eyes back and forth between us.

"I know a lot about Sam," Cromley said. "Not just about serial killers. I was on the committee, you know. We got him out. Tony Oakhurst and Sherron Konecki and all those big shots think it was them, they think they're all that and a bag of chips, they do the press conferences and all that shit, but I did the fucking work."

"And you think that gave you insight into Sam?"

"You really don't know anything, do you?" She reorganized herself on the couch, ready to deliver a lecture. "There are different types of serial killers. Almost all are men, with a brain-wiring glitch that gives them a sense of sexual satisfaction and power when they kill. Women so-called serial killers are usually predatory opportunists—for example, women who serially marry and then kill rich husbands. Real serial killers are different."

The way she said "real" made it sound like finding one was a prize.

In smug tones, Cromley continued, "There actually are some who forget their crimes. But Sam doesn't fit that particular profile. Those—"

"That's the second time I've heard that today."

"What?"

"Never mind. Go on, I'm fascinated."

Cromley's jaw set angrily. For a moment I thought she'd stop, but like anyone speaking on a subject dear to her heart, it wasn't all that easy to derail her.

"The ones who forget," she instructed me, "are ADD types. A lot of them self-medicate with drugs, and they kill like scratching an itch. Who remembers an itch after you scratch it? They have buttons and they kill when they're pushed. Then they stop until they're pushed again."

"Sam self-medicates with booze, and he thinks his buttons are these high-stress events. Getting out, his opening." I wondered if Sam was thinking, *Hey, yo, I'm sitting right here.*

"Sam," Cromley spoke as though I'd missed something right in front of my nose, "doesn't have ADD. He's more OCD. I mean, have you actually seen his work?"

"He went to my show," Sam stuck in.

"Oh, yeah?" Cromley's gaze didn't leave me. "Then you should know what I'm talking about. You can see obsessiveness in the paintings."

"You can see violence, too."

"That's a load of crap! Anybody with a brain would know that's allegorical! Idiots who take it literally . . ." Cromley blew out a breath. "The OCD serial killers, on the other hand"—if I didn't learn this, it wasn't going to be her fault—"elaborately plan their murders. That's as important as the actual killing. In fact, the crime can be considered to include the entire process, starting from choosing a victim. Sometimes they take trophies. Because they *like* to remember." She finished with an air of triumph.

"What if they're drunk?" I asked.

"You can't plan if you're drunk."

"You can kill."

"Only clumsily. You can't carry out a plan."

"Is that why you're helping Sam get drunk in the middle of the day? So he doesn't kill anyone? Even though he thinks it's when he's drunk that he *does* kill?"

"Fuck you!" Cromley flushed a bright purple-red, probably a color she had in a tube of paint somewhere. "Sam can drink whenever he wants. And he's not a killer!"

"He went to prison for it."

"That was completely different!"

"Sam?" I said. "Are you buying this?"

"Ellissa knows a lot," Sam murmured, not looking at either of us. "But I still think—"

"He still thinks it might be him and he'd feel better if you produced some evidence that it isn't!" Cromley snapped. "Isn't that what you're supposed to be doing? So why are you standing here?"

Because you didn't offer me a seat. "Actually, Sam hired me to prove it is him."

"Oh, for God's sake, whatever. Go do it."

"I need to talk to Sam. Before he gets any more loaded."

"I'm fine," Sam said. He put down his beer to prove it.

"Good. I wouldn't want you to get so crocked you went crazy and murdered your buddy here."

"Don't make jokes about that." Sam paled. "Ellissa helps me. I wouldn't hurt her."

"How do you know? Last night you were trying to tell me you're so crazy, you have no idea when, why, or whether you hurt anybody."

"Stop that!" Cromley jumped up as Sam melted into the couch. "Who the hell are you to call Sam crazy? Just because you don't get him? His head's in a different place. Somewhere people like you don't understand."

"I don't give a damn where his head is," I said. "He hired me to prove he's a serial killer, even though there's not a single shred of evidence that he might be. That's crazy."

"Why are you doing it, then? Why don't you just go away and leave him alone?"

I caught the fearful widening of Sam's eyes when she said that.

"Because," I said, "if he's right, he's even crazier."

7

I made it clear to Sam that my first choice would be to talk in his studio next door, but Cromley rose irritably from the couch, saying, "He doesn't like to be there all the time. Go ahead, talk. I have work to do. I can't hear when I'm working anyway." She stomped over to one of the easels and started setting out tubes of paint.

"Sherron is coming," Sam said over his shoulder to her. "With some collector. Maybe I should be there."

"I can't believe how you bend over backwards for that witch. We wouldn't have expected you to do that, you know. We'd have been much nicer."

"I know. But Peter said—"

"Oh, screw Peter." Sam flinched when Cromley said that. She went on, "And screw Sherron. She knows to come here if you're not there." Cromley found a palette board and started jabbing it with colors.

For all the crowded chaos in her studio and all her radiating, full-flood fury, the works-in-progress on Cromley's easels appeared to me desiccated, spiritless. All larger-than-life heads of women, they stared straight ahead out of the canvas without emotion. Cromley's style was realistic and carefully delineated, the photos she was working from pinned to the side of each easel. Her colors were off, in a way that should have been engaging: all a couple of ticks along the color wheel, so they were wrong, but balanced. But nothing about these paintings invited the viewer. They were distant, stifled, theoretical. A thought about a picture, it seemed to me, not the thing itself.

Sam turned back to me. "Come on, sit down. Have a beer."

"Forget the beer." But I did sit down. I glanced at Cromley, who was poking a canvas with a small stiff brush, her frown deepening as though the painting was disobeying orders. I said to Sam, "I need you to tell me everything you remember about the nights those women were killed."

"If I remembered anything, I wouldn't have come to you. I must have been drunk, I must have blacked out. I told you."

"Maybe. But I bet you haven't lost the entire day. I want you to tell me the last thing you do remember."

Sam put his beer bottle to his lips, discovered it was empty. He lowered it but didn't reach for another. "The first murder . . . that was months ago . . ."

"But it was the day after you got out. I'd think that would stick in your mind."

He laughed. "Like Ellissa says, my mind is different."

"Sam. Think."

"Yeah. Okay." The laugh flickered out. "I—I was at Peter and Leslie's that night."

"You remember that?"

"No, but I must have been. That's where I went when I got out, until I found an apartment. That's where the reporters all came. I didn't want to talk to them, but Peter said I had to, that he'd help me. So we did, until I couldn't take it anymore. I remember them all over the place, those reporters. But I think that was just the first day, I mean, the actual day I got out."

"Where'd you sleep that first night?"

"In the guest bedroom at their house."

"You woke up there the next morning? The day after you got out, the day of the first murder?"

He looked at me seriously, then nodded. "It was sunny. That room's too bright in the morning. I hadn't pulled the drapes when I went to bed because the cells don't have drapes and I kind of forgot. After that day, I pulled them."

"Then what?"

"Then what, what?"

"What did you have for breakfast?"

"Eggs."

"Cooked how?"

"Scrambled. No, no, fried, that's how Peter likes them."

"He cooked?"

"Yes. No, Leslie did."

"Who did, Sam? Peter or Leslie?"

"Leslie. Leslie cooked."

"After breakfast? Did you go out?"

Sam scratched his forehead, then got up and opened a fridge half hidden under a table. "You want another beer?"

"I'm not drinking. Sam—"

"Out. Did I go out."

"Did you?"

"*I don't remember!*"

"Oh, leave him alone!" Cromley threw down a brush and rounded on me. "Is this the best you can do? This is how you investigate?"

Sam looked as though he'd like to run and hide behind her skirt, but after a moment, new beer in hand, he came back and sat. "I'm sorry," he said, not looking at me. "But I really don't remember."

"Okay," I said. I didn't respond to Cromley, who stood behind the couch, flushed and practically sputtering. "How long were you at Peter's?"

"You mean, that day?" Sam wailed. "I said I don't know! Why—"

"Sam! Knock it off. I mean, all told. Until you got your own place."

"Oh. Oh. Sorry." Sam's thumb rubbed the cushion beside him, rhythmically working a single spot. "A couple of weeks. Maybe three. Peter helped me find an apartment. I wanted one in Queens near my old one, but Peter said not there. Not where—where Amy lived. He said we should look where the artists are, in Brooklyn. Because they'd accept me and it might be hard anywhere else. I'm a convicted killer, you know." He looked at me with an odd kind of hope in his face.

"I know that, Sam. Go on."

Deflated, Sam continued. "We found a basement apartment in Greenpoint. On a side street. So there aren't so many cars, or people going by, all that talking, laughing, footsteps—"

I interrupted his agitated account of urban life. "So until you found a place, you stayed with Peter and Leslie?"

"Yes. Leslie didn't want me there, but what could she do? Actually, Peter didn't, either."

"He said that?" That sounded unlikely.

"Oh, come on. He didn't have to. Peter's whole life got better with no crazy brother around. Big commissions. A-list parties, he used to tell me about them when he came up to visit. Him and Leslie, all lovey-dovey again. And suddenly, I'm baaaaaack, hiding in the closet when the doorbell rings."

"Sam!" Cromley said. "Stop it! It wasn't even like that. You just think it was. And besides, you have your own apartment now. You're an independent person. You don't have to worry anymore about what Peter thinks. Or Leslie." She perched on the back of the couch, glared at me, and began to rub Sam's shoulders.

Sam looked unsure. "But Peter always . . . Sometimes it helps me to think what Peter would want me to do."

"You're an independent person," Cromley repeated. "And Leslie? Please. She's just a giant walking ambition robot. Nothing to do with you."

Sam giggled at Cromley's characterization of his sister-in-law. "That's not nice. But anyway, if I'm killing skinny little blondes, she's not my type."

"Like me. I'm not your type, either," Cromley said.

No, but you could rapidly become mine. "All right, Sam, let's try last week," I said.

Sam's gaze stayed on the splattered floor. His fingers tapped his knee, fast and then faster. I was put in mind of a cat. Some cats, when you pet them, they might purr, but if the tips of their tails start to flick, you'd better notice. If you stop, fine. If not, a switch flips and you're suddenly in a maniacal mess of clawing, snarling, biting fur. I wondered how close Sam was to his switch, and what might happen when it flipped.

"Sam?" I asked again, and he looked unhappily up at me.

He was saved by a knock on the door.

A short silence, then a second knock, louder. "Oh, crap!" Cromley got up. "It's the Wicked Witch of the West."

She threaded the narrow path to the door. I expected her to yank it open, as she had for me, but her bearing transformed when she reached it. Pausing for a moment, she smoothed her skirt and her hair. Then she reached for the knob and opened the door in a calm, almost welcoming manner.

"Sherron!" she said in a tone that I supposed was meant to convey pleased surprise but that, to me at least, sounded as saccharin as it did desperate. "Come on in." She moved aside.

The woman in the doorway stood motionless, the way a prize stands on a pedestal when the curtain's pulled back. As all-of-a-piece and elegant as Cromley was disparate and unkempt, the newcomer gave the impression the multicolored smears on the doorjamb had been deliberately applied to highlight her ice-white hair, her ivory skin, her black sweater and skirt. She also gave the impression that she knew full well she gave that impression. She turned down the invitation with a tight smile, arched her long pale neck to look right past Cromley, and said, in a clear, low voice, "Sam."

Sam's eyes flicked to Cromley, to the floor, to me. To Cromley again. Cromley flushed. Unsteadily, Sam pushed himself up from the depths of the couch. Cromley spun and marched back to her easel. With a longing look at the beer he was leaving behind, Sam followed Sherron Konecki out.

8

I followed, too. What was there to be gained by staying behind with Ellissa Cromley, with her wild rage and pinched paintings? In the corridor, the black-and-white woman raised an eyebrow at me, gave me a slow up-and-down. The only colors in her calculated composition—she wore tiny diamond stud earrings, carried a black suede purse—were the pearl pink of her lipstick and the glacier ice blue of her eyes. She didn't object to my presence, but she seemed to be reserving that right.

Waiting a few steps down the hall was another man, a fellow with glasses, a bow tie, and a smile of boyish enthusiasm. He lit up when we came out. Sam, giving no one a glance, mechanically headed toward his own studio. After some fumbling at the lock, he pushed the door open and went in, the rest of us following, with me at the rear.

After Cromley's studio, Sam's was the relief of a silent empty sidewalk after the screaming of a cranked-to-eleven club. One of his diagnoses was OCD, and you could see it in the hyper-orderly layout of tables and easels; pads and pencils set out on tables; canvases squarely tacked on easels. Like some other outsider artists without technical training, Sam worked on unstretched canvas pinned to a backboard. In his case the canvas edges—there were three paintings underway—paralleled precisely the sides of the boards they were pinned to. Sketches taped to the wall hung parallel to each other, and the tape that held them followed their orientation, either long or wide. All of this seemed like it must be an old strategy of Sam's, to try to feel like he had some measure of control.

Not a word was spoken until the woman in black had closed the door behind us. She gave a brief smile of territorial satisfaction as she looked around the room, then turned to me. "Are you a friend of Ellissa's?"

"I don't think so. Bill Smith." I gave her my hand, which she glanced at before she shook. I guessed she was used to greeting artists and didn't want a paint smear on her cool, smooth palm.

"Sherron Konecki," she told me. "From Lemuria Gallery."

"I know," I said.

I'd never met Sherron Konecki, legendary Ice Queen of the New York art world, but the moment I saw her in the doorway I knew who she was. Konecki had owned and run the Lemuria Gallery for fifteen years. From the beginning, she seemed to have a crystal ball, an uncanny eye for artists about to hit. She'd sign unknowns other galleries would have nothing to do with, give them shows, make contacts for them, lease them cars and studio space, and lend them money—but never, it was said, a sympathetic ear—and when these bleeding-edge newcomers exploded on the scene, Lemuria was their gallery and Sherron Konecki was their dealer. Those early picks turned out to be right so often that the cause-and-effect balance had shifted over the years. These days, being discovered by the Ice Queen and signed by Lemuria was enough, by itself, to sanctify a career.

"You know me?" she said, with an amused smile. "Are you an artist, then?" She was readying the brush-off.

On my no, a small cloud of disappointment passed over the bow-tied man's face. Not hers, though. On hers, relief, like a swimmer finding the ocean clear of jellyfish. But following relief, suspicion.

"A collector, then? Or just a culture vulture?" She looked me over again, this time with the unmistakable implication that it might be a good idea for me to take a look at myself, too. Then she spun on Sam. "Are you letting people bother you? I told you I'd take care of people who want to see your work. You don't have to talk to anyone you don't want to."

"No, no," said Sam. "He's—"

"Sam and I go back a long way," I interrupted. "I just stopped up to say hello."

Konecki turned slowly back to me. "Really? And have you said hello?"

That I was now dismissed couldn't have been more obvious, but I smiled. "Sam and I are getting reacquainted. He's been away, you know."

She arched an eyebrow while she decided how she'd deal with me, allowed a few more moments to tick by. Sam, not good with suspense, crossed the room to look out the open window. I got the feeling he'd have kept on going right through it if there'd been a fire escape to run down.

"Well," the Ice Queen finally said. "A friend of Sam's." I wasn't sure whether the edge of incredulity in her voice was for the notion that Sam had friends, or that I might be one.

The clarification of my status had a different effect on the bow-tied guy. He came happily forward and offered his hand. "Michael Sanger," he said. "I'm so pleased to meet a friend of Sam Tabor's! I'm such a huge fan of his." He directed this expression of joy to me, Sam being as far away as he could get.

The Ice Queen stepped in to take charge of the situation. "Michael's a collector," she said. "He has an extraordinary feel for the new and important." A flash in her blue eyes, and then she had no more use for me. She called, "Sam! Come and meet Mr. Sanger." It was no suggestion, no invitation.

Sam, hearing it for what it was, turned immediately and trudged over. He shook Sanger's hand without looking at him, let Sanger's flood of praise wash over him without reaction. When Sanger asked, tentatively, almost reverentially, whether there was a chance Sam had new work and if so, whether he might see it, Sam didn't respond. But Sherron Konecki lifted her chin, such a tiny movement it might have come from a dressage rider working a champion horse. Sam at once crossed the studio again, to stand and wait, expressionless, in front of an easel by the window. Sanger and Konecki walked over to where they could see the work straight on, so I did the same.

The painting-in-progress was larger than the other work of Sam's I'd seen, maybe five feet on a side. The leafy branches of a maple tree cast shade on an emerald lawn and shadows on each other; through them, in places, translucent sunlight glowed with a radiance it was amazing to think had been made by mere paint. I was surprised, and impressed. This was better than the work in the just-opened gallery show, better than the sidewalk-art-fair paintings I'd described to Lydia: from six feet away, the picture was breathtaking. From six inches, where Michael Sanger was leaning in—I looked over his shoulder and then stepped back—the tiny battlefields, minute explosions, and agonized dying soldiers in swamps of ice and blood also took your breath away.

Like a punch in the gut.

"My God," Sanger said. "This is a whole new level. It's so focused, so distilled. And the shell picture"—this was the phrase the art press had coined for the overall painting, the large image that struck the viewer first—"is superb. Glorious in its own right. The light, the immediacy." He said this with a gleam in his eyes, a true admirer's thrill.

"Sam, it really is coming along beautifully." Sherron Konecki spoke like she was about to give Sam a gold star.

"Is this the direction you're moving in now?" asked Sanger.

Looking at the floor, Sam shrugged. His fingertips played on his thumbs. Konecki said, "Sam?" in a voice that was soft, but in the way of tiptoeing footsteps on creaky stairs.

Sam's hands stopped moving. He mumbled, "I guess. I don't know. I never know."

Sanger beamed. "Well, this one's marvelous. Do you have any sense of when it will be finished?"

Sam just shook his head.

"I'm afraid there's no way to tell, Michael," said the Ice Queen. "But if you'd like to put a reserve on it now—"

"Yes, yes. And if there are more like it . . ." Sanger turned again to Sam, who could only shrug.

"We'll have to see whether this starts a new series," Konecki said. "It's too early to know yet. Sam's not one of those capricious artists, always heading off in new directions before they've fully explored the aesthetic and technical potential of the work they've begun."

Lemuria handled a few of those artists, too, hummingbirds of style, medium, and content. The gallery's written materials called them fearless, future-focused, and unsatisfied to play it safe.

"Whatever comes next," Konecki went on, "I'm sure it will be extraordinary. What it will be, we'll just have to wait and see. But, Michael, you were one of the first to appreciate Sam's work. That's why I wanted you to see this. You can be first to see what comes next, too, if you'd like."

"I definitely would! Whenever you're ready, Mr. Tabor. I certainly don't mean to rush you. Would it be all right if I looked around the studio?" Sanger seemed unsure whether to address this question to Sam or his dealer, so he kept his head in motion between them.

Sam's face went a little grayer, but Sherron Konecki said, "Yes, of course. Though you understand the pencil sketches aren't for sale? Sam doesn't like to part with the sketches, on principle."

"Oh, no, that's fine. I'd just like so much to see them, if I may."

Konecki led Sanger to a wall of soft-pencil studies for the piece on the easel.

"Let's leave," Sam whispered to me when Konecki and Sanger had crossed the room. "While they're not looking. Let's go get a drink."

"Are you serious?"

"No. I think she has a taser. But what am I supposed to do? I can't paint with them here. What do real artists do when people are in their studios?"

"You're a real artist, Sam. Whatever you do, that's what they do."

"Just stand here? That's stupid. Why can't they leave?"

"What does Ellissa Cromley do?" I asked that because Sam's hands had started twitching again. I was hoping I could distract him, keep him calm, until they actually did leave. Not so he wouldn't make a scene—in fact I'd have been curious to see how Konecki handled that in front of an important collector—but I had more questions for him, and I wanted him to be in shape to answer them.

"Ellissa? She stops painting and has a beer with them. I think. That's what she does with me. I haven't been there when anyone else comes." He added, "It pisses her off that Sherron never comes."

"Is there a reason she should?"

"Sherron's always going there to find me. Like just now. And she knows Ellissa from that committee. She looked at her work when the committee started and decided she didn't like it, but Ellissa says she didn't *really* look. Ellissa says she's the one that got Sherron the golden goose—that's me," he clarified, in case I hadn't caught on, "and the least Sherron could do is *really* look at her work. Some of the other dealers sort of do, like if Ellissa's over here when they come and she invites them. But they really only stick their noses partway in. She says literally no one ever goes near her easels."

Probably because they're afraid of getting buried in a landslide, I thought, but only said, "Other dealers?"

"The ones who wanted me. Like Ellissa's gallery did. I liked some of them, but Peter said Sherron would be the best fit. I don't even know what that means."

"But the others still come here?"

"They like to look at my new work, how it's changing. They all say that, without saying why they think it would be changing. 'Because we got you out of prison, you lucky guy, we made you a free man even though you killed Amy. So go on, paint! Paint all kinds of new things, you're free! Except you're not free from us, we can pop in and bother you whenever we want and you have to put up with it because we got you out of—'"

"Sam. Sam! Stop." So much for my project of distracting him and keeping him calm.

Sam dropped his agitated arms and blinked at me. Across the room, Sherron Konecki and Michael Sanger started on a pile of drawings. Sam flinched when Konecki turned over a drawing and laid it on the previous one without aligning them, and then did it again.

"Shit," said Sam. "Maybe I should go to Ellissa's studio and get a beer. That really must be what artists do, because it's what Tony does, too."

"Tony Oakhurst? He comes to visit Ellissa, too?" I moved a little to my right so Sam would turn to face me and Konecki and Sanger would shift out of his field of vision.

"Don't be silly. She wouldn't let him in. Well, she would, because he's a super-big deal. But he doesn't come. They don't like each other very much."

"Why not?"

"He says her work is weak and gutless. She says he thinks that because she paints women and he's a big, fat sexist. He's really not fat, you know, but that's what she says. She says he's not my friend, he's just using me. I don't know what for. My mom always said I was useless."

Mom was a bad road to start down. I asked, "Does Oakhurst have a studio here?"

"In this building? God, no. Like I said, he's a super-big deal. That's him down there. The whole thing. Office, studio, apartment in the back."

Sam pointed out the window to a one-story, midblock building with rows of angled skylights. Once, it had been some kind of factory, the skylights providing cheap illumination for laborers. Now, if that was where Tony Oakhurst lived and worked, they provided light for a photographer known for his shadows.

Sam went on, "It must be nice, having a whole building. You can lock the door. Sometimes he calls me and tells me to come over for a drink. I like to go"—he lowered his voice—"except when Sherron's there. She's his dealer, too. He's the one who brought her up to Greenhaven to meet me. I once went over when she was there and when I went to the bathroom, they had a big fight. Well, Sherron was fighting. Tony was laughing, but he was serious, you know? It was about me. So I stayed in the bathroom."

Potentially distracting, and also intriguing. "About you?"

"Tony wanted Sherron to do something, I think to show some of his work, but she said no, it was over the line and would damage his brand. Like he's a department store. Or a cattle ranch." Sam laughed as though reacting to someone else's funny idea. "And Tony said, 'You can't be serious, you're showing Sam,' and she said, 'Painting's different from photography,' and he laughed and said, 'Bullshit,' and it sounded like Mom and Dad all over again, so I didn't come out of the bathroom until Sherron was gone."

Uh-oh, Mom and Dad. That didn't sound like a fight about Sam to me, but I got that our points of view were different. Something else occurred to me. "Sam, you drink with Oakhurst?"

"We hang out. *Now* you're going to give me the alkie lecture, right? You're going to tell me Tony's a bad influence, tsk, tsk, tsk, Sam. That's what Peter says, and Leslie, too, but she doesn't like anybody, especially anybody who says I don't have to listen to her and Peter."

Poor Oakhurst. Sounded like no one but Sam liked him. "How long have you been hanging out with him?"

"Since I got out. Kind of before that, even. He was on the committee. He used to come visit me upstate. He brought the COs fancy cigars. That's not allowed—you can't give them things—but he did. Him and Sherron, she came, too. Not together, except that first time he brought her. Ellissa came, too. After four years of only Peter, not even Leslie, suddenly every Wednesday, it's Tabor, Tabor, Tabor! The other cons made fun of me. 'Our baby boy's famous!' And you should have seen the guards staring at Sherron. I—"

"Stop. Go back. Oakhurst."

"I liked it when he came. We'd talk. He'd ask me all kinds of things about how it feels to paint. No one ever asked me that, except Peter when we were kids. It was cool to talk about." Sam's face darkened. "Except one day he asked me what it felt like to kill Amy. I didn't like that. I told him I didn't remember. I told him to stop asking that."

"Did he?"

"He asked it one more time, a couple of weeks later. I think he forgot I didn't want him to."

"Sam, you hang out with him," I said. "Could you have been with him the night of either of the murders?"

"Oh." Sam stopped. He looked out the window, then back at me. "I don't know. You think maybe? You think he'll remember?"

"I think I'll ask him."

Sam gave me Oakhurst's studio number. I called, gazing across the street at the skylit building while the phone rang. A young woman answered. Sounding bored, she told me Mr. Oakhurst couldn't speak to me at the moment. She was about to tell me he'd be available a week from never until I said Sam Tabor had told me to call.

"Oh," she roused herself to say. "Just a minute." She put me on hold, where Nina Simone was singing "Sinnerman." Nina had just started "My Baby Just Cares for Me" when the young woman returned to tell me, "Tony will be back in the late afternoon. Can you come by then? Say four o'clock?"

We said four o'clock and I hung up.

Sam and I watched Michael Sanger, across the room, lean close to inspect the top drawing on a pile. He didn't touch it, but Sherron Konecki lifted it to show him the one below it. Sam cringed.

"I don't want to have a beer with them," he said. "I want them to go."

I was contemplating whether clearing out Sam's studio for him was too much like babysitting when a knock came at the door. Sam looked shocked and thrilled, like he'd been spoken to by a burning bush. "Maybe it's Ellissa. Or Tony." He rushed to pull open the door. "Oh," he said. He regrouped, looking surprised but not disappointed. "Hi."

I started walking over so I could see who it was, but I didn't have to, because Detective Angela Grimaldi strolled right in.

"Sam." She nodded neutrally. "And Smith. Sticking close to your client, I see."

The Ice Queen had spun around at the knock. When she heard "client," she flashed her blue laser stare at me; then she fixed Grimaldi with it. "Who are you?"

Grimaldi's navy jacket was cut loose enough to hide her gun, but the gold shield she held out to Konecki told the story. "Grimaldi, Nineteenth Precinct. Just here for a look-see."

"What are you talking about? Sam's a free man. You have no right—this is harassment! Get out, now."

Grimaldi looked at Sam. "Who's this?"

Sam opened his mouth, but no sound came.

"I swear, if you're not out of here in ten seconds, I'll call the commissioner." Sherron Konecki whipped out a cell phone.

"You have his private number? Aren't you the lucky lady." Grimaldi sauntered through the studio. "Sam, you want to tell your watchdog why you invited me here?"

Sam looked like what he really wanted was to melt into the floor.

Konecki turned the glare to him. "Sam? What is she talking about? You *invited* the police here? Did they say you had to? It's not true. They have no right to bother you anymore."

Sam, his hands flailing but his arms not moving, looked at Konecki, at Sanger, at Grimaldi, at me.

"Sam! Come with me." Konecki turned her back and strode to the far corner of the room. There she stood, ramrod straight, waiting. Sam started in her direction.

It seemed to me his odds weren't good, so I went, too.

9

Back down on 39th Street, in front of the building that housed Sam's studio, I called Lydia. "The cat's out of the bag," I told her.

"That's good, it probably wasn't happy there. What are you talking about?"

I described the scene upstairs a few minutes ago: me trying to lay a lie on Sherron Konecki, suggesting Sam had asked both me and the NYPD to do a security assessment of his studio. For one thing, I was trying to honor Peter Tabor's request to keep this investigation as quiet as possible. Also, it seemed to me the suggestion of a simple paranoia in Sam might be easier for Konecki to take than his full-blown serial killer delusion. Or the small, but not nonexistent, possibility that he was right.

But Sam hadn't been able to play along. He'd tried for about a minute, but when your grip on reality is as tenuous as Sam's, a deliberate lie must be too slippery to hold. He'd spilled the beans—why I was there, what Grimaldi was looking for, what he was afraid would happen next. The Ice Queen had grown, almost unbelievably, paler as Sam babbled on. She'd said nothing, and her expression barely changed; but her glacier eyes would have frozen Sam to the spot if he'd met her gaze just once. Even when he'd talked himself out, he wouldn't look at her. She turned the ice rays on me, but she hadn't gotten me out of prison and she wasn't the source of my livelihood and fame, so all I got was a little frostbite around the edges.

"Well, maybe it'll fade to a tan," Lydia said. "What about the collector? Did he run away screaming when he heard about this?"

"He started by staying on the other side of the room like a good boy, politely looking through drawings while this drama went on in the corner and Grimaldi wandered around opening boxes and sniffing rags. But Sam couldn't keep his voice down. I'm not sure how much Sanger heard, but Konecki had one eye on him the whole time. So did I. Sanger's face was like some kind of cartoon worry-o-meter. When it hit 'dismay,' Konecki stopped the proceedings."

"How?"

"Adroitly. She interrupted Sam and said she'd heard enough. She told him her concern was for his work and his talent, and that Grimaldi and I were obviously dealing with this other situation, which would no doubt play out fine in the end."

"There's positive thinking for you."

"She said she and Sanger had another appointment, and this would be a good time for Sam to go home and get some rest so he'll be in top form for the Whitney opening."

"I'm surprised she's letting him out of her sight."

"What could she do? She had a big collector on the hook, with other artists she wanted to show him. Her car was waiting downstairs. She sent Sam home in it. He practically dove in through the back window."

"What makes her think he'll show up for the opening?"

"Because she told the driver there's a bonus in it for him if he parks outside Sam's building from now until then, sticks to Sam like glue if he goes anywhere, and delivers him to the Whitney at seven."

"That sounds kind of out of line for an art dealer."

"Sam actually didn't mind. The part he heard was, he gets to stay home all day. I think he may be secretly happy there's someone keeping an eye on him."

"So he doesn't kill anyone? It's not the right time for it."

"No, but if you're a werewolf, you worry that any light might be the moon."

"That's too deep for me."

"Anyway, Sam promised me he'd be at the Whitney. As Peter said, on time and with his pants on."

"Promised you?"

"But only if I promised him the same thing. So this is fair warning. You have a couple of hours to decide what to wear."

"I'm going, too?"

"And lucky they'll be to have you."

"Isn't it a big black-tie affair?"

"What, you don't have a tux?"

"What, you do?"

"No, but I have my funeral suit. And I'm heading out now to buy a black tie."

Lydia and I made plans to meet up before the opening and exchange accounts of the day. Then I called to make an appointment at my next destination. The wonder of a cell phone is, by the time I hung up, I was already there.

The office of The Tabor Group took up half a floor of a steel-and-glass 1960s high-rise in the West 40s. The place wasn't unfamiliar to me. Some of the meetings about Sam's case had been held here. I thought back to the scene around the conference room table: Peter, worried and uncertain; Leslie, angry and impatient; Susan Tulis, always professional, always kind. Sam hadn't been there; because of the nature of the crime and the possibility that he was insane ("Possibility?" Leslie had muttered), he'd been held without bail. When the team had needed to talk to him, we'd met at Rikers.

I gave the receptionist my name and settled in the waiting area, where the office's work glowed from backlit slide murals on two walls. The projects were recent ones, and they struck me as different from the work I remembered. The suburban office building on my left and the three private houses on my right seemed clean-lined, rigorous, and user-friendly, as the office's work had always been; but I also saw a startling originality and an audaciousness that were new since I'd last been here. New since Sam had gone to prison.

The door opened and Peter Tabor came through. Peter looked a lot like Sam, but more robust: five foot ten to Sam's five seven, rangy, not spindly, with compact muscles in place of Sam's droopiness; full, dark hair where Sam's was beginning to gray and thin. Peter's jawline was stronger, his cheekbones higher, his nose straighter. It was as though Sam had been the rough sketch, and Peter the improved and finished work.

"Smith." Peter shook my hand. "Come with me."

He led me to his office at the end of a glass-walled, wood-floored hallway, shut the door, and gestured me to a chair. I looked around; the place was messier than I remembered, more scattered papers, a pen on the floor. I picked it up and put it on the desk. Peter rapped on the glass that gave onto the drafting room, where sleek young people sat at sleek workstations in front of sleek computers. A tall woman with short black hair, high cheekbones, and heavy black glasses glanced up from leaning over a young man's shoulder. Leslie Tabor, Peter's wife and partner.

She said something curt to the young man, tapped his computer screen, and disappeared out of the drafting room. A few moments later she joined us in Peter's office.

"Smith." She offered me her hand. "Good to see you again."

I doubted she felt that, but aloud I agreed. As Leslie closed the door, Peter asked, "So, what's wrong?"

"Nothing critical," I said.

If I'd thought that would relax him, I'd been wrong. He perched on the edge of his desk and frowned. "Then why are you here?"

"Tell me, where was Sam the first couple of nights after he got out?"

"Where was he? At our place. He stayed with Leslie and me for a while, until I found him an apartment. Why?"

"Those first nights, he was there all night? He didn't go anywhere?"

"Not as far as I know. Les?"

Leslie shrugged. Arms folded, she remained standing, which struck me as a form of magical thinking: no need to sit, short meeting, just a question or two, no big deal.

"Would you have known if he'd gone out?"

"Well, not necessarily," Peter said, "if it was after we'd gone to bed. Though he'd have had to remember the alarm code, remember to turn it off, and then remember to turn it back on when he came in. I don't give great odds on that."

"That's true for, say, that whole first week?"

Peter spent a moment in thought. "The second night after he got out, I had a dinner with a potential client. I didn't get back until late."

I looked at Leslie.

"I had a Community Board meeting for one of our projects that same night. I got home around eleven," she said. "He was there. And the alarm was on."

"But he was alone for a while that night?"

"Oh, come on, Smith." Peter stood from his perch. "You know him. There's no way he went anywhere. The first day, there were reporters at the Greenhaven gate and at our house. The next couple of days were wall-to-wall people. I didn't let the press in, but even so, I couldn't come to work. Sam was freaking out."

"And God knows we can't let that happen," Leslie snapped.

Peter gave her a glance, then went on. "There were people there from the committee. Critics came, and artists. Sherron Konecki. Other dealers, too. And museum people, magazine people. I had to let them all in. We owed them."

I asked, "Other dealers?"

"People who'd helped get Sam out. Sherron jumped in and signed Sam right away, but dealers don't take no for an answer. Some are still looking to see if they can cut her out and steal him. That sour-faced woman, what's her name? She has a gallery, and the studio next to Sam's. She'd do anything to be his dealer. And, God, there was that jackass, Tony Oakhurst. Jesus, he wouldn't leave."

"He's a goddamn carrion beetle," Leslie said. "Have you seen his work? It's as creepy as Sam's." She radiated irritation, and I suspected Tony Oakhurst wasn't the only source of it.

"By the end of the day," Peter said, "Sam was practically hiding under the bed. Smith, what the hell is this about?"

"Sorry. I wanted to ask that before we got into anything else. It may or may not turn into a real problem, but I thought you should know. What he hired me for? He just announced it to his dealer and one of his collectors."

"Oh, shit. About the Martians, or whatever it is?"

"It's worse than Martians. Sam thinks he's a serial killer."

Leslie said, "Oh, Jesus Christ."

Peter frowned. "He what?"

"Two young women resembling Amy Evans were killed, each within a day of a big event of Sam's. His getting out, and his show opening. He thinks the events were what's called 'triggers' and that he killed them."

Leslie said, "You can't be serious."

"I am, because he is."

"What do you mean, he *thinks* he killed them?"

"He has no memory of either killing, but he doesn't remember anything else from the nights they happened, either."

"He was probably knee-walking drunk," Leslie said. "There are more nights he doesn't remember than ones he does. How does he even know this? That these women were killed?"

"It was in the *Post*, and on New York One. You didn't see it?" She shook her head. We both looked at Peter. He looked stunned, a little confused. A little like Sam. "I checked with the NYPD," I said. "The murders really happened. They wish the *Post* hadn't called it a serial killer this early, but they think it might be."

"The *Post*?" said Leslie. "The goddamn *Post*, and we're supposed to take it seriously?"

"It's what Sam hired me to prove."

"What?" Peter said. "That he didn't do it?"

"No. That he did. If it's true, he wants to be locked up before he kills again."

Peter stared, then gave a soft laugh. "I almost said, 'Is he crazy?' All these years, he can still surprise me. But now I get it. Locked up."

"Get what?"

"Sam wasn't unhappy in prison, you know. Leslie and I never thought this Free Sam Tabor thing was a great idea."

"You were part of it."

Leslie said, "Oh, give me a break. What choice did we have?"

"Seriously," said Peter. "Think how that would've looked, if we'd opposed it or even just stayed out of it. The jealous younger brother, finally rid of the wildly talented but crazy older brother and wanting to keep it that way. There were people already angry I'd known Sam's work all our lives and never told anyone about it. They said I had no right. No right! What about Sam's rights? Sam never *wanted* anyone to see it."

Leslie snapped Peter a look. "Enough. That's old news." Leslie turned to me. "These women who were killed, did he tell you anything at all? Their names? How he met them?"

"Their names were in the paper. He doesn't know anything else."

Peter said, "Because he didn't do it."

"When he saw it in the *Post*, he tried to turn himself in."

"To the police?" Leslie threw up her hands. "Oh, God in heaven!"

"The detective on the case thinks he's just looking for attention. She asked him for details, he didn't have them. The killer took trophies, he had no idea what they were."

"Trophies?" Leslie said. "What does that mean, trophies?"

"From the dead women. Some serial killers do that."

"God. Like what?"

"Jewelry, clothing, sometimes body parts."

Leslie blanched.

I said, "The detective wouldn't tell me what they have from these two cases. They save that to ask people like Sam, people who confess. She also checked out his apartment—"

"Wait." Peter held up a palm. "She had a warrant?"

"No, but he invited her in."

"Is that—even if he did, can she do that?"

"If she'd found anything she wanted as evidence, you might have an argument, but she didn't, so it's moot."

"No, it's not. People do this to Sam all the time. He lives in a fog. People take advantage." Peter ran his hand down his face, Sam's gesture last night. Peter probably wasn't even aware of it; and Sam, never knowing what to do in any situation, had likely copied it from Peter.

Jaw tight, Leslie said, "Smith. What did you mean about his dealer, that he announced it? He called Sherron Konecki to tell her he was a serial killer?"

"No. She was in his studio when the detective showed up." I told them about Grimaldi's entrance and Sam's inability to lie or keep mum.

"Hell!" Peter started pacing. "Michael Sanger, too? Do you have any idea who he is?"

"I gather he's a major collector."

"He's a high school English teacher who inherited a pile and got sharp investment advice. Now he's retired, he's a very rich man, and he's joined to Sherron at the hip. He's on the Whitney board, for God's sake, behind a donation of half a million dollars and a Kerry James Marshall. He's the one who got Sam into the *Violence* show."

"Sam said Konecki and Tony Oakhurst did that."

Peter's headshake seemed to me as much despair as negation. "Sam's a child in that world. That's probably what they told him, but seriously. Sherron's words may carry some weight, but Oakhurst? With all due respect, you don't think a museum listens to an artist? Sanger gently suggested to the show's curators that Sam would be a perfect late addition. Jesus, it would be a disaster if Sanger took this serial killer crap seriously."

"If it meant Sam could go back to painting alone in a basement, it might not be that bad."

Leslie looked at her husband. When he didn't speak, she said, "Damn it, Peter! Tell him the rest."

"Les—"

"Why shouldn't he have the whole story? It's not just about Sam anymore."

Peter met Leslie's fire-shooting eyes. He sighed. "Sanger wants to build a museum for his collection," he said. "Upstate. He's bought land and, because he's enamored of Sam, he got interested in us."

He stopped. Leslie waited for him to go on. He didn't.

"Christ!" Leslie turned to me. "A private museum's the goddamn holy grail of architecture, Smith. Sanger's museum could put us on the map. Where we should have been long since. But whatever great eye he has for cutting-edge art, he's still a high school English teacher. Not the kind of man who'd get excited about working with the brother and sister-in-law of a serial killer." Leslie glared at Peter, who didn't meet her eyes.

I said, "Sherron Konecki looked like she was doing major damage control."

Peter shook his head. "Damage control, mind control, Sherron can do it all. But it may not be enough. Shit! You see? This is the kind of thing that happens to Sam. Anybody else, the detective would have shown up while he was alone. It's just bad luck they were there. It's always bad luck with Sam." The desk phone buzzed. "Excuse me." He picked it up. "Yes. I don't know." He looked at Leslie. "Are we ready for the meeting?"

"Jesus, Peter. Did you ask if Asha's there with the numbers?"

"Oh, right." Peter asked Leslie's question into the phone. "Okay, let me know. Thank you." Back to me: "Sorry. We're short-listed on a big project and we're doing a run-through of our presentation. Okay. All right. I'll call Sanger. And Sherron. She knows Sam, so she knows. I'll explain to Sanger about the Whitney opening, how stressed out Sam is. Jesus, it never ends. Listen, thanks for coming. Whatever Sam said he'd pay you, send me the bill."

"That sounds like you think I'm through."

"Why wouldn't you be? Now that this is out?"

"Sam didn't hire me to keep it a secret. He wants to know if it's true."

"Today. Tomorrow, he'll be back to the Martians."

"The Martians haven't landed. Those women were really killed."

"Not by Sam. Smith, listen. What I said this morning about the haunted house? That only works if the monster's fake. As soon as it escapes and heads for your neighborhood, it's not fun anymore. If this gets out, people will drop Sam like a hot potato."

"And Michael Sanger will drop *you* like a hot potato."

"Yes, all right, that's true, and yes, it's a worry. You have a problem with that?"

"I'm only paid to worry about Sam's problems, not yours. I'm hoping I can prove where Sam really was, find something that makes it impossible for him to have killed those women."

"And if you can't?" Leslie demanded. "As long as there's even a hint that it's possible, it's a disaster. Sam killed Amy Evans—okay, he was drugged, he's an injured party, too. But a serial killer? A predator? Victim's rights! Me Too! Plenty of people already think he shouldn't be shown, killers of young women shouldn't be rewarded—"

"I've seen the press."

Peter said, "Then why go on with this?"

"Because Sam thinks he killed two women and he's afraid he'll kill another one."

"If I told you," Peter folded his arms, "if I said I was a hundred percent sure he was home all night both those nights, would you stop?"

"I might have, if you'd said that when I first asked. Now, no."

"That's my point! It doesn't matter how unlikely it is. You think it could be true. So will everyone else, and there goes Sam's career."

"If he had to choose between knowing he didn't do it and his career, there's no question what his choice would be."

"Sam doesn't always choose well. The whole idea's just another delusion and you know it. Leave it alone, let it blow over. He'll find something else to obsess about soon enough."

"I never saw him look as bad as he looked last night."

"You didn't grow up with him."

I regarded Peter. "Sam told me last night that the kind of paintings he does now are the same as he always did. What did you think about his work, when you were kids?"

"His *work*? They were just my weird brother's weird drawings, not his 'work.' Our parents wouldn't let him put them on the walls, not even in his room. Me, I drew stick figures and flowers because my kindergarten teacher said parents like to have pictures their kids made. Growing up with Sam, that was news to me, but I did it and they put mine on the fridge."

"Did that bother Sam?"

"I told him, just draw a flower. I didn't give any more of a shit about flowers and stick figures than he did. The stuff I liked was where no one but me knew what it was. I remember telling my mother once that a picture was five camels in a line. She gave me a 'that's nice, dear' smile and put it on the fridge. It was really two people and a dog in a snowstorm. Just do it, I told Sam. Every once in a while, a stupid flower. But he wouldn't. He had notebooks and sketch pads full of those other drawings. It was all he did."

"I didn't know about them when I was working for you."

"Damn right, you didn't. If anybody'd seen them, he'd never have gotten a deal. They would've said his work proved a predisposition to violence and he'd have been behind bars for the rest of his life."

"You just said that wasn't a bad place for him."

"I didn't know that then."

"And the predisposition to violence—would that have been wrong?"

"If two kids argued at recess Sam would run in the other direction. He's afraid of his own shadow."

"He committed a violent murder."

"On drugs!"

"And he drinks. Alcohol can give people courage, just like drugs do."

"That wasn't courage, it was psychosis. And alcohol gives Sam the shakes. He thinks he's high-functioning but he's a classic drunk. He slurs words and trips over his feet. If he'd been drunk instead of drugged when he took Amy Evans into that basement, she'd still be alive. Smith, please, when I—" Peter's phone buzzed again and he grabbed it. "Yes. Yes, all right, we'll be right there."

"I'm sorry, Peter," I said when he hung up. "I think you were right when you said Sam's latched onto me to keep him afloat. He needs to know I'm doing this."

Peter slipped his hands into his pockets. "Then how about this: Fake it. All he needs to hear is that you're on the case. In fact"—his face brightened—"tell him you found his alibis. Tell him he's—"

"Sam said he came to me because I'd never lied to him."

"Jesus Christ! What does it even mean, lying to someone who can't tell reality from a hole in the ground?"

"I don't know," I said. "But whatever it means, I'm not going to do it."

10

After another few moments where we stared at each other, Peter pulled open his office door and stalked down the hall. That left me alone with Leslie and her clenched jaw.

"Come on," she snapped. "I'll walk you out." In the reception area she opened the glass door, stalked through it into the hall, and kept going around the corner to the elevator lobby, where we couldn't be seen from the office. "Listen," she said. "I want to make something clear. Sam's through fucking things up for us."

"What do you mean?"

"Oh, come on. You heard Peter say Sam finally has a chance—well, that's true for us, too. But what he said about Sam living in a fog? I promise you, Sam is *not* the only one. When we met in school, Peter was a goddamn space cadet. A genius who couldn't find his ass with both hands. But I could see what he had. And I saw this, too—that I wasn't any kind of real artist and never would be. But together—" Leslie interlocked her fingers. "Peter needs me, or he'd stumble around in a haze of pretty sketches and never build anything. Architecture is full of people like that. Theorists. People who write and teach and never have to put their money where their mouth is. I wasn't interested in that kind of bullshit. I came into this field to make real buildings. Important buildings. I found out in school they weren't going to be *my* buildings. I can accept that because, with Peter, I can make it happen—and without me, he *cannot* make it happen. I'm the one who turns the pretty sketches into reality. That's why I picked him. But it never happened. Until now."

"And you're worried Sam will ruin that?"

"When Peter and I met, Sam was just Peter's weird older brother. He worked at a diner, for God's sake; no one told me he even painted. Any babysitting he needed, their parents did. Then they died and Peter somehow decided Sam was his job. Sam went from being that creep at Christmas dinner to a lead weight, and, Jesus, it's been one fuck-up after another. I could show you a list of missed opportunities as long as your arm, always because Sam needed this, or that, or new meds, or whatever. Even when he didn't, he was on Peter's mind. Have you ever seen a balloon deflated to where it just bounces along, two inches off the ground, instead of soaring into the sky?"

Her words were both melodramatic and sarcastic, but there was no question how seriously she meant them.

"I was going to leave him, you know," Leslie added. "We were going nowhere, just this nice little firm doing pleasant little work, and I'd had it."

"Sam told me you guys were having trouble."

"He noticed?" Her voice dripped venom. "Funny, Peter didn't. He was too busy tomcatting around and trying to hide it."

She must have seen my surprise, because she said, "Don't make the mistake of thinking I care about that. God knows that's not why I married him."

"Is that a fact?"

Leslie curled her lip in the direction of the office door. "Peter spends his day being the spacey, affable genius. At night, he wants . . . something else. Something a lot less warm and fuzzy. I don't play that."

"I see."

"I doubt it. I let him think I don't know what's going on, because I don't want to waste my energy on phony indignation, or him to waste his on bullshit remorse. I don't give a damn where he gets his rocks off."

"But you were going to leave him."

"Because the *work* was crap! Banal, second-rate. Beautifully detailed and built—that was me—but *meaningless*. I'd finally decided I was done. Then Sam was arrested. I had to stay through the whole damn thing or I'd be Hard-Hearted Hannah, and who'd hire that?

"And then something happened. Peter's work changed the instant Sam went to prison. Like he'd been reinflated. Can you see it?" She gestured through the glass at the backlit photos, didn't wait for me to answer. "Without Sam to worry about, Peter went to a whole new level. Critics are seeing it, clients are seeing it, Michael Sanger sees it, and I'll be fucked if I'm going to let Sam destroy that."

"Sam would never hurt Peter on purpose."

"So what? He has his hands full getting through the day. He doesn't have the space in his head to think about what he's doing to other people. Peter's about to screw up this meeting right now, I know it, because all of a sudden, Sam's got troubles again. You saw what a mess his office is. Every couple of weeks since Sam got out, I have to roto-rooter through it, and through the house, too, because Peter can't hold it together." She took a breath. "I'll tell you this: if Peter stays focused, the work coming out of this office will be brilliant. If he doesn't, it'll be shit." She locked her eyes on mine. "I will not let that happen."

"What are you saying?"

"You're Sam's friend. He trusts you. Keep him under control."

"That's not my job."

"It had better be someone's." Leslie spun and walked back through the door, to join Peter in the meeting.

I checked my watch, then headed back over to West 39th. Ike Cavanaugh, Ellissa Cromley, Sherron Konecki, and now Peter and Leslie—I seemed to be really good today at making myself unpopular. It was almost enough to make me want to put off Tony Oakhurst until tomorrow, to give the stars a chance to realign.

But I didn't believe in the stars.

—

The doorbell at Tony Oakhurst's building was answered by a pale, pierced young woman clothed in a black T-shirt, torn jeans, and ennui.

"Bill Smith." I gave her a card.

"The guy who called?" Languidly, she opened the inner door and said, "You can go in." Her tone told me she wasn't sure why I was getting the privilege.

At the far end of a huge, skylit room, two men stood over a long table sifting through photographs. I recognized Tony Oakhurst from magazine coverage and museum shows: tall and tanned, deeply lined face, thick black hair, worn and faded jeans, white T-shirt. The other man, unfamiliar to me, was shorter, paler, and balding. What hair he had left was combed back into a short gray ponytail. He wore an open black shirt, crisp black slacks, and spit-polished black wingtips.

The assistant drifted without haste to Oakhurst's side and spoke. Both men looked up and found me. "Just be a minute," Oakhurst called. "Feel free. You need anything, ask Amara."

He absently circled a hand in the air and turned his attention back to the table. The other man, who'd sent me a quizzical glance, dismissed me, too. The assistant, whom years of PI experience told me was Amara, went back to her computer.

I wandered the room. Whitewashed brick gleamed softly under the diffusing skylights. Lydia's brother Andrew is a commercial photographer, so I was familiar with the paraphernalia of lights, reflective and absorbent cloths and papers, umbrellas, tripods and monopods. Lenses covered a workbench, with camera bodies and filters between and beside them. Two other long tables held proof sheets, test strips, and various kinds of paperwork. Photos clipped to overhead wires swayed like laundry.

In a carpeted corner, a low glass cube sat between a pair of right-angled leather benches. The carpet was by Faig Ahmed; I'd seen his work in various gallery shows over the years. I'd never known anyone before this to actually put an Ahmed carpet on the floor.

Huge blowups of a few of Oakhurst's more famous photos filled the walls above the benches. He called himself a photojournalist—"I just shoot what I see"—but from early on his images of artists, musicians, actors, writers, cops, shop clerks, and strangers had hung in museums and galleries. There would be three in the *Violence* show at the Whitney, on the wall he'd offered to share with Sam.

I regarded the photos. Mick Jagger, ravaged and gloating, as though he didn't regret for a second selling his soul to the devil. Cardi B., from a recent magazine spread, looking ready to sell *your* soul to the devil. A photo labeled *Rick and Laurel*, all arms and legs, and more of them than could be accounted for by just Rick and Laurel. A days-old baby—famously, Oakhurst's own, from the second of his three marriages—with a horrified expression, as though he'd just realized what a mistake he'd made, getting born.

I was flipping through a coffee-table book of Oakhurst's work when I heard the meeting in the back breaking up. I looked up to see Oakhurst and the other man shake hands, turn, and head my way. I stood.

As Oakhurst neared, I could see the signature sardonic grin on his trademark stubbled face. "Smith? Good to meet you." A diamond earring in his left ear twinkled in the light. When he held out his hand, silver-and-turquoise bracelets jangled. His grip was maybe a fraction more firm than it needed to be. Crowds of tattoos ran up from both wrists and crawled into his T-shirt sleeves, to burst out again from the collar and slither up his neck.

The single snake wrapping my left arm might have turned green with envy, except it was already green.

"Be right with you," Oakhurst said. "Just let me see Franklin out."

Whoever Franklin was, the wide, gleaming smile he beamed at me was so full of pre-game hostility I just had to offer my hand. "Bill Smith," I said.

"Franklin Monroe. You're an art lover?" Monroe had a soft palm and a dead-fish grip.

"Very much."

"Ah. And Tony's work—it's . . . so unique."

"Yes, it is."

"Do you collect?"

I shrugged.

Oakhurst laughed. "Nothing to worry about, Franklin. Come on, let's go."

He steered Monroe toward the doorway, pulled the inner door open. They vanished. Eventually, still chuckling, Oakhurst reappeared and came striding over to me.

"Poor Franklin. That was pretty slick, saying you're an art lover."

"It's true."

"You scared him. He's afraid you're going to steal his limited editions."

"They're that limited?"

"They're . . . very specialized." Oakhurst regarded me. "Maybe sometime you can take a look at them. If you're serious."

For years I'd been hearing art-world rumors about the "specialized" nature of some of Oakhurst's images, images that were collected privately but never shown, even at Lemuria. Work darker than the photos in the book I'd been looking through, than in his other books, than in his shows. Work that, if Sam was to be believed, Oakhurst and Konecki fought over. I was far from sure it was a compliment that he thought I might be interested in that work.

Grinning, Oakhurst dropped onto the bench. "I normally wouldn't make that offer to a guy I just met, but I owe you one. I couldn't resist shining

Franklin on, since you gave me such a great opening. I told him you were here to look at the same things I'd shown him. Made him so nervous we closed the sale right there. Nice price."

"Glad to help."

"Like I said, maybe sometime you can see them if you want. But right now, you're not here to talk about pictures. You're a cop, right? And this is about Sam Tabor?"

"Not a cop. Private. I'm working for Sam." I sat, too.

"For Sam?"

"Some things he asked me to look into."

"Oh, I get it. Okay, you don't have to beat around the bush. He thinks he killed two girls."

"Jesus. Is there anybody he hasn't told?"

"Hey, I'm a friend of his."

"That may be. He also just announced it to Sherron Konecki, Michael Sanger, and the NYPD."

"Whoa. For real? And I fucking missed it?" Oakhurst threw back his head and laughed. "I bet Sherron shat ice cubes. So, what about you? Friend or foe?"

"Sam and I go back a long way."

"Doesn't answer the question."

"Employee."

"Fair enough. You want a drink? Scotch okay?"

"Bourbon, if you've got it."

He leaned, grabbed a bottle and glasses out of a low cabinet. Orphan Barrel Reserve, fancy bourbon for a scotch man. "Ice?"

"Not after what you just said about Sherron."

With a grin, he poured, handed me a glass.

"Thanks," I said. "You were one of the people who used to visit Sam upstate?"

"The minute his work first showed up in *Art Now*, I saw what he had."

"Which was?"

Oakhurst sipped. "His genius."

"Well, the art world agrees with you. Though I'm not sure Sam would."

"I'm sure he wouldn't. But I'm not talking about the same bullshit they mean. His technique, the tiny-to-big sleight of hand stuff, the shell paintings and the seed paintings. Yeah, yeah, yeah. Very cool, Sam. I mean 'genius' in the original sense. You know what that is?"

That was the game? Okay, I'd play. "That which dwells within. That which animates."

He grinned and raised his glass to me. "And that which animates Sam is different from that which animates the rest of us." Oakhurst circled his glass at the photos on the walls. "See here? This, my friend, is what you see when you pry open a turtle's shell. You're looking at what's inside. Mostly it's a lot of pain. But it's what's *real*.

"I can see it. A lot of people can't even do that, or more likely, they don't want to. So I can record it." He paused, gazing at his own photos. I wondered again about the "specialized" work. And about Leslie Tabor's branding Oakhurst a carrion beetle. "But Sam *creates* it. He has no idea, but it doesn't matter. He can't help it. He's doing what he has to do. I think the difference between Sam and the rest of us is he never had a shell."

Suddenly Oakhurst broke into a great, roaring laugh. "A naked turtle. What the fuck, right? You're asking what's great about Sam Tabor and I'm telling you he's a naked turtle. Remind me to lay this brilliant insight on Sherron. She can use it in his next catalog."

That wasn't actually what I'd asked, but I let it ride. "Listen," I said. "Sam says you and Sherron fought about him."

"You serious?" He paused. "Oh, what, that time he refused to haul his panicky ass out of the bathroom? God, Sam. That wasn't about him. I have work I want Sherron to show, but she says it's too over the top. The limited editions Franklin likes." He nodded toward the door. "I have other collectors, too, it's not like the stuff's going begging, but I want it *shown*. Sherron says she thinks it would be bad for my sonuvabitching brand, but I'm here to tell you she really thinks it'll be bad for *hers*. So I was making the point that anyone who shows Sam Tabor can't seriously be concerned about good taste. Which, by the way, is the enemy of good art." He took a slug of bourbon. "So, go back. What the hell do you mean, he announced he was a serial killer?"

"This morning, in his studio."

"To the cops, too, though? They were there? In the studio?"

"As it happened, yes, but he'd already tried to turn himself in."

Oakhurst stared. "My ass he did."

I shrugged.

"Jesus." Oakhurst raised his glass in the direction of the building across the street. "Fucking lunatic, Sam."

"He says you hang out together," I said. "Were you with him either of the nights those women were killed?"

"Aha. That's why you're here?" Oakhurst shook his head. "Sadly, no."

"Why sadly? Does that mean you think if you'd been with him things would've turned out differently?"

"It might just mean 'I'm sorry I can't provide an alibi.'"

"Why don't I think that's it? Do you think it really is Sam, this killer?"

Oakhurst finished his drink. He looked up at the photo of the baby, then swung his gaze back to me. "Here's what I think. When people have those naked-turtle moments? Those, my friend, are the only times, and the only people, worth giving a shit about."

11

I was on my way back to my place when my phone rang.

"Smith, it's Grimaldi."

"Detective. Always a pleasure."

"I bet you say that to all the cops. I'm calling to tell you you might be right."

"That's better than my usual average. About what?"

"I think I found another one."

I stopped. Stepping into a doorway to get out of traffic, I said, "Another what?" I knew, but I wanted to hear how she'd tell me.

"Woman, blond, stabbed, dead." A cop of few words, Grimaldi.

"Same type of knife? Same trophy?"

"I don't know yet. I'm getting the details. Until then, you only *might* be right."

"When?"

"A couple weeks before Tabor got out."

"Before?"

"Yeah. I widened the search. Thought that might put him out of the picture."

"Good idea."

"Gee, thanks," she said drily. "But since neither of us ever liked him for those other two, nothing changes. I'm just calling because I said I'd let you know."

"I appreciate it. Can you tell me why this one didn't show up on the radar before now?"

"I told you, I widened the search. Time and place both. This one was in freaking Hoboken."

Evening brought a chill to the spring air as I walked east to Chinatown to meet Lydia for a drink. Before we went to the Whitney we wanted to catch each other up on our days. The plan was to meet in front of her building, to lessen Lydia's need to walk far in heels while also lessening my chances of running into her mother. Our strategy succeeded for her, but not for me.

Lydia stood on the sidewalk by her front door in a sleeveless black dress, silver earrings, and shimmering black-and-red silk wrap. She waved. Beside her, her mother, grasping a string shopping bag, turned to see who the wave was for. She narrowed her eyes.

Walking up, I smiled at Mrs. Chin and said, "*Nei ho, Chin Taitai.*"

"Yah, hallo," Mrs. Chin muttered. She spoke to Lydia, looked me up and down, spoke again, and walked off.

"What did she say?" I asked.

"She said you look surprisingly respectable for once, but if we're going to a funeral I'd better go back up and change."

"What did she say before that?"

"You don't want to know."

At a bar a block away, Lydia, sipping her club soda, delivered her verdict on my day: "What a bunch of unpleasant people."

"Well, Sanger and Grimaldi."

"Grimaldi, okay. Sanger has too much money."

"You're just prejudiced against the rich. So—your day?"

"Nothing. I showed Sam's photo around and around. Mostly, a lot of headshaking. At the club where Annika was last seen, one of the bartenders, Malachi McCarty—"

"That's really his name?"

"Asks Bill Smith?"

"Touché. Please continue."

"He said, basically, *No, yeah, maybe, I don't know.* So did Kimberly Pike, a friend Annika ran into."

"At that same club?"

Lydia nodded. "They both think they remember a dark-haired white guy hitting on girls. Could've been the guy in the photo, or someone else. Could've been that night, or some other time. Could've sidled up to Annika, or maybe he didn't. As Kimberly said, that kind of thing isn't really memorable in a bar. It's what happens."

"Does it really?"

"Asks Bill Smith?"

"Unfair."

"Anyway, Kimberly and her date left early, and it was a busy night for the bartender, so neither of them could say. I called Tiffany's parents and Annika's sister and texted the photo to them, but more nothing. Which proves—wait, I know this one—nothing."

"A lack of bad news might be good news." I finished my beer. "Shall we go? You look spectacular, by the way."

"I was wondering how long it was going to take you to notice."

"Oh, I noticed right away. I just wanted to get the business out of the way so you'd be able to focus before you got drunk on my praise."

She blew me a completely deserved raspberry and we left. The heels and dress required a cab, so I hailed us one.

It was barely seven, but the streets around the Whitney were choked with limos and Ubers dropping off VIPs. "Early is the new fashionably late," Lydia informed me.

"Thank God I have you, or where would I be?"

"You know it," Lydia said, and kissed me.

I cut our cabdriver a break and had him leave us at 12th Street so he could turn and flee. As we approached the Whitney, we picked up chants and angry shouts.

"Protestors?" Lydia looked at me.

"Peter Tabor said this might happen. A group that calls itself Conscience in Art."

We turned down Gansevoort and there they were, behind NYPD barricades on the sidewalk across the street. A crowd I estimated at a hundred and fifty—a good turnout for a museum protest—carried signs that said VIOLENCE ≠ ART, CELEBRATING VIOLENCE CAUSES VIOLENCE, and PEOPLE BEFORE PROFITS, and their shouts said pretty much the same, sometimes in saltier language. Scattered through the crowd were signs aimed specifically at Sam, including what looked to be a bedsheet carried by three people that read, FOURTH FLOOR: MURDERERS' ROW.

"Are there other murderers in this show?" Lydia asked.

I shrugged. "All art criticism relies on hyperbole."

We walked through the police-cordoned path and up the steps to the entrance, protestors chanting, "Don't give in! Don't go in!" I resisted the urge to put a protective hand on Lydia's back.

"They have a point, though, don't you think?" she said. "The protestors?"

"They might if the show actually celebrates violence. I don't know if it does."

"Are you telling me to withhold judgment until I know what I'm talking about?"

"I'm not sure there's an answer to that that doesn't get me in trouble. Oh, wait, how's this—when have you ever not known what you're talking about?"

"Good job."

In the lobby, I gave our names to a mahogany-skinned young woman with cherry-red lipstick. She maintained a neutral expression as she scanned her list, then smiled brightly when she found us. She was walking a tightrope, I reflected: in case we were important, she'd best be nice to us, but if we were party crashers, she had to be ready to call in a surgical strike. Tomorrow and the next night would be cheese and white wine previews at descending member levels, and after that, the show would open to the public. Tonight was heavy hors d'oeuvres and fine champagne for donors, board members, art world titans, and other people the Whitney thought might benefit from understanding how much the museum esteemed them. In the lobby and throughout the open gift shop and restaurant, black-aproned waitstaff carried trays of champagne flutes or caviar on toast points, while a full bar stood by the windows facing the Hudson.

Packed in with the esteemed, Lydia and I rode the elevator to the fourth floor. The doors opened on a sonic blast of talk and music—a jazz trio, which seemed like a missed opportunity, given all the available violence-themed rap—underlaid with the tapping of heels on terrazzo.

We slid through the crowd, which was as much a show as the work on the walls. Spa-buffed men and women in black, white, black and white, or the occasional over-the-top pattern waved manicured hands in passionate argument, or stood as if transfixed by a construction or a canvas. I spotted Michael Sanger in earnest conversation with a heavyset black man, who might as well have been wearing Eau de Respectability. Both bore tasteful lapel ribbons identifying them as members of the Whitney board.

Navigating around the maze of temporary walls, Lydia and I passed a series of gray urban images etched on glass with video flames flickering behind them. We walked under the points of swords, scimitars, and spears swaying on fine chains from the ceiling, and skirted a bubbling crimson lake with an uncertain form bulging from the center. One wall was hung with dozens of small frames filled variously with cigarettes, bullets, and dollar bills. Around the other side of that wall, a crowd stood in respectful silence before three giant Tony Oakhursts, all of them images of the same bruised, bleeding, black male face: profile, three-quarter, straight on. I told Lydia who the artist was and she moved in to take a closer look.

As I studied the eight-times-life-size depictions of a man in pain, the aftermath of an event unshown, I felt a hand on my arm. I turned to see the ponytailed Franklin Monroe. With his tuxedo he wore a white shirt with black studs, but open at the neck and with the cuffs folded back over the jacket sleeves. His ponytail was tied with a black velvet ribbon.

"Smith, right?" When I admitted it he gave me a private, knowing smile. Nodding at the photos, he said, "So powerful, Tony. Always so powerful."

That was one attribute that was inarguable. "Yes."

Lowering his voice—pointless in that roar—Monroe leaned in and asked, "What did you think of the newest?"

I could see why Oakhurst had found baiting Monroe irresistible. His smug, secret-society air made him a balloon begging to be burst. Never mind that he'd apparently inducted me into the secret society. And that the secret society was one that paid Oakhurst what he'd called a nice price.

"I'm not sure about them," I said. "What did you think?"

"You're kidding. They're right up there with his best. Pushing the envelope! You didn't like them?"

"No, I didn't say that. I'm just—sometimes it takes me time to decide how I feel about things like that." Things like what, I could only guess.

Monroe's smile widened and grew more condescending at the same time. "I knew right away," he said. "I'm buying the whole series."

You didn't know until Oakhurst told you I was interested, I thought, but said nothing.

"It's always good to meet another collector of Tony's. Of the limited editions." Monroe's tilt of the head toward the crowd around us implied we were slumming amid the ignorant hoi polloi. "If you'd like to get together, give me a call." He reached into his jacket, withdrew a slim, ostrich-skin wallet, and handed me a card. "I can show you what I have. Tony's work, of course, but other things I think you'll like."

"Thanks." I took the card, wondering if I was supposed to give him a secret handshake, but with another small smile he faded into the crowd.

Lydia came back to join me. "Who was that oil slick you were talking to?"

"One of Oakhurst's collectors. He buys the work Konecki considers too dark to show. He wants me to come over and see what he has."

"Did you just wink at me?"

"Never. Come on."

We stepped outside Oakhurst's reverent semicircle. At the other end of the same wall milled a crowd that wasn't silent. Men and women murmured and nudged each other toward three tacked-up, unframed canvases. We watched people lean in for a closer look and jerk back as if bitten.

"I guess we're here," Lydia said.

"Go see," I said. "Before I introduce you."

Lydia slid through the crowd and approached one of Sam's paintings, a sagging-roofed barn in an overgrown field, late afternoon light warming its peeling red sides. She paused, looked it over, took another step in and leaned forward. After a few more seconds she calmly stood straight again, turned, and came back to my side.

"Oh. My. God," she whispered. "He's crazy."

"Told ya so. Come on."

I led her to where Sam was backed up against the wall, surrounded by hand-shaking, smiling admirers. He looked like a man standing on a shark-ringed island watching the tide rise. Well, at least he was sober enough to stand. He did, in fact, have his pants on, plus a jacket, white shirt, and tie. The tie was blue with yellow alligators on it. Anyone else, I'd have thought he was a Lacoste fan. Sam was probably a fan of alligators.

Peter was playing lifeguard on one side of him, Ellissa Cromley on the other. Peter welcomed people to Sam's little island, introducing Sam, who mechanically shook hands. Cromley glowered, scanning the crowd as if for pirates on the horizon. Tony Oakhurst, in white T-shirt and black jeans, kept breaching the crowd like an orca, camera snapping. Leslie Tabor, tight-jawed and stunning in black silk pants and a tuxedo jacket, stood just beyond Peter, a landing craft moored offshore.

Even farther offshore, I noticed Ike Cavanaugh riding at anchor. He was positioned across the room, wearing a rumpled gray suit, scowling at Sam and Sam's admirers, waiting, maybe even hoping, for some kind of trouble. I pointed him out to Lydia.

"He looks like the charmer you told me he was," she said. "Who would have invited him?"

"I doubt anyone did. He must have badged himself in. He could always say he was with an NYPD security detail, something like that."

Lydia eyed Cavanaugh. "Well, he's not helping the sartorial reputation of cops worldwide."

We shouldered through to Sam, in a chorus of "Hey!" and "There's a line here!" When Sam spotted me, it was as though he'd seen a rescue ship looming.

"Smith! Get me out of here."

"Don't do it, Smith," Peter said, low but clear. "Stay with him, keep him calm, but do not let him leave."

I moved directly in front of Sam to give him a brief break from his fan club. Lydia caught on and planted herself beside me. We made an effective levee, though I knew it couldn't last. I introduced Lydia to Sam, and to Peter, Leslie, and Cromley. Sam gave her the mechanical handshake he'd been handing out. Peter, two-handed, thanked her for coming. Leslie shook her hand in a cold, businesslike way. Cromley, narrow-eyed, offered her the single pump you'd give an enemy before a duel. Lydia smiled, her eyes returning to assess each person after the formalities were over. Peter's eyes, I noticed, also assessed her. Leslie, I noticed, noticed that, too.

Sam turned to me. "Come on, Smith. I hate it here. Can't we leave?"

"Not yet," I said. "Soon."

Tony Oakhurst, grinning, darted out from the crowd again. He snapped my photo, lingered a little longer over one of Lydia, and dove back through the surf.

"Can I at least have a drink?" said Sam.

Peter shook his head.

"No," I said. "Later for that, too."

"Not much later," Sam said. "I'm beginning to lose it. You know I lose it."

"You're not going to lose it. Just a little longer. Then you can go home."

"I don't want to go home. I want to get a drink."

"Okay, that, then. We'll get a drink." I ignored Peter's frown. "Right now, shake hands."

Lydia and I stepped aside, and a ruddy woman with a David Hockney painting silkscreened on her dress thrust ring-encrusted fingers at Sam, gushing about his courage in telling truths everyone else denies. Sam gawped at her bejeweled talons. Peter nudged him. Flinching, he stuck out the mechanical hand.

The woman was replaced by a jolly Asian man, followed by a pair of slim, handsome black men in tuxedos. Then the sea parted, and onto Sam's little island, like some 17th-century privateer striding onto captured ground, stalked Sherron Konecki.

Konecki was in bone white, including enamel-and-silver earrings, kidskin clutch, and stilettos. Again, no color in her makeup except the subtle pink on her lips. Nothing to distract from those piercing, glacial eyes.

Her gaze swept us all. Tiny muscles in her face registered her reactions: forbearance for Peter, dismissal for Leslie, disdain for Cromley, disgust for me, mild interest for Lydia. Lydia smiled brightly, which threw Konecki off, just for a second. She returned a thin smile, focused on Sam, and spoke.

"The wall looks brilliant, Sam. Hanging the barn in the center, I was right about that, I see. Your work is the talk of the show. You're having quite a success."

What Sam looked like he was having was a heart attack. His face had gone ashen and his fingers drummed fast on his thumbs.

"Now, come with me," Konecki said. "There's someone I want you to meet."

"No! No." Dread in his eyes, Sam surveyed the churning art-lover ocean. "I want to stay here. No, I don't want to stay here. I want to leave!"

"Sam," Peter said. "Just a little longer. Then we'll take a break, we'll go to the lounge. You don't have to go with Sherron"—he gave Konecki an apologetic glance, which she icily shot back—"but let's just stay here until Michael Sanger comes over. He got you into this show. You need to thank him."

"Thank him? I hate him! I hate everyone who had anything to do with this."

Peter's face registered end-of-his-rope despair, a state I imagined was familiar. Leslie shook her head grimly, as though watching a predicted, preventable disaster unfold. As for Konecki, I could almost see her mental GPS recalculating the route to what she wanted.

"All right, Sam, I'll bring Emilio over here. He's an important curator, and you really should meet him."

"No," said Sam. "Let's go."

"Sam," said Peter, his voice controlled.

"Sam," said Konecki, cool and commanding.

"Sam," said Cromley, cajoling, almost cooing.

None of these approaches worked. Sam's agitation mounted. I was on the verge of grabbing his arm to lead him away before he did actually lose it when Tony Oakhurst reappeared, camera slung across his body and a glass in each hand. "Hey, beautiful."

Planting a kiss on Konecki's cheek before she could jerk her head away, he handed a glass to Sam. Sam's whole face lit up. He seized it and in a second he'd thrown back half the contents. He sputtered and coughed, and Oakhurst said, "Hey, champ, slow down. I had to smuggle those up here."

"Jesus, Tony," Leslie barked. "What the hell?"

Peter reached to take the drink from Sam, but Sam twisted away, grinned, and drained the rest.

"Can I have that one, too?" He pointed at Oakhurst's own glass. Oakhurst laughed and held it out. Sam grabbed it and managed to gulp down a fair amount before Peter got a hand on it. In the tug-of-war, scotch sloshed out and down Oakhurt's T-shirt. He seemed delighted. Sam laughed, jerked the glass from Peter, and slurped down what was left. He loosened his tie, slipped it off, and waved it over his head like a lasso.

"For God's sake." Leslie yanked down Sam's circling arm. Through gritted teeth, she hissed at Oakhurst, "Asshole." Oakhurst pressed his palms together and cocked his head in mocking apology. Leslie pulled Sam. "All right, let's go."

Sam stumbled but kept laughing.

Konecki's imperious "What are you doing?" got no response. Sam, looking like he was enjoying himself, allowed himself to be towed through the objecting crowd. Oakhurst elbowed people aside to shoot Sam's exit as though it were a choreographed event and he its official photographer.

Peter, on the verge of following, stopped to apologize to Konecki. She was livid, her complexion a fiery contrast to her pale dress and hair. Cromley, on Konecki's other side, tried a placating smile. In a voice that sounded as if she meant it to be both confident and soothing, she said, "It doesn't matter if he leaves. Sam's work speaks for itself."

Skewering Cromley with a look of barefaced contempt, Konecki spun and stalked off.

I gestured to Lydia, and we cut through the crowd after Sam and Leslie. I caught a glimpse of Cavanaugh, across the room. His sneer seemed to take in not just Sam's departure but the entire evening. He caught me looking at him and flipped me the bird.

Behind us, Cromley, suddenly alone, cried, "Wait!" as she saw her ticket to legitimacy, even importance, in this crowd disappearing toward the elevator.

12

Lydia and I caught up with Leslie and Sam. "I've got this," I said to Leslie. "You can stay."

She practically spat her answer: "Why would I want to stay?"

Cutting through the press of people, Peter reached us at the elevator. He grabbed Leslie's shoulder; the band was too loud for me to hear what he said, but her voice was louder and her answer was "For God's sake, do you want Sanger to see him like this?" She waved Peter away. "You stay. Go make nice."

When the elevator door opened, though, Peter got in with us. We were squashed in tight with other early leavers, usually a situation that would drive Sam to the edge, but he was giddy with relief and guzzled scotch.

Things changed when we hit the lobby. Through the thicket of suits and cocktail dresses waiting for the elevator or perched on stools in the glassed-in bar, I saw that the museum's doors faced a larger, louder, more amped-up group of protestors than when we'd come in.

I stopped our progress. "We can't take him out that way. Come over here. I don't want them even to see him."

We retreated back toward the elevator, Leslie gritting her teeth, Peter looking around in concern and Lydia in attention, and Sam seeming happily unaware of anything except the alcohol coursing through him and the knowledge that he was being allowed to leave. I crossed the lobby to speak to a security guard.

"That's him?" the guard said, eyeing Sam while I explained the situation. "Shit, he don't look like much. Hold on."

He spoke into the two-way radio on his shoulder, then said, "Yeah, come on, this way."

I waved to Lydia, who had the Tabors corralled. She'd taken off her silk scarf and tied it onto her purse strap. Slipping the thin strap across her body to keep her hands free, she shepherded Sam, Peter, and Leslie over to join me and the guard. He led us to a staff door, pressed a code, and took us through scuffed back corridors, where signs read ABSOLUTELY NO SMOKING and YIELD TO ART IN TRANSIT. We left by the door beside the huge, closed loading dock in the back.

Outside, we found ourselves facing the chain-link fence that cut the West Side Highway off from the loading dock. Our choices were left, which would take us around to the front of the museum, or right, past one of the neighborhood's few remaining actual meatpacking plants and over to the club-filled party streets of the Meatpacking District. We started that way.

Not quite in time, though.

Maybe someone outside had caught sight of Sam through the front windows and guessed where we were going; or maybe the protestors had sentries back here; or maybe it was just another of Sam Tabor's bad-luck breaks. We'd gone about ten steps when a woman's voice shouted, "Hey, he's back here!" Another took it up: "It's him! It's him! Oh my God, it's him!" A man: "In the back!"

A few seconds earlier and we could've retreated inside; a few seconds later and we'd have been on the next block, out of sight. But the door had locked behind us and here we were.

People surged around the corner of the building. Voices yelled, "Killer!" and "Murderer!" Fists were shaken and fingers pointed. This antiviolence crowd was out for blood.

Sam looked around in drunken interest. I grabbed his arm. He tried to pull away.

"Get out of here," I snapped to Peter and Leslie. "Lydia and I have this."

"I'm staying with him," Peter said.

"Like hell you are!" Leslie yelled over the rising roar. "So we can be photographed in this shitstorm? Smith can handle it."

As though to illustrate her threat, Tony Oakhurst materialized, grinning, camera clicking everywhere. Cell phone flashes started going off, too, and chants arose: *Sam, Sam, the killer man* and *Whitney, say no! Tabor must go!*

"Beat it!" I said to Peter and Leslie.

Leslie manhandled Peter off to the right, where the museum butted up against the packing plant. She had to push him at times, but finally they disappeared around the three refrigerator trucks pulled up to the plant's loading dock for the night. Good. It wasn't that I gave a damn about their bad publicity. I just didn't want to have to worry about them, too, when push came to shove—as it literally did a moment later, when the back of the crowd surged against the people at the front and someone stumbled into Lydia. She heaved him away, he fell against a woman, and the woman, cursing, threw a water bottle not at him but at us. It bounced off my shoulder.

"Come on," I said to Lydia, and we retreated to the building wall, shoving Sam up against it. Lydia kicked off her shoes, becoming shorter and more lethal. We stood in front of Sam, a levee again. Laughing, Sam kept peeking out and ducking back behind us. I stepped forward and roared to the crowd, "Back off!"

A woman yelled, "You're shielding a killer!"

"Should I move so you can kill him?"

I lost her answer as a guy with a combed Brooklyn beard stomped up and screamed in Lydia's face. Big mistake; he should've screamed in mine. I'd have flung him away. Lydia kicked him in the balls so hard he keeled over and heaved.

"Oh my God, they're beating people!"

"Animals!"

"Do something!"

I was hoping someone would call the cops to protect them from us animals. I could do it, and if things got any worse I would, but taking out my phone would show my gun and we didn't need that kind of escalation. Sooner or later, the cops around the front of the building would figure out they'd lost half their flock.

Another wave of people came surging around the corner, and more missiles started flying. Water bottles, gravel, trash. Sam stuck his head out from behind me just in time to get hit in the face by a rock.

His response was electric. Like a rabbit bit by a snake, he leapt and took off. Lydia and I both tried to go after him. The crowd rushed us. The people with the bedsheet sign had made it around from the front and stormed forward, entangling everyone except their actual target, who raced away.

Smaller, more supple, and faster than I am, Lydia ducked down. She hoisted up the bottom of the bedsheet sign and scooted under it. Slicing through the crowd, she pushed a woman aside, kicked a man in the shins, and ran off, barefoot, after the jackrabbit Sam had become.

I hoped her tae kwon do calluses would be enough. In case they weren't, I scooped up her shoes. Brandishing them like a crazy man, I roared and bellowed and kept the crowd busy so they wouldn't notice who was missing. It wasn't fun—two more water bottles clonked me; this was a well-hydrated mob—but I didn't have to keep it up for long. Cops finally came charging around from the front of the building. They waded in, pushing, shoving, yelling at everyone to calm down. I dropped my arms and pressed back against the wall.

Cops lofted billy clubs but didn't bring them down on heads. Command must have figured the threat would be enough for these arts folks, and they were right. People on the perimeter started to melt away. As the crowd got smaller, the shoving eased off. The yelling continued, but now it was focused on the cops, not me. I slunk low, crab-walked against the building, swung up onto the meat plant loading dock, and squeezed between the plant's roll-down doorway and the first truck. I inched along until I was past the third, then jumped down and broke into a run as, behind me, voices shouted about free speech, police violence, power, and the patriarchy.

13

Once I'd gone a few blocks and the yelling had faded, I stopped and checked my phone. Nothing. No point in calling Lydia. If she'd found Sam, she'd have let me know. I tried Sam's number. He didn't answer. That probably meant he was still running. If he found a place to stop, he might not call me, but chances were he'd answer if he saw I was calling him. If he had his phone with him. If it was on.

So, assuming he was still in motion, where would he go?

He'd keep moving until he couldn't hear the sounds of the crowd anymore. Then he'd fall into the first bar he found.

Or try to. Here in the Meatpacking District, the cobblestone streets that had seen a century of meat wagons, teamsters, and slabs of beef now saw Google staff, venture capitalists, and fashionistas. The old bars had faded away, replaced by new ones with velvet ropes and bouncers. No way Sam would have gotten in any of these doors even if he hadn't been disheveled, bruised or maybe even bleeding, and already drunk.

But a couple of blocks east of here, there were still some old-fashioned watering holes. Did Sam know that? Did Lydia? I texted them both to call me. It also occurred to me to phone Tony Oakhurst, who, as Sam's drinking buddy, might have some idea where he'd go. Oakhurst didn't pick up so I left a voice mail, and also a text. *Looking for Sam, call me*. If he was still busy documenting the antiviolence melee, he might not check his phone for a while, but it seemed worth a try.

As I started working my way east and north, my phone rang: Peter. I debated, but he might be able to help. "Smith."

"What the hell's going on? Where are you guys? Is Sam okay?"

"He bolted. You have any idea where he might go?"

"You mean you lost him? What the fuck, Smith?"

"Any ideas?"

"I can't believe this. Those people are after his head! How could you lose him?"

"Let me know if he shows up or gets in touch," I said, and cut the call. I had no faith that Sam would have the wherewithal to get in a cab, or on the subway, and navigate to Peter's Park Slope town house, but I didn't want to hear that question from Peter again. I was already hearing it from myself.

I made quick trips in and out of a few bars, showing Sam's photo, getting nothing. As I came out of one on 15th off 8th, I got a text from Lydia: *Lost him. 16th and 7th.*

I texted, *Stay put*, and sprinted over. I spotted her on the corner, leaning on a wall. Her dress was rumpled, her hair damp with sweat, and her panty hose were shredded on her bare, grimy feet.

"If you tell me I look like a hooker, I'll slug you," she said as I jogged up.

"I wouldn't be the first?" I handed over her shoes.

"You wouldn't be the fifth. Bare feet bring all the perverts out. Stand still." She hung onto me with one hand and, hopping around, tugged the panty hose off and slipped the shoes on. "Though honestly, it's more comfortable than wearing these. Sam turned up this block, but when I got to the corner, he was gone."

I looked up and down the avenue. "I'm thinking he'll be desperate for a drink," I told Lydia. "Hoping, actually. That would mean he's probably in a bar here somewhere."

"All right," Lydia said. "We'd better start looking."

"You don't want to go home and change or something?"

She smiled. "I don't know if I want to kiss you for that or pop you one. I love that you're worried about me, but we have a client in trouble. Let's go."

"I know which I want to do," I said, and kissed her.

She smiled. "Good choice. Now, like I said, let's go."

We started after Sam, Lydia heading south, me north. Our plan was to each cover at least ten blocks, including weaving up and down the side streets for a block in each direction.

I got nowhere. From Lydia's telephone silence, I knew she was doing about as well. I showed Sam's picture on my phone to bartenders and bouncers—in these places, peacekeepers more than gatekeepers. Two of the bartenders knew him, but no one could tell me they'd seen him tonight. "Doesn't mean he hasn't been here," one bartender said. "But if he was, I didn't notice."

On a normal day, that would be Sam, forgettable; but with two drinks already in him and an air of diving for cover, he'd have stood out to any good bartender, if only as someone to keep a wary eye on. Still, I asked, "Can I take a look?"

"Knock yourself out."

I didn't find Sam, so I left my card and a ten-dollar bill, as I had in each bar, asking the bartender to call me if Sam came in. I was pushing through the door out to the street when Lydia called.

"Found him?" I asked.

"No. But something interesting. That photographer friend of Sam's. Tony Oakhurst? I saw him down the block, going into a place I'd just come out of, a place where the bartender knew Sam. He looked like a man on a mission, so I stopped and waited. He came out a minute later, skipped the next place I'd tried, and turned up the side street."

"You think he's doing what we're doing."

"And I think he knows where to look."

"Stay on him. Where are you?"

She told me. I pocketed the phone and ran.

Two texts later, I caught up with Lydia on 13th and 6th, outside a place called Bar Six. "Oakhurst went in a couple of minutes ago," she said. "He didn't come out, so I went in, just as far as the bar. He and Sam are in the back."

"Good," I said. "Come on."

I held the door for Lydia and followed her in. The place was dim, but not a dive. A neighborhood bistro: photos on the walls, their reflections in the mirror behind the bar on the left, a long banquette on the right, small tables in the back, mellow conversation-buzz in the air. As we walked through, Lydia got the up-and-down from the barflies, and then I did, too. A couple of them were probably wondering if I was responsible for her raggedy look, and if she needed help. A couple of the others were more likely considering whether it would be worth it to try to cut me out and get in on the action themselves. Without question, Lydia registered all of it the same as I did. She continued to the back as though strolling alone on the beach.

At a table in the rear, Oakhurst and Sam were laughing over something. Sam's upper lip was speckled with tiny drops of dried blood; his nose was purple and swelling, with a cut on the left side. As we approached, they both looked up.

"Hey," said Oakhurst, swinging his hightops off a chair. "What's shaking? Come on, you guys, sit down."

"Did you get my call?" I asked Oakhurst, still standing. "Sam? Did you?"

Sam shrugged. He took out his phone, looked at the screen, and nodded.

Oakhurst gave me a grin. "I wasn't sure Sam wanted you to find him. I thought I'd wait and ask."

"Did you ask?"

"Not yet. Hey, Sam, you want these guys to find you?"

"Yeah, sure, why not?" Sam looked at Lydia. "What happened to you?"

"A client made trouble for me."

"That's not very nice of them."

"Come on, Sam," I said. "Time to go."

He looked at me like he didn't know what I meant. "Me and Tony are hanging out."

"Not tonight. Let's go."

"Hey," Oakhurst said. "Come on, you guys, sit down, have one with us."

"Another time. Sam, get up or I'll haul you out of here."

"Don't do that. I don't want you to do that."

"Then let's go. Night's over."

He lit up as though he'd just thought of an unanswerable argument and pointed to his glass. "I'm not finished."

"Finish."

Lydia gave me a glance when I said that, but I was figuring Sam plastered and reeling would be easier to handle than Sam balking and belligerent.

"I'm not finished, either," Oakhurst said. "It's okay, Smith. I'll get him home."

"No, you won't. Sam?"

Sam just sat staring at me, so I moved in, clamped his arm, lifted him from his seat. He staggered and snatched at his glass.

"Hey!" barked Oakhurst, also standing. "Leave the guy alone."

"Yeah!" said Sam.

I started tugging Sam through the bar. Lydia briefly stayed behind, staring down Oakhurst as I marched Sam out.

Oakhurst's "Well, shit!" echoed as we moved toward the door, but he didn't try to stop us.

14

Lydia joined us outside and I hailed a cab. Once Sam was lodged firmly between me and Lydia, I told the driver, "Two stops." I gave him Lydia's Chinatown address and Sam's, in Greenpoint.

After a block or two, Sam looked around. "Where are we going?" He seemed to have already forgotten he was pissed at me for pulling him out of the bar.

"We're going to drop Lydia off. Then I'm taking you home."

"Who's Lydia?"

"Next to you."

He turned to Lydia, regarded her, and nodded. "Hi. I'm Sam."

"Hi." Behind Sam's head, Lydia spoke to me. "You understand home isn't where I'd intended to spend the night?"

"Shit. You're killing me."

"I told my mother it would be an all-night job. She squinted at me."

"I'm going to shoot myself."

Sam threw me a swift, wide-eyed look.

"He's just joking." Lydia patted Sam's hand.

"I'm sorry," I told Lydia. "You have no idea how sorry I am." I checked on Sam. He was leaning forward, staring out the front window. I dropped my voice. "But if there ever was a stress night, this is it. I want to be with Sam every minute, so if a woman gets killed in New York tonight, he can't claim he did it." I took half a second to consider accomplishing the same thing by locking Sam in a closet at my place before I gave an apologetic palms-up.

"You want me to come?" Lydia asked.

"Desperately. But Sam lives in a studio. With a very small couch." I grinned. "And you need a shower and a change of clothes. I don't think he really has to be watched all night. He just needs to be reassured in the morning. Take this night and put it in your mother's memory bank, so next time you tell her you're on an all-night job, she won't be suspicious."

"Yes, she will. But I get it." Lydia sighed theatrically. "It's kind of like babysitting, but I get it." She patted Sam's hand again. Sam turned to her, smiled, and patted hers back.

After we'd dropped Lydia in Chinatown and Sam and I were on our way to Greenpoint, I checked my phone. Peter had called three more times. I called him back.

"Smith! What the hell? What's going on? Jesus! Why didn't you pick up? Why didn't you call?"

"Everything's fine. Sam and I are headed to Brooklyn. I'm going to stay with him tonight."

"Fine? That's all, 'everything's fine'? What the hell happened? Where was he?"

"In a bar with Tony Oakhurst. Where are you?"

"I'm home, so what? Oakhurst, shit. Is Sam all right? Let me talk to him."

I passed the phone to Sam. "It's Peter."

"Hi!" Sam said enthusiastically. "What's shaking? . . . Yeah, sure I'm okay, I feel great . . . In a cab . . . I don't know, wait." Sam turned to me. "Where are we going?"

"Home."

Back to the phone: "Home . . . No, no, I don't want to go to your house, Leslie won't like it . . . But she'll come home and she'll get pissed off . . . No. No! Smith, tell him." He thrust the phone at me.

"What's wrong?" I asked Peter.

"I wanted him to come here but he won't."

"I told you, I'll spend the night at his place."

"No disrespect, Smith, but you lost him once already. Bring him here."

"Not if he doesn't want to go. No disrespect, Peter, but I'm working for Sam, not for you. Sam? Peter says he'd rather you stayed with him tonight."

"No! No-no-no-no-no." Sam's hands curled into fists and his head began to shake violently.

"Stop," I said, grabbing his arm before he could make himself sick and throw up in the cab. "Peter, he doesn't want to do it. We'll be in Greenpoint. Talk to you in the morning."

The cab rolled over the Manhattan Bridge and into Brooklyn, dropping us at Sam's address—a converted attached two-family, now six apartments with, most likely, an absentee landlord who didn't care much whom he rented to as long as they had first month, last month, and security deposit. Sam managed to make it down the four steps from the sidewalk to his door under the stairs, but I had to take his keys from him or we'd never have gotten in. Once we did, he fumbled for the light, flipped it on, and stood, letting out a huge sigh of relief.

Sam's apartment was as Grimaldi had described it. Small, low-ceilinged, nearly furniture-free, it was that staple of New York City real estate, the L-shaped studio. Like his Manhattan painting studio—which was larger—it was neat to the point of irrationality. To the left of the door was a kitchen, where bristles-up brushes sat in a coffee can in the sink. To the right, a couch faced a folding chair tucked precisely under a card table that held lined-up pencils and a carefully squared pile of sketch pads. Pavement-level windows nestled in the front wall over the sink and over the couch. The bathroom, with another window, opened off the kitchen, and the alcove in the back held a mattress covered with military-tight sheets and blankets.

On the right wall, facing the chair at the table, an unfinished canvas was pinned. Apparently, despite what he'd said, and although he now had a huge studio in Manhattan, Sam was still painting in a basement.

I shut the door, walked around Sam, and sat in the folding chair. Sam stood and stared and didn't start moving again until his glance fell on a half-empty scotch bottle beside the coffeemaker on the kitchen counter. He headed over, picked it up. "Hey, you want a drink?"

"Sure."

Sam took two coffee mugs from a cabinet. He poured a few fingers into each and handed me one. It seemed to me like one more drink and Sam would pass right out. Fine. I'd stay the night, as I told Lydia, more as a witness than a guard. Not really babysitting, and anyway, that was my rule, so I didn't have to follow it.

It didn't take long. Sam sat down on the couch. He reached for his neck as though to loosen his tie, but it was gone already. Discovering that made him grin. Settling in, he drank studiously, steadily, the way he'd work on a project. He didn't speak. I didn't say anything, either, sipping slowly, watching him. I wondered how much of the evening had registered with him, how much he'd filtered out, and whether the filtered-out parts would appear in canvases like the one pinned to the wall.

From my chair I could just about make out the pencil lines Sam had transferred from sketches taped around the canvas. I strained, but I couldn't tell what anything was, and I didn't want to get up and look more closely, in case movement might interfere with Sam's losing consciousness.

He must have noticed me looking, though. "You like it?" he asked. "Oh, that's right, you don't like my work."

"I can't see it very well."

"You wouldn't like it anyway. It's a sailboat. A windy day on the ocean. Waves and sparkly sun. Doesn't that sound nice?"

"Sounds great."

His face darkened. "I think the sharks think so, too. And the giant squids. And the electric eels, and the rogue waves, and the rocks, and the orcas, and—"

"Sam. Stop."

He did. He stared at me, then down at his glass. He finished the drink. A few moments later, he said, "I don't feel so good."

"Time for bed."

Sam nodded and pushed unevenly to his feet. I helped him lurch over to the mattress. He threw himself down, rolled in a blanket, and curled up facing the wall.

I checked that the door and the windows were locked, including the small, pebbled-glass one in the bathroom. I hauled the couch a few feet over until it blocked the doorway. If Sam tried to get out, he'd have to go through me. Not that I expected him to try; this was to prove to him that he hadn't. I took off my funeral-suit jacket, my tie, and my shoes, and stretched out the best I could on the couch, my head on one arm and my legs hanging over the other. As Sam started to snore, I looked at my watch. Just past eleven. I'd been hoping it was later; it was going to be a long night.

Sam wasn't a serial killer; I was pretty sure of that. Was there a way to convince him, short of finding the real one? That wasn't my job, and I was willing to bet the NYPD would do it, and sooner rather than later. Would that be enough for Sam, though? Or would he carry this fear with him, let it creep into his days, put it in his work, for the rest of his life?

When my phone rang, I jumped. Sunlight was edging in the windows. I grabbed the phone and rasped, "Smith," thinking the night hadn't been so long after all.

"Grimaldi. Your client doesn't answer his phone. You know where he is?"

I swung my legs down, rubbed my stiff neck, peered past the card table to the back of the room. "Tucked in his bed."

"You sure?"

"I'm looking at him."

"He been there all night?"

A chill ran through me. "Yes. Why?"

"Why the hell do you think? We have another one."

15

Grimaldi's closing words had been "Keep him there. I'm on my way." I didn't see any reason to wake Sam before she arrived, so I pulled myself off the couch to head for the bathroom. Sam's jacket and pants were lumped on the floor, and I practically tripped over his shoes in the kitchen. So he'd gotten up in the middle of the night.

The window in the bathroom was open.

I did what I needed to do, finishing with sticking my head under the faucet. In the kitchen, I filled the coffeemaker with water, found coffee in the fridge, rinsed last night's mugs. When the coffee came through, I poured it into both mugs, took a big gulp from one, and, crouching by the bed, shook Sam, because the open window was a reason to wake him.

"Huh? Wha?" His eyes widened. "Smith? What are you doing here?" Propping himself on an elbow, he looked around, maybe to assure himself he was right about where "here" was.

I handed him a mug. "Where did you go last night?"

He looked at the coffee, past me at the scotch bottle, back to me. "What's in this?"

I said, "Coffee. The bottle's empty. Answer my question."

"There's another one in the cabinet."

"Forget it. Where did you go last night?"

"Go? When?"

"After I was asleep."

"I tiptoed. So I wouldn't wake you up. I took my shoes off. I had to take a crap."

"You went out the window."

"Out? The window? What window?"

"In the bathroom. I wouldn't be able to fit through that, but I'll bet you can."

"The bathroom window? To the alley? That would be silly. There's nothing there."

"You opened it."

"I stunk up the place."

"Then what?"

"Then what, when? Then what, when, where, why, how."

"Sam. After you opened the window. Then what?"

"Then the bathroom didn't stink anymore, so I went back to bed. I took my clothes off, but I guess it was kind of too late, huh?" He pointed to the pile beside the mattress. "Looks like I ruined them. I hope so. I never want to wear them again. I never want to go to that kind of party again! That was—"

"Okay, Sam. Take it easy. I—"

Someone banged on the door. Sam's eyes went wide.

"It's okay," I said, standing. I moved the couch away from the door as the banging came again. I peered out the peephole, but I didn't see Grimaldi. I did see a cop, though. It was Ike Cavanaugh.

I pulled my shoes on, slipped outside, and shut the door.

"What the fuck?" Cavanaugh sneered. "I should've known. Is he in there?"

"What are you doing here?"

"I came for that bastard. He killed another girl."

"He didn't, and it's not your case."

"Oh? You see another cop around here anywhere?"

"You have a warrant?"

"I don't need a warrant to arrest his sorry ass!"

"You do to come inside."

"Move or I'll take you, too. What's your deal, anyway? You his bitch? Christ Jesus, I bet you get off watching him kill girls. Too much of a wuss to do it yourself but you love to watch him do it, right?"

He grabbed my shirt. I could smell booze and coffee on his raspy exhale. In another life, he and Sam would probably have been drinking buddies. I slammed his hand away, pushed him aside, and backed up the steps to the sidewalk. Cavanaugh followed. I was prepared to stay close but keep retreating; I really didn't want to get into it with a pissed-off cop, but hating on me kept Cavanaugh's focus off Sam. I was backing along the sidewalk and he was lurching toward me when a black Taurus screeched up and rocked to a stop. Grimaldi swung out and ran toward us, thick curls flying.

"Ike, what the hell?"

"Well, look who's here. About time, missy."

Grimaldi's face turned a ferocious red. "Get out of here, Ike."

"Screw you. You're going to give him a kiss and send him to bed. He killed another girl!"

"If he did, I'll take him up. If he didn't, I'll find out who did. Either way, you're going to get out of my grille or I swear I'll call your captain."

"He thinks you're screwing this up, in case you're wondering," Cavanaugh said. "He wishes it were me on the case."

"But it's not. How about I call *my* captain and let the two of them duke it out?"

"You'd do that, Detective Women's Intuition Genius, wouldn't you? Rat out another cop. Fuck you!"

Grimaldi took out her phone.

Cavanaugh growled, and his hands folded into fists. He took a step toward her, his beef with me forgotten. She lifted the phone and he hesitated. Would the satisfaction of decking her—which I wouldn't have called a sure bet anyway—be enough to make up for the deep shit he'd be in if he attacked another cop in front of a witness?

Apparently not. He spat on the sidewalk and retreated to a dented blue Regal, cursing us both. He might have harbored hopes of waiting there until Grimaldi brought Sam out—or left without him—but she just stood with her back to Sam's building and her phone lifted, staring at him. Finally he drove away.

"Do *not*," Grimaldi said to me before I could open my mouth, "think I'm doing you or your weirdo any favors. I just don't want Ike screwing up any case I might have. Also, if you try to fuck him up for assaulting you or any crap like that, I'll say I saw the whole thing and you're full of shit."

"You'd lie to protect him? You were about to call his captain."

She shook her head and started down the steps. "You must be one lousy poker player. Now let me in."

"You have a warrant?"

"You're shitting me," she said.

"He's my client. I can't just—"

At which point my client, in jockeys and socks, opened the door. "Hi," Sam said to Grimaldi. "I know you. I don't remember why, though. I'm Sam."

"We've met. Detective Grimaldi, NYPD. I want to ask you some questions."

"Ohhh." Sam took a moment, then nodded. "Oh. Now I remember. I tried to turn myself in and you wouldn't arrest me. But you came here and you came to my studio." He smiled. "You scared Sherron. That was cool. Are you going to arrest me now?"

"Now I just want to talk. Can I come in?"

"Sure."

"Sam, I'm not sure you want to let her in."

"Wow, you sound just like Peter. *You're* not sure what *I* want to do. Even if I just said what it was." He stood aside. "Come on in. What's your name again?"

"Angela. So, Sam, where were you last night?"

"Last night? I was here."

"All night?"

Sam thought. "No. No, first there was that awful party at the museum. Then I had a drink with Tony."

"And after that you came here?"

"Yes. With Smith." He nodded at me. "And someone named Lydia, but we dropped her off."

Grimaldi looked at me, but I didn't clarify Lydia's status. I did, though, have to clarify something, because Grimaldi would find out anyway.

"Not right away," I said.

"Not right away what?" Sam asked, interested.

"We didn't come here right away. I had to find you."

"Oh! Right. You came to where me and Tony were hanging out, at that bar."

"You had to find him?" said Grimaldi. "After the thing at the Whitney?"

I told her about the mob, the rock—she glanced at Sam's cut and swollen nose—and the search for Sam.

"So he was alone for about an hour?"

"I don't know if he was alone, but he wasn't with me."

"Around what time?"

"Maybe eight to nine. What do you have for time of—"

She held up a silencing hand. Back to Sam: "Where were you before Smith found you?"

"I ran around. I tried a couple of bars, but the door guys wouldn't let me in. So I kept going and then I remembered about this bar me and Tony go to, so I went there."

"Who's Tony?"

I had every confidence Grimaldi knew the answer to that and just wanted to see what Sam would say.

"Tony Oakhurst. He's a photographer. He's a friend of mine."

"Okay. Can I look around?" Grimaldi started strolling through the apartment without waiting for an answer.

"Not without a warrant," I said. Sam said nothing, probably replaying in his mind the shouting, the flying missiles of last night's mob.

Grimaldi had reached the door to the bathroom. She peered in without entering, shrugged, and came back. "I can get one, you know. Okay, so after Smith found you," she said to Sam, "you came here and you were here all night?"

Still not looking at her, Sam took a couple of beats. A lot of people would have gotten impatient and asked the question again, maybe louder, but Grimaldi just waited. Finally, Sam looked up and nodded.

Grimaldi turned to me. "You can confirm that?"

Now for the other clarification. "I fell asleep. But I had the couch up against the door."

She looked to the bathroom, where the open window could be seen through the doorway. "That a fact?"

I didn't answer.

"Okay," she said, facing Sam squarely. "Here's why I'm here. A woman was killed last night."

It took Sam a moment. He went white. "What? I killed someone else?"

"I didn't say that."

"But you came here. So I must have. Where? Who?"

"You tell me."

"I can't. I don't remember."

Grimaldi took a photo from her jacket pocket. "When did you meet this woman?"

Sam peered at the photo. I did, too. A young woman with short blond hair and gold earrings smiled at the camera. I wondered how long it had been between that smile and her death last night.

Sam asked, "Is that the woman I killed?"

"Where did you meet her? When?"

"I . . . I don't know."

"Do you recognize her?"

He shook his head.

"Tell me about last night."

"I told you."

"I want all the details. Every little thing. Starting from when you left the party."

Sam looked at me.

"Just tell her whatever you remember," I said. "Or we can tell her to leave."

"No. Why? Then we won't know if I did it. Can I sit down?" He pointed to the folding chair.

"Sure," Grimaldi answered, dropping onto the couch. I stayed standing.

Sam settled and took a breath. Then, with a concentrating frown: "What were we talking about?"

"Last night. What happened—"

"When we left the party! I remember." He nodded to himself. "I waved good-bye, with my tie. Leslie made me stop and pulled me like I didn't want to leave and she was making me. That was funny. We went down in the elevator. With Peter, too. Ellissa didn't come, or Sherron, either. You mean that?"

"Yes," said Grimaldi. "Go on."

Sam took a breath and continued, not stalling out again. He needed to be steered back from side roads a couple of times, accounts of people he didn't like and bars he did, but he went over it all: leaving through the back, facing the crowd, being hit by the rock, running. Going from bar to bar, being refused by bouncer after bouncer, with enough specifics that Grimaldi would probably be able to fill the timeline in. Finding Bar Six, Tony coming in soon after, me and Lydia after that. I was surprised by how detailed his memory was.

"Okay," Grimaldi said when he was done. She slapped her hands on her thighs and stood. "Those the clothes you were wearing last night?" She pointed at the pile by the bed. "And those shoes?" Sam nodded. "Can I take them?"

"Help yourself. I never want to see them again."

"Sam—" I started.

"In plain sight," Grimaldi said. "And with the owner's permission." I noticed she didn't say "suspect." She pulled on nitrile gloves and plucked Sam's shirt, pants, jacket, and shoes from the floor. Beaming at me with a you-lose smile, she said, "I'm out of here. Don't leave town."

"I'll be right back," I said to Sam and followed Grimaldi out. Once the door closed behind us, I said, "What's the rest of it?"

"The rest of what?" She trotted up the stairs.

I followed. "Come on, Detective. You didn't like Sam for those other killings, but you came straight here on this one."

She regarded me. "The vic," she said. "Kimberly Pike. A friend of one of the earlier vics."

"Oh. Shit."

"It may not be as bad as it sounds. Or it may be worse. She went to that protest with a couple of friends." Grimaldi opened the trunk of her car and took out two black plastic bags. She stuffed Sam's clothes in one and his shoes in the other and slammed the trunk. She turned to face me. "Seems a private investigator named Lydia something had come around with a photo of Tabor, asking people if they'd seen him with Annika Hausman."

Aha. "Lydia Chin. She's my partner."

"Goddamn it, Smith! Aren't you the guy who said he wasn't going to mess with my witnesses?"

"Unless I had to."

"And you absolutely had to?"

"Remember," I said, "Sam didn't hire me to prove he didn't do these killings. I'm supposed to find out *whether* he did."

Grimaldi peeled off the gloves. "In other words, you couldn't find him a bulletproof alibi."

"Right."

"I see. And?"

"The best we got was that, according to Kimberly Pike and one of the bartenders, Annika might have been hit on by an average-height dark-haired white guy. They couldn't identify Sam from the photo, but they couldn't say for sure it wasn't him, either."

"Jesus. And you didn't tell me this?"

"Tell you what? That we showed them a photo and they weren't sure?"

She took out a notebook. "How do I find your partner?"

I gave her Lydia's address, her phone number. "So," I said. "Last night?"

"Last night, what?"

"Oh, come on. Do we have to play this game?"

Grimaldi seemed to be thinking about what to tell me. She shrugged. "So, last night, Kimberly Pike and her friends decided to go to the Whitney to make the point that whether or not Tabor did Hausman, people who kill people shouldn't get famous off it."

"That's not why Sam's famous."

"Not for nothing, but I don't give a shit why he's famous. My question is, was this one of these coincidences we all find unbelievable but there you go, or did her knowing the other vic get her killed? On the coincidence side, you've got the fact that she's another short-haired blonde, which we know this killer likes, and that there were other people there who knew Hausman and nobody killed them. On the other side, you've got pretty much everything else."

"Including physical evidence? At the scene?"

Grimaldi sighed. "Not that, no. Unless there's something on Tabor's clothes. Pike was stabbed, like the other ones."

"Same kind of knife?"

"Don't know yet. There's blood on Tabor's shirt."

"From the bloody nose. What about the trophy?"

"You asking did the killer take one?"

"And was it the same as the others."

"All right, yes and yes. Not going to tell you what it was."

"Not going to ask. But how about this—you said there was another one, in Jersey, before Sam got out. Same MO? Same trophy?"

"Jesus," she said. "I told you I'd call you when I know."

"This mean we're on the same team?"

She took a long pause. "Depends. If we're not playing games, tell me this. Can you say for sure that except for that hour you lost him, you and your weirdo were together all night?"

I let the weirdo part go. "No. When I woke up this morning, the bathroom window was open. Sam says he opened it when he crapped in the middle of the night and then went back to bed. It's small, but it might be just about big enough for him to squeeze through. He was flat-out wasted when he fell asleep, though. The idea that he got it together enough a few hours later to go out the window, make his way to—" I realized I didn't know where Kimberly Pike had been found.

Grimaldi let me hang there for a moment, then said, "Back to the Whitney. Pike was found near there."

I thought. "An hour there, an hour back, two subway lines—I don't see it."

"Or an Uber. At that hour, twenty minutes each way."

I thought about that, too. Sam was just about crazy enough to take an Uber to a murder scene. "Why would she still be there, though? Waiting for him?"

"Maybe she wasn't waiting. Maybe he just went back there because he's crazy, and he ran into her coming out of a bar or something."

I had to admit that wasn't impossible.

"I already have someone checking with Uber and the cab and black car companies. I can get a warrant for Tabor's phone, too. Though I agree, that's a long shot. It's more likely, if it was him, it was in that hour when you lost him."

"You must be able to narrow time of—"

"You'd think so, but we can't. Pike was found this morning in one of the meat trucks at the packing plant next door. Which is why we have no forensics—trace evidence in a meat truck, bad joke. The refrigeration unit was off, but it was still goddamn cold in there. We have no accurate time of death."

16

I expected to find Sam huddled on his mattress with the bottle of scotch he'd told me was in the cabinet, but when I came back inside, he'd put on a sweatshirt and a pair of jeans, made his bed to military standards, and, pencil in hand, was squinting back and forth between the canvas on the wall and one of the sketches taped up beside it. Three utility lights clamped at even intervals on an overhead pipe washed the wall with scalloped arcs and crisscrossing shadows.

Sam glanced over at me as I came in. Turning back to his work, he said, "Go away."

"Sam—"

"I don't like people here when I'm working. Did I kill that woman?"

"I don't think so."

"I do."

"Grimaldi doesn't, either."

"Bullshit. Then what did she come here for? You don't know where I was after I ran away."

"I know up till then you'd had two drinks and after that you couldn't get into any bars until the one I found you in."

"I could've been drunk enough to kill someone on two drinks."

"But not drunk enough to forget it."

"You thought I left here last night. I'd had more by then. You thought I went out the window."

"I asked if you did. There's a difference."

He straightened and looked me square in the face. "And did you get the answer?" When I didn't reply he said, "That's what I thought. Now go away." He bent over his work again. "Go find out if I killed that woman. And the other ones. If you don't find that out, you're fired." He laughed and started making minute pencil lines on the canvas.

I poured the rest of the coffee and watched him from the kitchen while I drank it. He ignored me, focusing on what he was doing as if I'd already gone. He didn't react at all when I rinsed my coffee cup, pulled on my jacket, stuffed my tie in my pocket, and left.

—

As I walked to the subway I lit a cigarette and called Lydia.

"Hey! Have a good night out there in Brooklyn?" she asked when she picked up.

"No, and a worse morning." I told her what had happened, ending with, "Grimaldi wants to talk to you. I gave her your number."

She ignored that. "Oh my God. Oh, God, Kimberly Pike? Bill, we saw her last night."

"We did?"

"Around the back, when we were trying to leave. She was the one who kept screaming, 'It's him, it's him,' to get everyone else to come around back. Oh, that poor woman. I talked to her. I showed her Sam's picture. She might not have gone to the Whitney if I—"

"Or she might have. Or whoever wanted her dead would've found her wherever she was. You didn't do this."

She took a long silence and I gave her the space for it. I smoked and held the phone to my ear. Finally, she said, "Bill? You think someone wanted her dead? Her, specifically?"

"I don't know about that," I admitted. "But another murder in Sam's orbit—Grimaldi says she's just barely willing to entertain the possibility it's a coincidence, but there's no way she thinks it is, and I don't, either."

"No," Lydia said, "me, either. What details do we have?"

Back to business. Good. I knew what she was feeling and that she'd have to work through it—and that the best way to do that was actual work.

I told her about the refrigerated truck. "That means time of death could be anywhere between nine last night, when Pike's friends say they lost her in the crowd rushing around to the back, to about six this morning, when the driver found her."

"They don't lock those trucks?"

"I guess not once they're empty."

"Bet that driver will from now on. Was she left there on purpose, do you think? To confuse the time of death?"

"Possible, though it also could have been just a place to hide her."

"Is there anything linking Sam to it, other than who she was?"

"Grimaldi says not yet. She took Sam's clothes from last night to test."

"She came with a warrant?"

"No. Sam just handed them to her when she asked."

"I'm beginning to see what Peter means about everyone taking advantage of Sam. You couldn't stop her?"

"I could've, but what's the point? I'm not his defense attorney. He wants to know. I don't think he did it, but I can't guarantee that."

"You think he needs an attorney?"

"Not yet. If we're right, he won't." My phone buzzed. I checked the screen. "Hey, I'll call you back. Peter's calling me."

"Good luck."

"Peter," I said, answering the call. I'd reached the subway and stood off to the side at the top of the steps. I dropped the cigarette butt and ground it out.

"Smith! Where are you? I just called Sam, he said you left. What the hell is going on? He says some detective came this morning. Named Angela? And you just let her in?"

"Angela Grimaldi. NYPD. Sam let her in."

"Of course he did! He's clueless. Your job—"

"Another woman was killed last night. That's what Grimaldi came about."

Silence, then, "What? And why—"

I thought of Sam: *what, when, why, where, how.* "A friend of one of the other two, and at the Whitney. Are you in your office?"

"Yes."

"I'm on my way." I hung up in case he wanted to argue.

I called Lydia to tell her to meet me at Peter's office. Then I backtracked a couple of storefronts to a bakery, where I grabbed a sweet roll and more coffee. I had a feeling it was going to be a caffeine-heavy day.

17

Lydia was waiting for me, as arranged, outside the subway exit when I hit midtown.

"You look like you spent a sleepless night on someone's couch," she said as she kissed me.

"I wish it had been sleepless. I wouldn't ache any worse, and Sam would have at least half an alibi."

"Half?"

"Even if I hadn't fallen asleep, there's still that hour I lost him."

"*We* lost him. And you can't really think that he could've done this, no matter when he was alone."

"I don't, but that doesn't matter."

"Grimaldi, you mean."

"Not even her. If he didn't do it, she won't find anything. But that won't convince Sam. I wanted to be able to prove to *him* he couldn't have killed anyone last night." I shook my head. "But my thinking was theoretical. That's why I let myself fall asleep. I wasn't actually expecting anyone to get killed."

She squeezed my hand, said nothing as we walked to Peter and Leslie's office building. After a few moments, I smiled and said to her, "By the way, you look great." She wore the leather jacket again, over a blue striped shirt and black slacks.

"I slept very well, thank you. Since I had nothing else to do except sleep."

"You're not going to let me forget that, are you?"

"Not a chance. How often do I arrange to spend the night at your place?"

"Not often enough. I'm going to talk to your mother about it."

"You do that."

We rode up, arrived at The Tabor Group's glass entrance, went in, and asked for Peter. A minute or two later Leslie threw open the waiting room door. "My God," she said, stopping in the doorway when she saw me. "You look like a homeless person. Did you have to come here like that?"

"A woman's been killed," I said. "The cops came to talk to Sam. Peter called me, all pissed off. I thought it might be better to get here fast than go home and make myself presentable. If that bothers you, don't look at me, look at Lydia."

Leslie did, giving Lydia a sharp glare. Lydia returned a bland smile. Leslie snapped, "Come on," and stalked down to Peter's office, followed by Lydia, me, and the furtive stares of the sleek young people behind the glass wall.

Peter's mood was no better than Leslie's, but his office was a lot less chaotic than the day before. Leslie must have done some of the roto-rootering she'd told me about.

"Smith! What's going on?" Peter demanded as Leslie clicked his door shut. "Who was killed? Why did the police come to Sam? What did they say?"

I could see people in the drafting room cautiously eyeing the office through the window wall. Clenched jaws and red faces on the bosses might herald a tough afternoon.

"Her name was Kimberly Pike," I said. "She was a friend of one of the other two victims, and she was found at the Whitney." I sketched them the morning, starting with Cavanaugh.

"Oh, Jesus, I remember him." Peter ran his hand down his face. "He still has it in for Sam?"

"Why wouldn't he?" Leslie snapped.

Peter just looked at her, his shoulders slumping. I went on, told them about Grimaldi and Sam, Sam's impressive memory, the open window. I finished with, "Grimaldi took Sam's clothes from last night, to test."

"What the fuck?" Peter came back to life. "You fell asleep? And you let that cop take his clothes?"

I could hear the bell ringing for another round between me and Peter, but Leslie jumped in. "What difference does it make? They must already have some kind of evidence. Something makes them think he's guilty, or they wouldn't have come."

I said, "Grimaldi says except for who the victim was and where she was found, they don't."

"Why would she tell you?" Leslie retorted. "They must have something."

"What makes you think that? Because she came to Sam? There's enough circumstantial evidence to make that reasonable."

"I don't believe it."

"Les, you're wrong," said Peter. "If they actually had anything, they'd have arrested him."

"I agree," I said.

"Who gives a shit?" Peter wheeled on me. "What the hell good have you been so far? If you hadn't lost him last night in the first place, and then fallen asleep, he'd be off the hook now. Or if you hadn't been so eager to get rid of us. If I'd stayed, I wouldn't have lost him."

"I wasn't the only one who wanted you out of there." I looked at Leslie, who just glared back.

"Jesus," said Peter. "You're useless. You're fired. Get out."

"Nice try," I said. "You keep forgetting I don't work for you." I didn't mention that Sam had already threatened to can me. "But the 'get out' part, fine. Just one thing. Where were you last night?"

"Where was *I*?"

"Where were you—both of you?"

"Are you insane?" Leslie demanded.

"I don't think Sam did this. Or the three earlier ones, either."

"Three?"

I nodded. "The first was in Hoboken about two months before Sam got out. Same MO, same trophy." Actually, Grimaldi hadn't confirmed that to me yet, but I wanted to see what would happen if I said it. What happened was interesting: a flash of confusion in Peter's eyes—and what I could have sworn was a veil of despair in Leslie's.

Peter said, "Before? That—doesn't that prove Sam's innocent?"

"No," Leslie said, rousing herself. "It just proves he didn't do that one."

"True," I said. "But it's getting clearer, even leaving that one out, that the others are related to him in some way."

"Obviously," Leslie said. "And the simplest way would be, he did them."

"Les!" Peter turned to her. "What are you saying? You know he didn't."

"Peter." Leslie gave him steely eyes. "I think it may be time to face facts."

"What facts? What are you talking about?"

"We'll discuss it later." She turned the steel on me. "Last night—since you have the balls to ask—we got away from that riot as fast as we could. Peter took an Uber home to Brooklyn. I went back into the Whitney to see if I could smooth Michael Sanger's fur. Then I went home, too. Now get the hell out of here."

She jerked open Peter's office door and stood there. As soon as Lydia and I had walked through, she slammed it shut.

"Can we stay and be a fly on the wall?" Lydia asked. "I bet they're about to have a doozy of a fight."

"Except we wouldn't be flies on the wall," I said, nodding and smiling at the young people behind the glass, whose stares had followed us out of Peter's office and down the corridor. Eyes quickly dropped back to computer screens. "More like fish in a bowl."

"Too bad," said Lydia as we reached the elevator. "I'd sure like to know what they're hiding."

"You think so, too?"

"Oh, my God. The question is, are they both hiding the same thing from us? Or are they each hiding something different from each other?"

18

"And by the way," I said as Lydia and I melded into the foot traffic on 46th Street, "I couldn't fail to notice up there that you had nothing to add to the conversation."

"You were doing so well."

"The way a worm does on a fishhook."

"Your grasp of metaphor is weak today. What now?"

"Before anything else happens, I need to go home and take a shower. Then we need to talk about what we're going to do next. I want to look into some things, but I don't want to step on Grimaldi's toes."

"Coming from you, that's unaccustomed consideration for the sensitivities of a cop."

"No, she just scares the crap out of me."

"Uh-huh."

"Coming?" I started for the subway.

"You seriously think I'm that cheap? That after you blew me off last night I'm going to trot along to your place now just because you're going to be naked and dripping wet?" She matched my steps down the subway stairs.

"The thought never crossed my mind."

"It better have."

I kept my arm around her all the way on the swaying ride downtown. At my place, she waited for me to unlock the street door, then sprinted up the two flights to my landing. "Go ahead," I said from a flight and a half behind her. "You have a key."

"No, it's okay, I have plenty of time."

"Very funny," I said, reaching the landing and unlocking the door. Inside, I disarmed the security panel, pushed the door shut, reached for her, and followed up the subway kiss with one that took a good deal of the plenty of time she claimed to have.

"You know," she finally said, breaking away, "there may be a better place for this."

"You don't like my doorway?"

"I love it. I love all doorways. Let's go through that one." She nodded toward the one leading to the bedroom.

———

Eventually I got my shower. As I was finishing up, Lydia stuck her head in the bathroom. "Your phone's ringing. It's Sam."

"Go ahead and pick it up."

I shut the water, grabbed a towel, and came out to hear, "All right. Stay where you are. We're on the way. Yes, really. Yes, him, too. Of course he will. Don't worry about that. Yes, right now. Wait, here he is."

I reached for the phone. "Sam? What's up?" But Sam had clicked off. So I repeated to Lydia: "What's up?"

"Sam wants us to come out there. Someone broke into his apartment."

"Shit! Is he okay?"

"He wasn't there. He'd gone out for a drink and discovered it when he got back. He ran right back to the bar. I told him to stay there." She looked at me. "He was afraid you wouldn't come because he fired you. He fired you?"

"Christ. No, he didn't fire me." I started to pull my clothes on. "He said he would if I didn't either clear him or incriminate him. If I can't do either of those things, I'll fire me, too."

We jogged the two blocks to the lot where I keep my Audi. I stuck the phone in the hands-free and tried to call Sam as I drove, but he didn't answer. In a little over twenty minutes I pulled into a loading zone in front of Victor's, a bar a couple of blocks from Sam's building. Sam, just months in the neighborhood, hadn't wasted any time establishing his local. He was on a bar stool, halfway into what was clearly not his first scotch, when we pushed through the door. He turned to face us. I wouldn't say he lit up, but some of the misery in his eyes seemed to fade.

"What happened?" I asked.

"I'm sorry I fired you."

"That's okay. What happened?"

"Will you still work for me?"

"Yes. What happened?"

He nodded, apparently reassured. He swirled his scotch, watched it circle, and seemed to forget why he needed me to work for him.

"Sam? What happened?"

"Oh." He looked up. "They broke into my apartment."

"Who?"

"I don't know. I didn't stay around and ask them."

"You mean they were still there when you got there?"

"I don't know. I didn't see anyone."

"Did they take anything?"

"I don't know. I ran out right away."

"How did they get in?"

"I don't know."

"What—"

"I don't know!"

"Okay," I said. "Okay. Let's go have a look."

Sam pulled back. "What, go there? Are you crazy? You can go if you want. I'm staying here."

Lydia said, "Forever?"

Sam looked at his drink. "Why not?"

"Sam," I said, "we need to know why they came. What they wanted." Though what Sam could have that anyone would want, except maybe sketches and the unfinished canvas, wasn't clear to me. "You're the only one who'll know if anything's missing."

"What if they're still there?"

"Lydia has a gun. If they're dangerous, she'll shoot them."

Sam turned to Lydia. "You will?"

"Of course." She gave him the kind of reassuring smile that would never have worked on her mother, but Sam's shoulders relaxed a little. He looked at me.

"What about you?"

"I have a gun, too. But Lydia's a better shot."

Lydia pulled her jacket back just enough to show Sam the gun at her hip. She raised her eyebrows. He met her gaze, grinned, threw back the rest of his drink, and jumped off the bar stool.

"See ya, Vic!" He saluted the bartender and headed for the door.

I pulled out my wallet to cover Sam's drinks, but the bartender waved me off. "He runs a tab. Good tipper, too. A crazy nut, but a good customer."

"Glad to hear it." I walked out into the sunlight, where Lydia and Sam waited for me. "Come on, get in. We need to move the car anyway."

"We'll meet you there," said Lydia. "I'll walk with Sam."

Sam smiled.

I met her glance, nodded, and watched them walk away, heads together in a friendly chat. They were waiting for me when I pulled into a place a few doors up from Sam's. When I joined them, Sam handed me his keys.

"You go." Only when Lydia started down the steps after me did he say, "Be careful."

Gun drawn, I unlocked the door, eased it open. Unsurprisingly, it was latched, but the bolt wasn't thrown. Sam hadn't taken the time to do that before he'd run. Still, this lock was no high-security device. Even if it had been bolted, I might have been able to pick it; anyone better than I am would have had no problem. Lydia moved in right behind me. Sam, up on the sidewalk, watched anxiously.

Once we were inside, it took about thirty seconds to ascertain that the place was empty. All we needed, besides a glance around and a walk through the kitchen to the bathroom, was a peek in the closet, accomplished with a dish towel on the doorknob just in case. The windows, this time, were all closed and locked. There wasn't any way to hide under the bed. The unfinished canvas was still pinned to the wall, with the sketches taped around it. Nothing, to my eye, looked disturbed.

"Okay, Sam," I called, sliding my gun into its shoulder holster. "No one's here. Come on down."

Sam took the steps from the sidewalk warily. He walked through the door and flinched. He sidestepped over close to Lydia.

"Tell me," I said. "How do you know someone was here?"

Sam pointed to the table. "The red pencil. It goes over there."

"That's it?"

"I never put the red one on that side. Never. And they're not lined up right." The pencils were, in fact, a degree or two off of parallel from each other. He spoke as though this were wild chaos. "And the coffee cups. In the dish drainer. I left them with the handles between the wires."

"All right," I said. "Let's look around. Carefully. Tell us anything else you notice."

Sam turned to Lydia. She smiled, kept her gun out, and stayed at his side. While they checked the place out, I did the same, looking for small changes, missing sketches, even missing tape. My only conclusion was that the place was even more organized and orthogonal than it had been when we'd walked in last night.

Sam prowled in small steps, peering at the bed and the kitchen counter, into the cabinets and the closet and the laundry basket. He had nothing more to say until he came to the bathroom. "They opened the medicine cabinet! See? You have to move the toothbrush to do that, and they put it back in the wrong direction."

"That might just mean they moved the toothbrush." *Or you put it back in the wrong direction*, I didn't say aloud.

"Why would they move the toothbrush?" he asked, not belligerently, just with interest. I had to admit I didn't have an answer. I couldn't see any prints on the mirror; if someone had actually been here, they must've worn gloves. I used a towel to keep my own prints off the glass and pulled the cabinet door open.

"See anything missing? Out of the ordinary?" The cabinet held nothing but dental floss, Band-Aids, comb, aspirin.

"I . . . No, everything's good."

"Okay," I said. "All right, Sam. Maybe someone was here, but they're not here now. You might want to get bars on the windows and change the lock on the door."

"I might want to not be here anymore! What if they come back?" He looked at Lydia. "Can you stay here with me?" Before she could answer, he shook his head. "No, that won't work. If you're here, I can't paint."

I thought. "You want to go to Peter's?"

He spun to me. "You're as crazy as I am! The Crazy Brothers! *No*, I don't want to go to Peter's. I can't paint there *and* Leslie hates me. They'll fight and then pretend they're not fighting and everything's fine. Mom and Dad used to do that. I hate that." He scowled, then brightened. "I want to go to my studio. Yes! Good idea. Come on, let's go there." He frowned. "But they know the combination. Peter and Sherron. They can come in. But!" He looked at us in hope. "But if no one tells them that's where I am, they won't! You won't tell, right?"

Lydia said, "No, Sam, we won't tell." I nodded my agreement.

"Okay," Sam said. "That's a good idea. Let's go."

Remembering how Cromley had buzzed me in, I almost pointed out that the security in that building was a little soft. But the idea of going there was cheering Sam up, and I didn't believe he was actually in danger. If anyone had been here, and I wasn't convinced of that, they'd waited until Sam was out. They'd come for something, not for him.

I asked, "Do you want to take anything?"

"Like what? Everything's there. Oh, you mean like the scotch! Good idea."

"I really meant like clean clothes."

"What for? No one's going to see me." He opened a cabinet and took out the bottle he'd told me was up there. Lydia raised her eyebrows, I shrugged my shoulders, and, using Sam's keys, locked the place up. We all got in my car for the drive to West 39th Street.

19

As we rolled over the bridge, I caught glimpses of Sam in the rearview mirror, oscillating his fascinated glance from the windshield to the windows on either side as though he'd never seen the Manhattan skyline before. If he remembered the dread that was taking us there, I didn't see it. No one spoke, but Lydia, with a look, conveyed her question to me: Had anyone really been in Sam's apartment? I shrugged my answer. Given Sam's OCD, it was possible that the items he saw as having been moved actually had been. Given the lunacy of last night and this morning, it was also possible that he had been less assiduous than usual and what he was seeing—and reacting to with fear—were marks of his own loosening of control. As usual with Sam, what you saw depended on where you stood.

At the studio building, I parked in another loading zone, this time sticking the DELIVERY sign in the windshield. It's surprising how often this gives me half an hour or so before some traffic cop begins to question why an Audi would be making a delivery. Lydia and I took the elevator up with Sam. Before he could get his studio unlocked, the half-opened door down the hall flew wide and Ellissa Cromley rushed out.

"Sam!" She threw her thin arms around him. Sam staggered, but he looked pleased. "Are you all right? Oh my God, look at your face! Why didn't you answer my calls? Where did you go?"

Sam tilted his head.

"I called you!" she said. "Like a million times! I was so worried last night, that mob! You shouldn't have gone out there. By the time I got out I couldn't get to you, and people said you'd run away. Then the police came. And then some woman got killed. Everyone in the building is talking about it. But I know you didn't do it."

Cromley gave me a reproachful glare, including Lydia in it in case she was guilty of Criminal Disregard of Sam, too. I answered with a steady gaze, Lydia offered a warm smile, and Sam, missing all this, took out his phone and poked buttons.

"Oh," he said. "You did call. I guess I had it off since last night." He looked at me. "Hey, you called today, too." I didn't know if I was supposed to respond to that, but before I could he said, "Oh, look! Tony called, too! And Peter." He looked at Cromley. "I think I did kill that woman."

He turned to the door, and before Cromley could respond, he'd managed to punch the right numbers into the keypad. He ambled into his studio, leaving the door open for the rest of us to trail in his wake. Lydia and I did, but Cromley apparently wasn't in a sociable mood.

"Don't call them back!" she yelled from the hallway. "Tony or Peter. Do not call anyone back. You didn't kill anyone. I need to tell you something. Come over later." She swept me and Lydia with the glare again. "When you're alone." Her skirt swirled as she spun and stalked back to her own studio. Her slamming door echoed in the hallway.

"Wow," said Lydia. "What did I ever do to her?"

"Nothing, but you're about to and she knows it."

Sam looked bewildered by Cromley's exit. He shrugged and lifted his phone. He listened to his messages with a growing smile. When he lowered the phone he said, "That's what she says on her voice mail. Ellissa. That she wants to tell me something. And you know what? Tony says that, too. And Peter, too. Everyone wants to tell me something. And you know what else? I don't care! I want everyone to shut up. I have work to do. Good-bye." He took a close look at Lydia and gave an apologetic nod, though I got the idea he was apologizing more to himself than to her. "Yeah, you, too. Bye-bye."

He stood, head tilted, smiling, until we caught on. We walked to the doorway, Sam right behind us. I turned to speak but had to jump back as Sam shut the door in my face.

Lydia laughed, probably at the close call my nose had had. "I think that's what they call a mood swing, yes?"

"He does have those," I agreed. "But he likes you."

"He may be crazy, but that doesn't mean he doesn't have good taste."

"Which, according to his buddy Oakhurst, is the enemy of good art. But you know what I want to know?"

"What all those people want to tell him?"

"Exactly right."

We looked at each other, then started down the hall to Cromley's studio, to begin asking.

20

Our knock on Cromley's door produced immediate results. When it opened, the sight of Lydia and me produced predictable ones.

Cromley's triumphant look morphed immediately into a scowl. "I thought it was Sam."

"Sorry to disappoint you," I said. "Can we come in?"

"Why?"

"Why not?" Lydia said, walking past Cromley as though she'd been invited. Cromley's eyes widened, but she stepped aside, and I decided to let Lydia take the lead on this one, since she obviously had a better sense than I of how to play it.

"What do you want?" Cromley asked, recovering. She shut the door.

"Actually, I want to see your work," Lydia said.

A beat. "You do?"

Lydia nodded as she threaded the path to the easels by the window. "Bill told me about it. I don't know much about art, but I'm interested in any work by women and people of color that interrogates the straitjacketing patriarchic norms."

I was impressed as all hell. Cromley gave me squinty eyes, probably dying to know exactly what I'd said about her work but not wanting to ask for fear of looking like she was dying to know. Lydia, hand behind her back, gave me a quick "stay away" gesture. I worked at keeping my expression neutral.

Cromley turned to the easels by the windows as Lydia picked her way from one to another, returning to each and finally stopping at one and saying, "Tell me about this. What is it you want me to see?"

While Cromley hurried to where Lydia stood, I took my phone from my pocket, checked it, and turned my back as though listening to my messages. I gave it a few minutes, during which I couldn't make out Cromley's or Lydia's words, but I could hear Cromley's tone changing slowly from defensive anger to near eagerness. I pocketed the phone and turned back toward them in time to hear Lydia say, "I understand completely what you're getting at. I also see why you had to open your own gallery. It would be hard to get any established dealer to take a chance on work like this."

Well, I thought, *that's true.*

"Bill," Lydia said, "why don't you go take care of that other business? I want to talk to Ms. Cromley for a while."

"Ellissa," Cromley said generously. Her generosity did not extend to me, though; she waited pointedly beside Lydia, saying nothing else.

Contrary to popular opinion, I can take a hint. "Good idea," I said. "I'll text you." I left, closing Cromley's door behind me.

I stood in the paint-spattered corridor, thinking. Since Lydia had been referring to no particular business, I was free to take care of any business I wanted. I was pretty sure she'd annihilate me if I went to talk to Tony Oakhurst without her, but everyone else was fair game. I'd just taken out my phone again to call Grimaldi and see if she had the details on the Jersey victim yet when Sam burst out of his studio.

"They were here!" he shouted, waving his arms. "They were here, too!" He showed no surprise at finding me hanging around the hallway. I got the feeling, not for the first time, that in Sam's world, offstage characters had no separate lives but waited in the wings for a cue to return to his drama. He grabbed my sleeve and started hauling me into his studio.

"Look!" he said, yanking me over to the table that held the sketches he'd been so on edge watching Konecki and Sanger go through. They'd been neatened to Sam-approved standards, but a drawer in the table gaped open. Boxes of pencils lined it, with erasers stacked at the back behind them.

"Tell me what I'm seeing," I said.

Sam took a breath, preparing to explain to the ignoramus. "I needed a pencil, so I came to get one. See how the pencils are all different numbers? So are the erasers, sort of. They don't have numbers, but different erasers work better on different pencils. I keep them where they go. But see how that one, that light grayish one, is with the white ones? And see how they're all kind of pushed over on that side? Someone stuck something in there and then took it out, but they didn't put the erasers back right. See?"

I saw. The erasers, like the pencils in Sam's apartment this morning, weren't quite straight, the ones in the middle not quite centered. And a light grayish one was on the side with the white ones. Their shades were very close, so I could see how someone could make that mistake. Someone; but not Sam.

I wondered if the disruption could be accounted for by something as simple as the drawer sticking, so I slid it in and out. I guess I should have expected that it had been oiled within an inch of its life. Nothing in it moved even a millimeter.

"Someone put something there," Sam insisted. "And then took it out again."

"Sam—"

"I know! I know, it's crazy, why would anyone do that, break in here and put something in my drawer and then take it out again? It's crazy. But that's what happened. Somebody came in and—"

"I believe you."

He stopped. "You do?"

"Shouldn't I?"

"You should." He nodded quickly, up and down, up and down. "But sometimes you don't."

"Sometimes you don't make sense. I think this time you're right." I took out my phone, turned on the flashlight, and examined the drawer. "Can I move this stuff?"

Sam made a face but said, "Okay."

I lifted out the contents, inspected the drawer again. I slid it out of the table, checked it and the table's underside for anything taped on, or signs of anything recently removed. Nothing. Whatever had happened here had left no trace except out-of-place erasers.

I put the drawer back and clicked the flashlight off. "Do you keep anything in there, or maybe attached to the drawer or the table? Something someone might have been looking for?"

He gave me a look that said there were times when *I* didn't make sense. "I keep pencils there. And erasers. Stop, don't put them back. I'll do it."

"Nothing else?"

"What else would I keep in there? That's the pencil and eraser drawer."

Of course it was.

I texted Lydia. *In Sam's studio. Someone's been here.* "Okay, Sam," I said. "When was the last time you opened this drawer and everything was normal?"

He thought. "The day before yesterday."

"What about the rest of the studio? Anything else wrong?"

"Oh. I don't know." He swiveled his head like a searchlight, as though he could inspect the whole studio from one spot.

"Can we look?" I said.

"Walk around, you mean?"

I raised my eyebrows. Reluctantly, he started forward, and we reprised the slow assessment of his apartment from earlier in the day. Probably because the studio was one big room with no place to hide, and probably also because

I wasn't Lydia, Sam didn't insist on my staying right at his side. He scrutinized drawers, studied paper piles, and peered at pads. He finally declared everything except that one drawer intrusion-free.

"All right," I said. "Now. Who has the door code? Peter, and Sherron Konecki, right? Who else?"

"Well." He put some thought into the question. "I think maybe Tony. Yes, Tony. And Ellissa, I remember I told her. We traded."

"And if Peter knows, Leslie might, too?"

"Ugh. You think?"

"Could be."

Sam frowned. "So you mean it was one of those people who broke in here? Wow. I thought they liked me. Well, except Leslie. I guess it must have been her."

"Your logic's off, Sam, but you might be right. We'll find out. Meanwhile, I have a friend who's a locksmith. You want me to call him?"

Sam emphatically did.

Ernesto Luz ("Luz for Locks!") was, as it happened, not far away and finishing up a job. He promised to rush over. I described the combination lock we were looking at. "Can you reprogram it?"

"If you got the paperwork."

"If not?"

"Then we replace it. I got a couple in the truck."

Just after I hung up the call, someone knocked on the door.

Sam jumped.

"Should I open the door?" I asked.

"I don't know," Sam said but I did anyway, and when it turned out to be Lydia, he smiled.

"I got your text," she said. "What happened?"

Sam said, "Do you still have your gun?"

"Sure, I have it. Do I need it?"

"No," I said. I pushed the door shut behind her. "Someone was here." I explained about the pencil-and-eraser drawer, showed her.

"Oh," she said. "We're positive?"

"We are."

"Sam? Are you okay?"

Sam nodded.

"Ernesto should be here any minute," I told her. "How did you do in there?"

"In where?" Sam asked.

"Ellissa's studio," Lydia said. "And not so well. She could talk about her work and her gallery all day"—I caught Sam's eyeroll when Lydia said that—"but she wouldn't let on anything about what she wanted to tell Sam. Except she hinted it was important. Sam, you need to find out what it was."

"You mean, go talk to Ellissa?"

"Yes."

"No. I don't care what it was. Nobody can tell me anything today. Nobody. Anything. Anybody. Nothing. Even you guys. Go away. Wait, not now! After the locksmith comes. Then go away."

I said, "Sam? Maybe Ellissa knows who broke in here."

Sam took a long pause. "Oh. You think maybe?"

"I do."

He frowned, then grinned. "Okay, go ask her."

"She won't tell us."

"Tell her I want her to."

"I think—"

The buzzer let us know someone was downstairs.

"Probably the locksmith," I said, asked at the intercom, and turned out to be right. I buzzed Ernesto in, opened the door, and waited.

He greeted us as he ambled from the elevator. He glanced at the lock and said to me, "You got the paperwork? The manual got the owner's code in it."

"Sam?" I asked, but Sam shook his head.

"Okay, then I got to replace it. Costs more."

"Go ahead," I told him.

While Ernesto set to work on the door, Lydia and I tried to set to work on Sam. "If Ellissa knows who was here," I said, "we could—"

"Shhh!" Sam said. "I want to watch. Besides, it was Leslie. And it doesn't matter, whoever it was. If we change the lock, they can't come back."

Having solved the intrusion problem with Sam-logic, he refused to listen to another word from either of us. He bent, hands on knees, to focus, with that laser-like attention he could bring, on Ernesto's dismantling of his hardware.

"Give it a few minutes," Lydia said softly. I didn't see another choice, so I leaned on the studio wall and wished you could still smoke in New York buildings.

Sam's concentration, being like a laser, could also suddenly switch off. After a while he straightened, looked around as though reorienting himself, and walked back to his easel by the window. He started sharpening pencils, peering at his painting, glancing at the street. I was about to start another offensive, when he jumped back.

"Oh no!" Sam pointed out the window. "Oh no!"

"What's wrong?" Lydia charged over, me right behind.

"Sherron! Sherron just came out of Tony's. She looks mad. She can't come here. I won't talk to her." He raced to the front of the room. "Lock the door! Oh, no, there's no lock!"

Ernesto looked up. "Soon," he said. "Ten minutes."

"Too long!"

I watched Sherron Konecki practically stomp across the street to the door of the building we were in. "Get lost," I told Sam. "I'll deal with Sherron."

"Okay. Say I'm not here. Say you're waiting for me and you don't know where I am but I won't be back for hours. Say that."

Sam ran down the hall and made it to the bathroom just before the elevator door slid open and Sherron Konecki, in black skirt, hose, and heels, ivory sweater, and obsidian pendant, stepped from it. A dozen clicking steps and she stopped short at Sam's door.

"What in the hell are you doing?" she demanded.

Changing the lock would have been gratuitous, so I said, "Someone broke in."

"You can't do this without my permission. I lease this studio. What do you mean, someone broke in? Is everything all right?" By the way she peered past me, it was clear Konecki meant the drawings and the large canvas—her assets. "Where's Sam?"

"Not here. We're waiting for him." The bathroom door, I noticed, cracked open a tiny bit.

"How did you get in if he's not here?"

"He was. He left. He said we should take care of the lock and he'd be back later."

"It's not his lock to take care of."

"He said he'd never come back here unless the code was changed. He didn't have the manual, so we decided to put on a new lock."

"Of course he didn't have the manual. My office has it. You should have called."

"Sorry, didn't occur to me. I figured it was an emergency. Finish up," I told Ernesto, who seemed to be trying to hide a grin. Stepping out past him into the hallway, I said to Konecki, "Sam will call you later."

"Don't you patronize me. Who appointed you Cerberus?"

The answer seemed too obvious to state, so I said nothing. Konecki glared, letting out a small hissing sound like a pipe about to blow. She spun and stalked down the hall. The bathroom door clicked shut, but Konecki didn't go that far. She stopped at the next door, where her knock was answered with the speed of someone who'd been waiting for it. She disappeared into Ellissa Cromley's studio.

21

I walked down to the bathroom and knocked. "It's okay, Sam," I said. "She's gone." Ding, dong, the witch is dead.

Sam emerged. "I heard you, you know. I had the door open a crack. You lied." He grinned as we walked back to the studio. "You said I said I would never come back here. I thought you didn't lie."

"Only to you, Sam. To everyone else, I lie all the time."

For some reason that made Sam's grin widen.

"Who's Cerberus?" Lydia wanted to know.

"Guardian of the gates of hell," I told her, and added, "a dog with three heads."

"Oh." She narrowed her eyes, regarding me.

"Go ahead," I said. "Though it's a cheap shot."

Lydia said, "You're right, I'm better than that. Where did she go?"

"Konecki? To Cromley's studio."

Sam frowned. "No, she wouldn't go there. Except to find me. They hate each other."

"I saw her go in. Maybe this has something to do with what Ellissa wanted to tell you." I had no idea if that was right, but the opportunity was too good to pass up.

"Oh." Sam thought. "Oh, well, then, maybe I will go see Ellissa." He looked at me and added, "After Sherron leaves."

That was likely to be the best we were going to get. Ernesto stood up. "Okay, papi," he said to Sam. "It's ready."

"Ready for what?"

"You got to program the number you want."

"I choose it?"

"Sí, papi. You don't got to tell nobody."

"Except Lydia," I added quickly. I caught Ernesto's eye.

"Oh," Ernesto said. "Yeah, somebody else got to know. Maybe Lydia."

Sam pursed his lips and nodded. "Okay, Lydia. But not Peter, or Sherron, or anyone else."

With Ernesto's guidance, Sam chose his code. He tried it twice, then again, grinning like a kid with a Christmas toy. "Come on," he said to Lydia, "I'll show you." She joined him at the door, and the two of them poked buttons and whispered to each other.

I paid Ernesto and took the paperwork. "He's funny," Ernesto said, packing up his tools.

"You don't know the half of it. Thanks for coming so fast."

"For you? Never a problem. Bye, Lydia."

Lydia waved and Ernesto headed for the elevator.

"Sam," I said, holding out the manila Luz for Locks envelope, "put this somewhere safe. In case you need to change the code again. You're in charge."

Sam gave the envelope a strange look. "I'm never in charge of anything."

"You are of this."

After a hesitation, he took the envelope from me, walked it to the window wall, and put it in a drawer in the back table. He looked at it as though he was unsure that was where it went. Then, resolutely, he closed the drawer.

A moment later, where that envelope belonged was no longer Sam's biggest problem. The elevator door slid open. Ernesto stood aside to let two people get out before he got in. The two new arrivals walked toward us. One was a uniformed NYPD officer. The other was Angela Grimaldi.

"Smith." Grimaldi nodded. "He in there?"

"Sam?"

"Who the hell else? He got a lawyer? Call him. I came to take him up."

"Sam?" I said again, as if there were a question. "Why?"

"On suspicion of homicide—Kimberly Pike. Why do you think?"

"You have new evidence? This morning you had nothing."

She nodded. "New physical evidence."

"On the clothes you took?"

"His? No. On hers. And that's all I'm giving you. Now, move."

Sam joined us at the door. "Hi, Angela."

"Hi, Sam. I'm sorry, but you're going to have to come with me."

Sam's eyes went wide. "Are you arresting me?"

"I'm afraid so."

"Sam," I started.

"Quiet! I did kill her, didn't I? Last night. Whatever her name was. I killed the other ones, too, right? But now I won't kill anybody else, because you're going to arrest me!" Sam looked at me, and then at Lydia, almost glowing. "I did kill them, and she's going to arrest me. Arrest me!" he demanded, turning back to Grimaldi.

She gestured to the uniformed cop. "Read him his rights. And cuff him in front." The uniform, whose nameplate read SEGURA, looked a little perplexed, but he did his job, muttering Sam's Miranda rights and clicking on handcuffs.

"I guess you can get forensic evidence off a body in a meat truck after all," Grimaldi said to me.

"What's the evidence, specifically?"

"Are you serious?"

"All right. But listen. Someone broke into Sam's apartment this morning. And into here sometime yesterday or today, too. That's why we changed the lock."

Grimaldi looked at Sam. "That true?"

He nodded earnestly.

"Did they take anything? Either place?"

Sam shrugged.

"Did you report it?"

Sam shook his head.

"Why not?" Grimaldi directed the question to me.

"It would've been hard to prove. I wasn't even sure it was true at the apartment until I saw what happened here."

"It was," Sam chimed in.

Grimaldi asked, "So, what happened here?"

I showed her the pencil and eraser drawer. She listened and looked. When I finished, she said, "That's it? Are you as crazy as he is?"

"If it were anyone else, I'd agree with you. But he knows."

She shook her head. "Well, good luck getting a crime scene team in here. I'm not requesting one. No way you're making a fool of my ass with this."

"I'm just thinking, whatever you have, something more's going on—"

"Stop it!" Sam said loudly. "Stop trying to talk her out of it. She's arresting me. She knows I killed those women. You didn't figure it out, so you're fired. Come on, Angela, let's go. Bye, Lydia."

Grimaldi lifted her eyebrows at me. "I guess you're fired." She looked around. "Are you Lydia? Smith's partner? I want to talk to you."

"Lydia Chin. Yes, Bill told me. Whenever you want."

Grimaldi shook Lydia's extended hand and then nodded to Segura, who gripped Sam's arm. The three of them marched down the hall to the elevator. Grimaldi pressed the button. As they got in and the elevator door started to close, she said to me again, "Call his lawyer."

22

I called Susan Tulis.

"Yeah, I heard he was out," Susan said, when I told her I was calling about Sam. "He's Picasso now, right?"

"He may be back in. He's just been arrested. I'll fill you in and I'll cover your bill, but right now he needs someone down there to help him keep his mouth shut. I get the feeling he's about to sing even though he doesn't know the tune. Or the words."

"Stick to straight narrative. Your metaphors are always baroque. I'll send someone. But find somebody else to pay me, because I want you working for me, not the other way."

Susan was the defense attorney who had called me in on Sam's original arrest six years earlier. We had a retainer arrangement: she paid me a dollar a year and that meant I was working for her any time she said I was, actual bill to be determined later. It made sense to invoke it here. Anything I learned working for Sam's attorney would be protected by attorney-client privilege, but there was no such thing as PI-client privilege. Plus, Sam had fired me.

Susan said, "Give me the details."

I told her what she needed to know about why I was working for Sam again, finishing with his recent arrest.

"Okay, I'm on it," she said. "And tell me this, not that it matters. Do we think he did what they picked him up for?"

"I don't. But he does."

"Ah, yes, that's our Sam."

When I hung up, Lydia said, "Susan's in?"

"She's in. And she doesn't think any more of my use of symbolic language than you do."

"I always admired her. What now, boss?"

"I'd better call Peter and tell him what happened. Then how about we drop over next door and shake some trees?"

She sighed. "You just don't know good advice when you hear it, do you?"

It turned out we were able to go next door sooner than we thought. Peter, The Tabor Group's receptionist told me, was home sick, and Leslie was out. I left a message that it was urgent one of them get in touch with me, clicked off, and said to Lydia, "I do have Peter's cell number. But, you know, the guy doesn't feel well. Maybe we should give him a break, just for a little?"

"You mean, just while the Wicked Witch of the West is still at Dorothy's?"

"Now who's using unauthorized analogies?" We stepped into the hall and shut the door. "Lock up, you who knowest the code."

"It's *giraffe*," Lydia said, poking buttons. "He made the letters into numbers."

"What do you do for the *r*?"

She gave me a baffled look so like Sam's I had to laugh. "The one and then the eight. No one ever said it had to be one letter, one number."

"Of course. My mistake."

It took a couple of loud pounds to get Cromley's door opened. When it flew wide with the customary yank, Cromley stood there, red-faced.

"Oh, God. What the hell do you want? Get lost."

Seeing Lydia didn't seem to soften her reaction to me. Or maybe it had, and that was why she hadn't socked me. The hand that wasn't on the doorknob was balled in a fist.

"We have news. You'd better let us come in."

"Why?"

"Really," Lydia said, "it's a good idea."

Cromley stood, clench-jawed, for another few seconds, then stepped aside. We walked past her on the narrow path and she slammed the door. Looking at the piled chaos of rolls and boxes, cans and brushes, I was reminded of Tony Oakhurst's turtles. What would Cromley be like, I wondered, without her shell?

We reached the clearing by the paint-smeared couch, where Sherron Konecki stood glowering. If I'd been wearing an outfit that snazzy, I wouldn't have sat down in this room, either.

I said, "Hope we're not interrupting anything."

"You are," Konecki snapped. "What do you want?"

"We thought you'd both like to know the police just arrested Sam."

"*What?*" That panicked burst came from Cromley. Konecki's eyes widened just a little, but she said nothing.

"On suspicion of murder. The woman who was killed at the Whitney last night."

After a moment, Konecki asked calmly, "Why?"

Cromley looked at me helplessly.

"They have physical evidence. The detective wouldn't be more specific."

Cromley found her voice. "But—"

With a sound like the ice you're standing on starting to crack, Konecki laughed. "Well," she said to Cromley. "There you go. Our arrangement's off."

Cromley, both hands now in fists, said desperately, "Sherron!"

But Konecki turned and slid past me and Lydia. She strode to the door and pulled it open. Pausing in the frame of the doorway—*Woman Leaving Room, in Relief and Anger*—she asked me, "Does he have an attorney?"

"Yes."

She arched a single eyebrow. "A good one?"

"Yes."

"If he needs anything, call me."

Konecki shot Cromley another triumphant look before she stalked down the hall to the elevator. Cromley made no move to follow but stared after her, looking like she was about to cry.

"That was interesting," I said. "What arrangement would that be, the one that's now off?"

Cromley swiveled to face me, staring poison. "None of your damn business! Get out."

I said to Lydia, "The two least likely contestants ever on *Let's Make a Deal*. One of them pleased that their arrangement fell through, the other upset. What does that suggest to you?"

"That one wanted it a lot more than the other."

"But the one who didn't want it was going to do it anyway."

"So the one who wanted it must have been very persuasive."

"But her persuasiveness went up in smoke with the news of Sam's arrest."

We both looked at Cromley.

"What are you talking about?" she said. "Sherron and I had a deal and now she's rethinking, so what? Get out."

"Rethinking, based on Sam's arrest," I said. "For being a serial killer. Oh, but you don't think he is, do you?"

"He's not," she retorted, but it sounded automatic and she didn't meet my eyes.

"You're a bad liar," Lydia said gently. "You had something important to tell Sam. You also told Sherron Konecki something, maybe the same thing, or else she told you something, that got you two in business together even though she didn't want it. Sam's on his way to jail; you'd better tell us."

"Are you crazy?"

"Sam is," I said. "But he's not a killer."

"Yes, he is! He was in prison for it!"

I regarded her. "'That was completely different.' That was your answer when I made that point yesterday. Now you've changed your mind?"

Cromley flushed. "You don't know what you're talking about. Get out! I want you both out of here right now, or I'll call the police myself."

I didn't know how empty Cromley's threat was, but there were other people we needed to talk to and I judged the chances of us getting anything from her to be at zero. I'd have called it in negative numbers, but as Lydia had said, Cromley was a bad liar. She slammed the door behind us as we left.

23

"I want to call Peter," I said as we walked back down the hall. "But from Sam's studio. With the door open."

"So we can see if Cromley leaves," Lydia said, keying in Sam's combination.

"I have an idle interest in two things." We stepped into Sam's studio. "One, if she does leave, where she's going, with whatever information she has that Konecki doesn't care about anymore. And two—"

"What she had in her hand."

"You saw that, too?"

"Who do you think you're talking to?"

"I withdraw the question."

"Something small," Lydia said. "Something she didn't want us to know about, but something she didn't want to leave where Sherron could grab it. And something, therefore, that has to do with the arrangement that's off."

"You're reading my mind."

"Who do you think you're talking to? Now, read mine."

"You want to—"

We heard the door down the hall click open.

Lydia gave it a couple of beats. "Okay," she said to me conversationally. "Bye. Talk later." Sauntering out to the hall, she almost bumped into Cromley on her way to the elevator.

Cromley stopped. "What are you doing in Sam's studio?"

"Bill has some calls to make," Lydia said pleasantly. "I'm leaving, myself. We have other cases besides this one, and until Sam's arraigned or released, there's not a lot we can do here. Unless you want to tell us—"

"As if." Cromley strode ahead of Lydia and just about punched the elevator button.

When the elevator door closed in front of them, Lydia was looking at her phone and Cromley was looking like it was a good thing the elevator wasn't a pressure cooker. She'd have blown the top off.

I walked to the window to see where they went. Lydia's plan, of course, was to follow Cromley, but as it turned out, she didn't have to go far. They issued onto the sidewalk, Cromley in the lead. Lydia stopped and looked at her phone some more and Cromley, without a glance at her, stalked across the street to Tony Oakhurst's studio.

My phone rang.

"See that?" Lydia said when I answered.

"I did. A lot of cross-pollination going on this afternoon. If she goes anywhere else, stay with her. Let me know."

"I have something else you want to know. 1-2-1-3-1-4-1-5."

"What's that?"

"The code to Cromley's studio. It'll save you lock picking time. Sam told me while he was showing me his."

"Why?"

"Because I asked him nicely."

"You're a genius."

"No, I'm just nice. Listen, you'd better hurry. She might come storming out of Oakhurst's and back upstairs any minute. It seems to be the thing to do today."

Knowing Cromley's code did a lot more than save me lock picking time. I'm not bad, but combination codes test the limit of my skill; I might not have gotten in at all. I found the code Lydia had given me depressingly, though not surprisingly, unimaginative, but it worked.

I closed the door behind me and stood just inside Cromley's studio, wondering where in the hell to start. I was looking for the small thing she'd held in her fist that had unfavorably but unquestionably impressed Sherron Konecki. It was possible Cromley had taken it with her, maybe to talk to Tony Oakhurst about, or maybe just so she'd know where it was. But it was also possible she hadn't. From all accounts, Cromley and Oakhurst didn't like each other. Oakhurst was intimidating in a way Konecki wasn't, for all her imperial posturing and all his hail-fellow friendliness. He was a large man with a jump-and-the-net-will-appear reputation and a penchant for metaphorically prying off turtle's shells. A thin, angry woman with a case to make, whatever it was, might have chosen to leave Exhibit A behind.

On the other hand, I thought as I stood there, she might have left a five-hundred-pound gorilla behind, sleeping among the piles and boxes, and unless it snored, I wouldn't find it. Searching this kind of disarrayed haystack for a needle that might not even be here could well be a fool's errand.

But I'd been on those before. I moved into the room, trying to be methodical. I opened drawers holding jumbles of paint tubes, lifted papers that seemed to have bumps in the middle of the stack like the pea in the princess's bed. I looked in cans of brushes and on tables thick with pencils and erasers. I guessed Cromley didn't have a pencil and eraser drawer.

And just after that thought, I heard Sam's voice in my head. *She says literally no one ever goes near her easels.*

I threaded my way to the back of the room, where Cromley's three easels stood by the windows. The paintings on two of them didn't look like they'd changed since yesterday, but though I couldn't be sure, it seemed like more scarlet, cardinal, and crimson had blossomed on the center one, the one Lydia had been looking at. I stood before it, looking not at the painting but at the area around it. The table, the palette, the brush tray. The cleaning rags.

With great care I opened each bunched-up rag. Cromley had quite a few, mounded in a volcano-shaped heap, but here, as with her lock combination—and her canvases, if I reverted to art critic mode—her imagination was limited. What I was looking for was wrapped in the rag buried at the bottom of the pile.

At least I assumed it was what I was looking for: a small box, the velvet-covered kind you get from a jeweler. Using a rag as a glove, I opened it. Inside, on satin, rested three single earrings.

I wrapped the box in its rag and stuck it in my pocket. I trod the barely cleared path back to the door, cracked it open, and peered into the hall. I saw no one, so I slunk out and giraffed my way into Sam's studio.

24

As I shut Sam's door behind me, my phone rang.

"Get out," Lydia said.

"I'm way ahead of you. I'm already out and lounging around at Sam's, mission accomplished. She's on her way back?"

"Waiting for the elevator."

"Okay, come on up. We need to talk to her."

I cut the call and waited. The elevator bell dinged; that would be Cromley. By just about the time Cromley would've walked—or stomped—down the hall to her studio, I heard her door open and slam. Then the bell dinged a second time. I stepped into the hallway, closing Sam's door behind me, and watched Lydia emerge from the elevator.

"You found something?" Lydia said, walking toward me.

"I did." I took the box from my pocket, unfolded the rag, and showed her the contents.

"Oh, God, Bill," she breathed. She met my eyes. "The trophies? From the killings?"

"Or what looks like that. I think we want to know what they really are, where they came from, and why Cromley had them." I stuck the box back in my pocket for the walk to Cromley's studio.

It took some hard pounding on Cromley's door to get even a shouted answer from inside, and when it came, it was "Go away!"

"No," I yelled back, and kept pounding.

Finally the door was jerked open. Cromley, ashen-faced, stared from me to Lydia and back. "What the fuck do you want?"

"To talk about these." I took the box from my pocket again, unwrapped it, and opened it.

For a moment, Cromley froze. Then she threw a wild look at the pile of rags behind her. Whipping her head back to me, she croaked, "Where did you get those?"

I nodded toward the easels.

"*What?* How—" She charged to the back and starting flinging rags into the air. Finally she spun to face us. "You bastard! You fucking bastard. You broke in? You fucking broke into my studio? You son of a bitch. You can't do that. This is *my* studio. You can't just come crashing in here and taking my things."

"Your things," I said. "These are your things?"

Lydia and I stepped in from the hall and I shut the door.

Cromley stopped, looking sick. "Of course they are. They're mine, I wear them. Give them back." She grabbed for the box, but I pulled it out of her reach.

"They don't look like your style," Lydia said.

"What the fuck do you know?"

"Not much," Lydia said. "Why don't you tell us?"

"Tell you what?"

"Where you got them."

"Some store somewhere, I don't remember."

I looked at Lydia. "I don't know about you, but I'm too tired for this bullshit. Let's go."

I turned and opened the door again. Cromley choked out, "Wait! Where are you going?"

Leaving the door open, I turned back and said, "To see Detective Grimaldi. I'm betting these are either the trophies from the killings Sam claims he did, or something put together to pass as them. And I'm betting Grimaldi will know which, and will really, really want to know why the hell you had them."

In a voice that had devolved from choked to strangled, Cromley said, "Close the goddamn door."

I shrugged but closed it. Cromley opened her mouth to speak, but before she did, I could practically see a lightbulb go on over her head. She gave me a sly glance. "If you show them to the detective, she'll want to know where you got them. And I'll tell her you broke in here and stole them. That wouldn't be so good for your license, would it?"

I laughed and Lydia smiled. Lydia said, "You watch too many movies. Bill's license has been hanging by a thread for years. One more B and E won't make any difference."

"Especially," I added, "if it produces evidence in a multiple murder case."

"But that can't be evidence! You didn't have a warrant or anything."

"I don't need a warrant. I'm a thief. And you didn't have one when you stole them from Sam's studio, either."

"That wasn't stealing. He's my friend."

"Oh, so that is where you got them?"

Cromley's eyes widened. She made a tiny sound.

"Tell us," I said.

She didn't respond.

"All right, never mind. We can let the police decide what's evidence and who stole what."

Cromley stumbled to the clearing and dropped onto the cruddy couch. She put her head in her hands.

Lydia walked over and sat down beside her. "It's okay," she said gently. "I'm betting you were trying to help Sam. That's what I told Bill."

After a moment, Cromley lifted her head and wiped her damp eyes. She gave me a glance of pure hatred and then shifted to face Lydia.

"That's right," she said, just above a hoarse whisper and only to Lydia.

"Can you tell me about it?"

Cromley swallowed. "This morning. I checked in Sam's studio when I got here, but he wasn't there. I was working, waiting for him to come back, and I heard his door close. I didn't hear the elevator or him opening the door, but sometimes I don't hear things when I'm working. Because I'm concentrating, you know? So when I heard it close, I ran out. He wasn't in the hall. I thought, oh good, maybe he was just getting here, not leaving, and I knocked, but he didn't answer. He sometimes doesn't hear either, when he's working, so I went in."

Cromley paused. Sam's miserable voice came back to me, complaining about people coming and going in his studio.

Softly, Lydia prompted, "But he wasn't there?"

"No one was there. I thought, oh shit, I missed him, and I just sort of stood there. Because I was so worried about him and he didn't answer my calls or texts, you know?" For some reason that got me another glare. "And while I was standing there, I saw the drawer was a little bit open. The one where he keeps his pencils."

Lydia nodded.

"I got—a kind of chill? It wasn't open much, just a little, but it wasn't like that when I went in the first time and Sam never leaves the drawers open, or the cabinets, or anything. It's his OCD."

Lydia nodded again.

"I thought, he must have been seriously upset when he was there—I mean, kind of crazed, to leave a drawer open. So I went to close it so it wouldn't upset him when he came back. But it was a little stuck. So I opened it to see why. And I found that box." Cromley stopped as if that were the end of the story.

"What did you do?"

A tiny flash of the Cromley fire flared at Lydia. "Obviously, I took it."

"Why?"

"Come on."

"To blackmail Sam?"

"No! Are you crazy? He's my friend. I just—I thought it was safer with me than with him. He might go running to the cops with it or something."

"If he's a serial killer and these are the trophies, then he *should* go running to the cops. Or you should."

"He's not! He . . ." Cromley trailed off and shifted around as though she'd abruptly discovered the couch was as uncomfortable as it looked.

"If he's not," Lydia said, "why does he have the trophies?"

"We don't even know that's what they are!"

"No, you're right, we don't. And as long as the police don't have them, we don't ever have to know. We can just pretend they're not."

"Or," I said, "we can pretend they are."

Cromley snapped her head up and gave me the foreseeable sneer. "What the hell are you talking about?"

"I'm not as nice as Lydia, so I don't even believe you were trying to help your friend Sam when you took the box in the first place. I think you realized what gold it was the minute you saw it. You grabbed it, called Sherron Konecki, and told her she'd better come over."

Cromley's face blazed. "That had nothing to do with anything."

"Crap," I said. "You showed it to Sherron, told her where you got it, and made some kind of deal based on it. The fact that it might be evidence that could get a crazy killer convicted—I mean, your friend Sam—and save other women's lives didn't bother you at all."

"Bullshit. Who asked you? You're an idiot. I don't know why Sam ever thought you were any good."

Lydia grinned. "Actually, Bill's wrong a lot. That's why he needs me. He's screwing up again?"

"Damn right."

"How?"

Cromley folded her arms. "You serious with that good cop bad cop bullshit? You think I'm stupid? Go to hell, both of you."

"She wasn't blackmailing Sam," I said to Lydia. "For what? And why bother? He already adores her." Hard to fathom, but demonstrably true. "He'd give her anything she wanted. But he doesn't have what she wants. Sherron Konecki," I said to Cromley. "You'd do pretty much anything to get into her world, wouldn't you? What was the deal? Her gallery would take you on and you wouldn't tell anyone about the earrings?"

Cromley rolled her eyes. "That's the most idiotic thing I ever heard. You really don't know how things work, do you? If I made her sign me, so what? Even if I made her give me a show. She could sell me or not sell me, whatever she wanted to do. She could just shake her head a tiny bit when people looked at my stuff, say I was overpriced right now and they should wait, or I passed my peak already, or I wasn't developing along the lines she'd hoped—whatever bullshit. Gallerists do it all the time, fuck over an artist to make the collectors feel loved. It doesn't cost her anything except storage space to sign an artist. Just her having me wouldn't do me any good."

"You could threaten to tell people about the box unless she made you big."

"And she could say she can lead the collectors to water but she can't make them buy."

"True," I conceded. Susan Tulis would've loved that one. "But you did have some kind of a deal. Something that evaporated once Sam got arrested."

"What a pile of crap."

"Oh, boy." I looked at Lydia. "What do you think? I'm ready to go."

She stood. "Yeah, me too. So long," she said to Cromley.

"Where are you going?"

"Where we were going before," I said. "To the cops."

"You can't!" Cromley jumped to her feet. "I told you where I got the box. We had a deal."

I couldn't resist: "What a pile of crap. Seriously, you want to be arrested for withholding evidence? In a multiple murder case? The NYPD doesn't screw around with that kind of thing. Besides, there's something else."

"What? What else?"

"Sam was with me, or with me and the cops, or with his bartender, out in Brooklyn all morning. If this box was left in his studio when you heard the door close, Sam didn't leave it."

Cromley stared in stupefied silence.

"And if that's true, someone else is killing women and trying to frame your friend Sam."

Cromley frowned in what looked like genuine confusion. "But not the killer."

"But not the killer, what?"

"The killer didn't leave the box. If it's real. Though I guess, if it's fake . . ."

"What are you talking about?"

A small smirk; Cromley's inner know-it-all glowed momentarily through the dark clouds of anger. "The killer didn't leave the box. If it's real. He wouldn't give up his trophies."

"To throw the police off the scent, to frame someone else?"

"No way. Killers who take trophies do it so they can relive the crime. They're as important as the crime itself; they bring it all back. He probably has ritual times he looks at them. Maybe he touches them, maybe he doesn't, maybe he even puts them on if his ear is pierced. No way he'd give them up."

"Now that's interesting. If you're right—"

"Of course I'm right."

"*If* you're right, it could mean these are fake. Or it could mean they're real and they're Sam's, and he was just moving them from one hiding place to another. Which did you think when you took them?"

The smirk faded; the clouds closed over.

"Never mind," I said. "Why did you go see Tony Oakhurst?"

"Asshole."

"Me or Tony? Because I don't care what you think about me, but I want to know why you went to see Tony. To make a deal with him, too?"

"What the hell kind of a deal?"

"Did you tell him you'd give the trophies to the police and his friend Sam would go to prison unless he paid up?"

"Are you kidding? What does Tony care? He'd go to the prison and photograph Sam behind bars and Sherron would sell the damn photos for a fortune."

"I think you're right about that," Lydia said calmly. "But you went to see him and you came back angry."

"He pissed me off."

"How?"

"Never mind. Anyway, he'll be sorry."

"Why?"

"Because screw him. And screw you, too. Give me back that box and get out."

"Why did you go see Tony?"

"Give me back the box."

I looked at Lydia. "Stalemate?"

"Looks that way."

"Anything else for us?" I asked Cromley.

She started to sputter. "You—I—"

Lydia and I left. The sputtering turned to shouted curses as we walked down the hall. The slamming of her studio door could be heard as the elevator opened.

25

"Boy," Lydia said as we rode down in the elevator. "She really doesn't like you, does she?"

"Why should I be different from the rest of the world? You might want to look into your heart and see what you're doing wrong, that she likes you so much."

"I think she changed her mind on that. Probably because of the company I keep. We're really going to the cops with that box, right?"

"We sure as hell are. Even though every word of that story might have been a lie. She's bragged more than once that she knows everything there is to know about serial killers. I think she's capable of putting together that collection of earrings for the sole purpose of blackmailing Sherron Konecki into whatever their deal was. We don't know that earrings are the trophies in this case, much less that these are them, but Konecki doesn't, either. If they are, her golden goose heads back to prison and there go her eggs."

"You'll never change, will you?"

"You wouldn't want me to."

"So we're saying maybe it's not as complicated—or as long term—as Cromley making Konecki represent her. Maybe she just wanted a big payout right now."

"Could be. And Konecki agreed because if Sam's actually doing these killings, eventually he'll get caught—and because it's him, it'll be sooner rather than later. She needs to sell as much of his work as she can while he's still worth a fortune."

"Wow. That's cold," Lydia said as the elevator let us out in the lobby. "He'll keep killing, but she'll get rich?"

"They do call her the Ice Queen. But now it looks like he's been caught, so there's no point in this deal."

"But Bill, Konecki aside, Cromley's story might actually be true. That she found the box in Sam's drawer after she heard his door close. But Sam came running out in a panic when he got here and saw the drawer open."

"He sure did."

"Which means someone planted it there."

"Unless he did and he forgot."

"I guess that could be. But if it wasn't Sam and if Cromley's right, it wasn't the killer, it's someone else, who knows who the killer is and wants to frame Sam."

We walked out into the afternoon. "Before we go up to Sixty-Seventh Street," I said, "I want to try Peter's cell. It might be that Susan called him already and told him Sam's been arrested, but if not, he should know."

I lit a cigarette and made the call.

Peter answered his phone in a dull monotone. "What is it, Smith?" He must have been really ill if he couldn't summon the strength to be irritated at me.

"Sorry, Peter," I said. "I know you're sick, but there's bad news."

"Tell me." He sounded like a man whose bad news cup had run over long ago.

"Sam's been arrested. For the murder last night at the Whitney."

A pause. "Oh, Jesus." In the silence, I could picture him wiping his hand down his face.

"They have some kind of physical evidence. I don't know what it is, but someone from Susan Tulis's office is there, so we'll know soon."

"Physical evidence," Peter repeated, as though he didn't quite get the meaning of the words. "They can't. That he killed her? How can they? He didn't."

"I don't think so, either, but we need to find out what the evidence is." I didn't tell him about the potential physical evidence wrapped in a rag in my pocket. "Call Susan and she'll tell you whether he's been booked and where he is."

"Susan. Yes, okay. Jesus. Let me know what you hear." He hung up.

"How did he take it?" Lydia wanted to know.

"He sounds like someone who'd have to get better just to die."

"Well, it's bad news to hear when you're sick, that your brother's been arrested for murder."

"Or when you're well. I wonder if there's more to it."

"To what?"

"He was fine yesterday, but now he really sounded like hell. I wonder if Michael Sanger ditched them or something. You up for one more stop before we go uptown?"

"You're pushing the withholding-evidence envelope. Let me guess—Tony Oakhurst, right?"

"Everyone else seems to be doing it."

Amara, the ennui-filled assistant, answered Oakhurst's door. She gave us enough of a frown so we'd know who was in charge, but didn't tell us outright to get lost. "Is Tony expecting you?"

"He'll want to see us."

Unconvinced, she raised a pierced eyebrow. "Hold on." She left us between the outer and inner doors, but not for long. "Yeah, okay," she said grudgingly when she returned. "You can come in."

This time Oakhurst came striding right over. "Smith," he said, and then, giving Lydia a quick appraising glance, said, "hi. Saw you at the Whitney, but I don't think we've met. Tony Oakhurst."

"Lydia Chin. Bill's partner."

"Lucky Bill." Oakhurst let the glance linger, then turned to me. "So what the fuck is going on? Ellissa Cromley blew in here to say Sam's been arrested."

"For the murder at the Whitney last night. You heard about that?"

"On cable news this morning. You know—if it bleeds, it leads. Damn. I guess we left too early, huh?" He grinned.

"If you don't mind, I'd like to ask you a couple of questions. Can we sit down?"

"Is that one of them? Sorry. Yeah, sure, come on." He led the way to the benches. Lydia looked at the photos on the wall the way Oakhurst had looked at her.

"Anyone want a drink?"

Lydia and I both declined, Lydia because she rarely drinks, me because after this, we were going up to the 19th Precinct, though I didn't mention my reason to Oakhurst.

"Seriously? Neither of you? Well, I do." Oakhurst leaned to the cabinet and, I guess since I hadn't asked for bourbon, took out the Macallan 18. "What can I do for you? Or for Sam, poor guy?"

"Tell me first, why did Cromley come over here?"

"Like I said, to tell me Sam had been arrested."

"Not for nothing, but I got the feeling you two aren't close. Why would she bother?"

"I think she wanted to gloat. That she knew something important about our pal Sam that I didn't."

"That was it?"

Oakhurst shrugged. "How the hell do I know? Maybe she wanted to case the joint for something to steal to pay the rent on that dismal gallery of hers."

Lydia asked, "It's dismal, Ellissa Cromley's gallery?"

"Are you kidding? With her on the selection committee? You need a good siesta, go to one of their openings."

I said, "She sure was pissed off when she left here."

"Christ, Ellissa was born pissed off." He sipped. "I took the news about Sam pretty well. I mean, it's not completely unexpected, right? Maybe it bothered her that I didn't clutch my pearls and faint." He winked at Lydia.

"Maybe," I said. "Okay, what about Sherron Konecki? Why was she here?"

Oakhurst's laugh held a sharp edge. "You have me under surveillance or something?"

"We happened to be in Sam's studio."

"Just staring out the window, watching the comings and goings?"

"Something like that."

"Sherron's my dealer. I called and asked her to drop by. I have new work I wanted to show her."

"She looked pissed off when she left, too."

"She didn't like it."

"Enough to leave here furious?"

"I can only hope. What are you getting at?"

"I'm not sure."

"Well," Lydia took over smoothly, "it's been a very strange day. Someone broke into Sam's apartment in Brooklyn, did you know that?"

Oakhurst shifted to give her his full attention. "No, I did not. Did they take anything?"

"Doesn't look like it. Broke into his studio here, too."

"You're shitting me."

"No. And they don't seem to have taken anything there, either. Ellissa Cromley didn't tell you that?"

"Goddamn it, no, she didn't. She knows?"

I said, "Maybe she thought her big news was more important. Or maybe she was keeping something in reserve so she could come back and gloat again."

"That would be like her. Anything else 'strange'?" Oakhurst asked Lydia.

"When Sherron Konecki left here, she went over to talk to Cromley."

"The two of them aren't close either, are they?" I said.

"They can't stand each other. Ellissa thinks Sherron is a frigid-ass bitch, and Sherron thinks Ellissa is a talentless suck-up. They're both right."

"Well, she went over there. And then Cromley came storming over here. And of course, in between, Sam got arrested."

"Holy shit." Oakhurst finished his drink. "Yeah." He rolled the glass between his palms. "So, why did Sherron go to Ellissa's?"

Lydia gave him innocent eyes. "We were hoping you'd know."

"I don't, and, God, would I like to. Right after she was here?"

"Directly from here. What did you say to her that would have sent her charging over there like a mad bull?"

Oakhurst laughed. "Let me get this straight. You think my new work pissed her off so much she went right away to see someone she generally crosses the street to avoid?"

"We're just trying to get at the answers here," Lydia said with a smile.

"Why don't you call Sherron and ask? Or Ellissa? I'm sure Ellissa would be happy to talk at you for hours."

"Call" must have been the magic word, because Oakhurst's phone started to ring. He pulled it from the back pocket of his jeans and said, "Franklin . . . Yes, I did, I have something I think you'll like . . . Now? Well, okay, if you are. Yeah, actually, ten minutes works for me. Great, see you then." He clicked off, slid the phone back in his pocket, finished his scotch.

"Okay," he said. "Tell you what. I'll call Sherron and find out about this little love affair between her and Ellissa. But I can guarantee you, asking her while she's still fuming will just get me reamed out. She needs time to calm down. I'll let you know what I find out. And call me if anything else 'strange' happens, okay?" He clunked his empty glass on the glass cube and stood. "Sorry, but I have a collector coming over. Your pal Franklin." He nodded at me. "Amara, could you let these guys out? Thanks." He shook my hand, then Lydia's. For her, he used both of his, plus a lopsided smile. "Talk soon."

Oakhurst strode to the back while Amara drifted over and unlocked the inner door, waiting in bored silence for us to leave.

26

As Lydia and I headed for the subway, she said, "He'll call her after she calms down? And he'll let us know?"

"Yeah. And the hoot owls are flirting with the chickens."

Lydia rolled her eyes.

"But it's interesting how interested he is in what went on between Konecki and Cromley," I said. "Personally, I'm more interested in what went on between Konecki and him. And Cromley and him. By the way, I feel compelled to mention that you flat out lied to him. We know why Konecki went to see Cromley."

"He leered. I have no obligations to men who leer. And he was lying to us, too. Cromley didn't just come to tell him Sam got arrested. I think she told him about the earrings."

"He was definitely lying. I'm not so sure about the earrings, but I did get the feeling that whatever she wanted from him, she didn't get it."

"Not her day. I'd like to say, though, that I'm getting tired of being the good cop. Can we switch it up a little?"

"No one would buy it."

"You could practice. In the mirror."

"Even I wouldn't buy it." I took out the phone and made the next call.

"Grimaldi."

"Smith."

"Booked, got a lawyer, headed downtown. Anything else I can do for you?"

"I have something you want to see."

"What is it?"

"Evidence. Though I'm not sure of what."

"Why do I want to see it? Never mind, you're not gonna give up. I'm at the precinct. Can you be here soon?"

"Sooner."

We took the subway, faster than a midday cab would have been. The 68th Street stop was a block from the 19th Precinct.

"Nice building," Lydia said as we approached.

"Only on the outside. The inside is as crapped-up as any other cop house."

"Is that a metaphor for something?"

"Life."

Upstairs in the squad room, Grimaldi was behind her desk. One other detective, a big, broad-shouldered, brown-skinned man whose nameplate read IGLESIAS sat at a desk across the room, two-finger typing at his computer. Everyone else was gone. Must've been a big day for crime on the Upper East Side.

"Smith," Grimaldi said. "And Ms. Chin. Good of you to come."

"Am I hearing sarcasm?"

"Only about you. Ms. Chin I wanted to see."

"Lydia. I'd be glad to answer any questions," Lydia said, "but I think you should see what we have first."

"Curiosity's killing me."

I brought the rag-wrapped box out of my pocket. Grimaldi took it, used the rag to open the box, and burst out, "Shit! Oh, shit! Is this what I think it is?"

"I don't know. Are earrings the trophies here?"

She shot me a look. "Okay, they are. Son of a bitch, where did you get these? Wait. Sit." Grimaldi moved some papers, put the box on her desk, photographed it and the contents. "Where's the other one?"

"The other what?"

"I have four vics, and you're giving me three earrings."

"That's what I found."

"In the box? In the rag?"

"Yes."

"Where?"

"Ellissa Cromley's studio."

"Who?"

"Next door to Sam's. His friend."

"Oh, yeah, okay, her. Where's she now?"

"Still there, as far as I know."

"She give you this?"

"No. It was hidden. I found it while she was out."

"She know you have it?"

"Now, yes."

"Female serial killers killing women." Grimaldi bit her lower lip. "Very, very rare."

"She says she stole it."

"You believe her?"

"Yes."

"Long story?"

"Yes."

"Then wait." Grimaldi pulled open a drawer, took out two plastic evidence bags, scribbled on them, slipped the box into one and the rag into the other. "Stay here. Get yourselves some coffee. No phone calls. Or texts. I don't want *anyone* knowing what the trophies are, get it? Unless you called the *Post* already?"

I raised my hands. "No one." Lydia shook her head.

Grimaldi scooted out the door while Lydia sat down in the guest chair and I got myself a cup of coffee from the pot on the counter. It was good;

in my experience, cop coffee gets a bad rap. I pulled a chair over from an absent detective's desk. Lydia and I didn't speak until Grimaldi got back. Coming through the door, she said, "Gabi?"

"No phone calls," Iglesias said without looking up from his keyboard. "Or texts."

"You don't trust us?" I asked.

"Why would I? That stuff's on its way to Jamaica"—Jamaica, Queens, home of the NYPD Crime Lab—"but if they're not the trophies, I'll eat my hat. Look."

She walked to the case board, on the wall behind her desk. "This is Pike. This is the one earring she had on this morning when we found her."

Four crime scene photos, head shots of dead women, marched across the top of the whiteboard, with body shots and close-ups of wounds in rows below, and colored-marker lists, notes, and questions under that. In the photo Grimaldi tapped, the earring in Kimberly Pike's right ear was a match for one of the three in the box.

Grimaldi gazed at the board, then turned and dropped into her chair. "This better be good. If you've had those and you've been holding out—And where the hell's the other one?"

"I don't know where it is," I said. "That's what I found. And we haven't been holding out, though it would've helped if we'd known what the trophies were from the beginning."

"Helped what, besides me being busted back to beat cop?"

"I found those about an hour ago. If we'd been sure, we'd have called right away."

"That may be crap, but I'll make you a deal—I won't worry about it right now. Where exactly did you 'find' them? And what have you been doing in that hour that was more important than calling me?"

"How about we add to the deal you tell us what the physical evidence is you arrested Sam on?"

"How about you tell me what I asked or I *will* worry about you holding out on me?"

"When you put it that way." I told Grimaldi the whole story: Cromley hiding from us something we were sure she'd been showing to Konecki; the two of them having a deal that Konecki called off when I told them about Sam's arrest; me stealing the box when Cromley went to talk to Oakhurst; Cromley claiming she'd taken the box from Sam's studio; and Oakhurst denying knowing anything about anything.

"Your mama," Grimaldi said when I was through. "So, forgetting you just admitted to a felony, you're saying your wacko had the trophies?"

"Unless Cromley's lying, and she's not very good at that, they were in his studio." I didn't point out Cromley had committed the same felony; that didn't make me less guilty. "But that doesn't mean Sam knew about it. Cromley says she heard someone leave the studio in the morning, and then she went in and found the box. In the morning Sam was with me. And," I pointed out, "you."

"And he came squawking into the hallway when he saw his drawer was open, yeah, you said. He may be a better liar than she is. Or he may have stuck them in that drawer in, you know, a fugue state, and forgotten all about it."

"That would be easier to buy if one of those earrings weren't from last night."

"Why?" Grimaldi leaned back in her chair and steepled her fingers. "You don't think he had time? Why couldn't he have come up to the Whitney while you were sleeping, killed Kimberly Pike, put the trophy in the box and brought it to the studio, and then vamoosed back to Brooklyn?"

"That's a lot of careful thinking for a drunken guy in a fugue state."

Lydia said, "And the killer stuffed Kimberly Pike in the truck. Another step, more careful thinking."

"You, too?" Grimaldi said.

"Also, how did he find her?" Lydia went on. "I know you think he might have gone back to the Whitney for some crazy-man reason, and then run into her coming out of a bar or something, Detective. But what about the people she'd been with? Or even if she was by herself, a bar isn't empty just because you're drinking alone. It would've been hours after the end of the demonstration before Sam got back to the Whitney. Someone would've seen her. Or Sam. Or them together. Has anyone?"

"So far, no," Grimaldi admitted. "We can't put either of them in the area after the demonstration broke up. We're still canvassing the neighborhood. His, too, in Brooklyn, to see if anyone saw him running around in the middle of the night."

"You won't find anyone," I said. "He didn't leave."

"You hope."

She was right, but I ignored that. "If no one saw Pike later, she must have been killed during or right after the demonstration, when Sam was on the run and then with us. Unless you're thinking she hid out by herself somewhere for hours waiting for a secret rendezvous with Sam that they'd already set up?"

"Still possible," Grimaldi said, and then, "but yeah, I don't buy it, either." She turned to the board again, then back to us. "And you never saw that fourth earring?"

"No."

"No."

"All right. Why don't—ah, shit."

Lydia and I twisted toward the squad room door to see what had brought Grimaldi to her feet.

Ike Cavanaugh.

I stood, too, as did Lydia beside me.

"What the hell, Ike? You have some special radar for when Smith's around?" Grimaldi said.

"I came to see you," Cavanaugh grunted. He seemed to shove a path through the room although there was no one in his way. He thumbed at me. "What's he doing here?"

"I asked them to come in," Grimaldi said. "What are *you* doing here?"

"Who's she?"

"Smith's partner."

"They give you anything? Or they're just trying to get Tabor sprung?"

"What are you doing here, Ike?"

"I heard you picked up Tabor. I came to say congrats."

"Thanks. Now, good-bye."

"Don't give me that bullshit. This time there's evidence and he's not walking."

"If the evidence is good, he's not. If it's crap—"

"If it's crap, find more."

"If there's more, I'll find it."

"Only if you look for it. Instead of sitting here on your big fat intuition having a tea party with Tabor's friends."

Grimaldi looked at him. "Ike, how do you know there's evidence?"

"It's on the grapevine. You picked him up this afternoon."

"That's on the grapevine, sure. But the grapevine doesn't usually give a shit about details. What's to say I didn't just get convinced by him the hundredth time he tried to turn himself in?"

"You? Not goddamn likely."

"I swear to God, Ike, if I find you've been sticking your nose in my case, or second-guessing me, or—"

"Oh, don't get your thong in a twist. Everybody needs a little help sometimes."

"Get out."

"Listen, missy—"

"I've had enough of you, Ike."

"Ooh, I'm scared."

"Detective Cavanaugh?" That came from across the room, where Iglesias had stood up at his desk. "Ike? We haven't met, but I'm Detective Sergeant Gabino Iglesias, and I'd take it as a personal favor if you'd get the hell out of this squad room right now."

Cavanaugh looked at him, then threw a smirk at Grimaldi. "See? Good to have help, right?"

"I'm helping *you*, Cavanaugh." Iglesias came around his desk. "And myself, because I don't want to have to do the paperwork once Grimaldi here throws you out the goddamn window. Now, beat it."

Cavanaugh's already ruddy face flushed. "Fuck you all," he snarled, and pushed his way back through nobody, out of the room.

27

Grimaldi stood staring at the door while Cavanaugh's steps slapped down the hall. Then she turned. "Thanks, Gabi."

"No problem. Everybody needs a little help sometimes."

"On second thought, fuck you."

The big detective got himself a cup of coffee and returned to his desk. Grimaldi sat again and looked at Lydia. "Okay, Ms. Chin. Tell me about Pike. You spoke to her earlier yesterday, right? Did you see her at the demo?"

Lydia and I each took the chairs we'd vacated. "Yes, and yes," she said. "I spoke to her at the bar Annika Hausman was last seen at. She couldn't identify Sam's photo, but later around the back of the Whitney, she was screaming, 'It's him, it's him.'"

"So she did recognize him there?"

"I don't know if she recognized him. Anyone at the demonstration probably would've known what Sam looked like. She might have been just alerting the other protestors that Sam was around back."

"What else did she tell you when you spoke to her?"

"Nothing. She thought she remembered a dark-haired white guy hitting on some of the women in the bar, and he might have hit on Annika, but he might not have, or that might have been a different night."

"Fantastic. Did she see who Hausman left the bar with?"

"No, Kimberly left first."

"Anything else? Anything anyone said, maybe the bartender, another customer?"

"No. The bartender wasn't sure about the photo, either."

"Yeah," Grimaldi said, "that's pretty much what we got. This is her, by the way. Hausman." She pointed to the photo next to Kimberly Pike's at the top of the board. A blonde with a tousled cut and no earring in her right ear. Like Kimberly Pike's, Annika Hausman's pale eyes were open, staring at nothing. "Just so you know."

Again, Grimaldi took a moment, gazing at the photo. Then she turned back, leaned her forearms on her desk. "Okay. Now. Why did you think it was any of your business what was going on between Cromley and Konecki? So much your business that you burgled Cromley's studio?"

That one was obviously for me. "Sam's the connection between them. Otherwise they detest each other. They had some deal that Konecki called off when she heard you'd arrested Sam. Any friend of Sam's would be interested."

"Any friend. That wacko is lucky he has one."

"Two," said Lydia with a smile.

"Four, if you count Cromley and Oakhurst," I put in.

"Should I?" Grimaldi asked.

"Jury's out."

"Yeah, well, good for him. Never saw a son of a bitch so happy to be arrested. He just kept saying, 'I knew I did it, I knew I did it.' But you think he gave me one useful fact? Where they met, anything?" She shook her head. "Unless he's the second coming of Vinny the Chin, I still don't like him for it. Which means I still think there's a maniac out there killing girls."

"I agree."

"Yay. So, now that I picked up Tabor, my captain's all over my ass to close the case. Based on what we have, it's an easy damn case to close, and I have a couple other open ones. But I'm not feeling it. I look around at the evidence, and it don't add up to him. This is what Cavanaugh hates about me, you want to know. Ninety-nine percent of the time, the way it works, you ID a suspect, you go find your evidence, you bring them in, you lean on them, they give it up. Sometimes they fight you for it, sometimes they're proud of it, but the guy you ID'd, that's the guy. That's what you learn at the academy, that's what you learn when they partner you up with old-school guys like Ike. I can do that, by the way. When it's right.

"But at the same time, I also work the other way. From the evidence out, you know? And what we have here, it don't spell Tabor to me. Plus, I lean on him, he just looks unhappy, like he's worried he's disappointing me."

"He probably is. Or worried you'll let him go."

"Not up to me anymore, he's been booked. Unless I can bag someone else. Which I want to do, because I want the real maniac. But my captain, and Ike, and *his* captain, and a hell of a lot of people would be very happy with your wacko for this. So before my captain takes my ass off this case and calls it closed, which I'm telling you he's about to do, what I need from you is everything. Anything you have. You want him out. I want the real killer. So we're on the same page."

Grimaldi stopped and waited expectantly.

"You sound like you think we're hiding something," I said.

"You had the earrings," she pointed out.

"And we gave them to you."

Before this skirmish could turn into open hostilities, Lydia, who'd been staring at the crime scene photos, said, "The earrings."

"Yeah?" Grimaldi looked at her, then also turned to the board.

"Two things. One, where *is* the other earring? The one that's missing is from the first victim, am I right?"

"Yes. And I'm with you. Why the hell is it not in the box?"

"The killer could have lost it," I offered. Both women looked at me with a mixture of skepticism and pity I had to admit wasn't totally unfamiliar to me coming from women.

"Seriously?" Grimaldi said. "You kill someone, take a trophy, and then you lose it? You really think so?"

"Maybe that's why he got the box. So he wouldn't lose any more."

Grimaldi looked at Lydia. Lydia rolled her eyes. So much for me.

"Also," said Lydia, "Kimberly Pike's earring."

"What about it?"

"The other three the killer took were from the right ear. From Kimberly, he took the left."

Grimaldi jumped up, examined the board. "Shit! You're right. How did I miss that?" She turned to me. "You, though, you're going to tell me it means nothing? Like the missing first earring?"

"No. I'm going to ask if the knives were the same in all four killings."

"And that is a damn good question. Why should I answer it?"

"No reason. We can call Sam's lawyer. She'll tell us."

"Yeah, fine. Preliminary forensics says yes, but no. Similar, but the first three, the blades were longer. Those might have all been the same knife, or three identical ones. Possibly some kind of folding knife. Last night's was similar, but smaller."

"A pocketknife? They come in different sizes."

"Something like that. So, I'll read your mind. You're thinking the first three were one killer, and Pike was someone else. Especially since the earring is from the wrong ear."

"And she's the only one where the killer made any effort to hide the time of death."

"Or maybe he was just hiding the body. Which, okay, he didn't do with any of the others, either."

"And they were all killed in parks. Not on loading docks."

"True. But if it's a different killer, why is the damn earring from the wrong ear in the box with the other two? They know each other, these killers? It's a tag team? And where's the one from the first one? Where in the hell is that one?"

"Or maybe we assume the wrong-ear thing doesn't mean anything and there's only one killer," Lydia said, still looking at the board. "Maybe Kimberly Pike's killer went out of his way to confuse things by making her death look different. If I were that killer, trying to frame Sam, I'd take out the earring from the murder from before he got out."

"Okay. And why are you framing Sam?"

"I think the police are getting too close to me?"

"Hah. You must know something I don't. Oh, button it, Gabi," she said in answer to Iglesias's laugh.

"If you planted that box," Grimaldi turned back to Lydia, "you would've had to know how to get into Tabor's studio."

"Pretty much everyone did," I stuck in. "And while we're on the subject of physical evidence . . . ?"

Grimaldi said, "You're not going to give that up, are you?"

"It'll just save me the trouble of calling the lawyer."

"Ah, shit. Okay, because your partner here gave me the wrong-ear-earring thing. Even though that might not mean anything. Dark hairs, on Kimberly Pike's sweater."

"Sam's? You know already?"

"Rapid DNA. I get the fancy new tech because it's a high-profile case. You sound surprised."

"I am."

"And seeing as how Tabor says he didn't know her, I bet he is, too."

Lydia began, "It could just mean—"

"Don't start. Could've been from another time. Another place. She snuck into the Whitney party and brushed against him. She went to the any-gender bathroom right after he did. She stood behind him on the line for the bar. Hairs go flying through the air on a breeze all the time. It proves nothing, except it gives the DA something to hold him on and that plus these damn earrings in his studio plus him confessing to everyone and their monkey gets him sent back upstate and my maniac is still walking the streets and where the *fuck* is that other earring?"

28

"Well," Lydia said as we left the 19th Precinct, "that was enlightening. Wait, let me rephrase that. Cavanaugh's a pig."

"No argument."

"And Grimaldi's a mensch."

"No argument there, either. And you're a genius."

"No argument."

"However," I said, "while you were so enthralled watching Grimaldi and Cavanaugh butt heads, I had a thought."

"Hey, I don't usually have a front-row seat at a pissing contest."

"Would you really want one? Now, think about this. While we were with Oakhurst before, a collector called. Franklin Monroe. You saw him at the Whitney."

"The oil slick with the ponytail?"

"Itself a strike against. Oakhurst had called to invite him to come see some new work."

"Right, and he used that as his excuse to kick us out."

"Yes. I met Monroe at Oakhurst's yesterday, though. He'd been looking at Oakhurst's new work. He was annoyed because he thought I was another collector, which would mean he didn't have an edge. So what new work could Oakhurst have now, except something he made last night?"

"Ohhh. He *was* at the Whitney photographing the action, inside and out. But this would be something for his private collectors? The people who buy the work too dark for Sherron Konecki's gallery to sell? That he made last night?"

Our eyes met.

I said, "If that's what it is, I'd sure like to see it."

I called Tony Oakhurst. Amara's bored monotone told me that Tony was out—really out, even for me. She'd be sure to let him know I'd called. I tried his cell phone but got voice mail.

"Do you think he showed whatever he has from last night to Konecki and that's what got her so upset?" Lydia asked.

"That did cross my mind. Let's ask."

The young woman who answered the phone at Lemuria Gallery was as briskly professional as Amara was chicly lethargic, but no more helpful. Ms. Konecki was out; no, she didn't say when she'd be back; no, I couldn't have her cell phone number; yes, I could leave a message; yes, she'd get it as soon as she came in or called. Was there anything else?

"No Ice Queen?" Lydia asked when I lowered the phone.

"That was her assistant, Permafrost." I thought for a moment. "Well, there's one more thing to try. Monroe claimed he was always happy to meet a fellow collector."

Lydia made a face as I took Monroe's card from my wallet and dialed.

Two rings, then, "Go for Monroe."

"Franklin, it's Bill Smith." A second's silence, so I said, "We met yesterday at Tony Oakhurst's."

"Oh! Yes, sure. And again at the Whitney last night. Another of Tony's collectors. What can I do for you?"

"You just saw Tony, didn't you? You saw last night's work?"

Cautiously: "Yes, that's right. Have you seen it?"

"I'd like to talk about it. Do you have some time?"

I could practically see his teeth gleaming white as his voice smiled. "Any time's a good time to talk about art. I'm just back from his studio, actually. You have my address?"

"On your card."

"I'll be expecting you."

"I'm in," I said to Lydia as I pocketed the phone. "Want to come?"

"Do you need me?"

"Is that even a question? In this case, though, unless you really want to go, I think Monroe might be happier if it was just the two of us."

"You know what? I might be, too. I'm a little overdosed on creepy men right now."

This was my case. If I'd really wanted her to come with me—or had somewhere else I wanted her to go—she'd have done it. But I'd have a better chance with Monroe if he saw this as a meeting of the secret connoisseurs society, and I could tell Lydia had something else on her mind.

"Do you have a plan?" I asked.

"I think I want to go back to Sam's neighborhood. If someone really broke into his apartment, it would be useful to know who."

"Grimaldi already sent people there."

"To see if anyone saw Sam in the middle of the night. She didn't say they were asking about the break-in. Besides, even if they are, everybody needs a little help sometimes."

We kissed good-bye. I watched her hips swing as her confident stride took her to the subway entrance. Then I headed in the other direction.

On my way to Monroe's I grabbed a slice of pizza. I'd just about finished it when my phone rang. Wiping my hands, I checked the screen: Susan Tulis, Sam's attorney.

"Susan," I said. "What's up?"

"Just checking in. Sam's been booked downtown. I sent one of my best young associates. Lupe Veracruz. He made her crazy."

"How?"

"By happily telling everyone he saw that he was being arrested and he wasn't going to kill anyone anymore."

"God, Sam."

"Lupe finally told him if he shut up and let her do all the talking, she'd arrange for him to have paper and charcoal in his cell, otherwise not. He told her he didn't like her, but okay."

"Give her a bonus."

"I'll put it on Sam's bill. If she stays on the case, I may have to bill for a shrink, too."

"It's Sam. We'll probably need a shrink anyway. Maybe you can get a two-fer. Anyway, stay with it, Sam's good for it."

"That's actually one of my questions. Who's my client, Sam or Peter? Peter says he'll take care of it, like last time."

"You talked to Peter?"

"He called. He wanted to know what the evidence was. It was hairs, by the way. Sam's, on the victim's sweater."

"I know. I just came from talking to the arresting detective. I don't like it."

"I hate it. So, by the way, do Peter and Leslie, though it seems like for opposite reasons."

"She was on the call, too?"

"Of course. He kept saying it wasn't possible, Sam didn't know the woman and didn't do it. *She* kept saying it wasn't all the cops had, there had to be something else they weren't telling us about. Peter said that that sounded like she thought Sam did it. She said the cops don't make an arrest like this without more evidence than a few hairs. I said sure they do, and I doubted they had anything else, but if they did, they'd have to produce it eventually. I got the odd feeling neither of them was listening to me."

"I get that feeling with them all the time."

"After a couple of times around that barn, I signed off so they could go dance with each other."

I told Susan she'd better bill Peter, because she was more likely to get paid in this century. Although with Sam's OCD, for all I knew he paid his bills assiduously. I asked her to keep in touch and hung up. I gave the situation some hard thought as I covered the final blocks to where I was headed.

The Park Avenue address on Monroe's card turned out to be a prewar dowager of a building, all burgundy brick detailing, terra-cotta window surrounds, and haughty suspicion of the new glass tower across the street. I announced myself to the doorman. He announced me to the intercom handset, listened, and pointed me across a mirrored lobby filled with the gentle aroma of money. Ten floors later, the brass-buttoned elevator opened on a hallway wallpapered in tropical forest scenes. Its thick carpet led me to an elegant dark green door, where a sonorous doorbell brought me a toothily smiling Franklin Monroe.

"Well," he said. "Great to see you. Come on in."

I followed him through a marble vestibule into a large sunken living room. Hulking gray tweed sofas and oxblood leather armchairs squatted among gray walls hung with photos, paintings, and prints. None of the work was familiar to me, though I might have been willing to take a stab at guessing about half the artists, ranging through the last three centuries. The photos weren't anything I'd seen, either, but it was clear which ones were Oakhursts. The subject of everything hanging in this room was the same: pain.

Blood, wounds, agonized faces. A 19th-century woodcut of Death flying through the air with the body of a child, its mother wailing on the hillside below. Red paint smearing a 1970s collage of news headlines about bodies found, children lost, whole families slain. A beautifully delineated, hyper-realistic canvas of a severed hand on a tabletop, blood continuing to drip down from somewhere just out of the frame.

The Oakhurst photos, three of them, were stylistically unmistakable: shadowy colors, deep blacks, glares of white. In one, a terrified-looking young woman tied to a chair could just be seen over the hulking shoulder of a shirtless man. The subject of another was unclear, but it featured blood, flesh, and damp hair. In the third, a scarred arm rested on a filthy mattress with a needle still stuck in the vein. Behind it, a skeletal junkie, works fallen into her lap, mouth open as she drifted off, seemed oblivious to the man ODing beside her.

I found myself understanding Sherron Konecki's refusal to show these photos. I also found myself hoping they were made using props and models, but I had a bad feeling that wasn't the case.

"Drink?" Monroe asked, pointing me to a chair.

Not a bad idea. A cigarette would be good, too, but I didn't see any ashtrays. I sat; the chair gave a little too much, seeming to want to devour me. Monroe poured into heavy glasses from one of half a dozen crystal decanters on a cabinet. As he walked across the room to hand me a glass, I spotted three of Sam's pencil drawings framed and hanging by the fireplace.

"So? Not bad, right?" Monroe took his glass to an armchair opposite, crossed his legs on a leather hassock. There was a hassock in front of my chair, too, but I wasn't sure I wanted to get that comfortable. "I have a good many more, of course. I keep them rotating, out here, in there." He gestured vaguely with his glass toward a hallway I hoped I wouldn't have to enter.

"You have a great eye," I said, giving him the compliment a collector treasures most. "The Oakhursts, the Santlofer"—that artist was a friend of mine; I'd have to talk to him about the direction he was moving in now, if Monroe's charcoal drawing was any indication—"and the Tabors. I didn't know you collected him, too."

"Tony introduced me. Those are sketches for *Red Barn*. A lot more powerful than the painting itself, don't you think?"

No, but more rare. "I thought Tabor didn't sell the pencil sketches, on principle. That's what Sherron Konecki told Michael Sanger."

Monroe smiled his tooth-filled smile. "Right now, he doesn't. Sherron's fine with that. She can pump up demand while there's no supply. But you know she'll talk Tabor into selling. Money talks, stick-up-the-ass principles walk. Michael's an idiot to fall for that, but he's generally an idiot."

"Is he one of Tony's private collectors, too?"

"Michael?" Monroe snickered. "He doesn't have the balls. He's an aesthete. That's another word for asshole. Sherron started out by dumping her hard-to-sells on him. When he discovered Tabor, he turned into a money fountain."

"If Tabor has yet to be talked into selling the sketches, where did you get those?"

"Tony asked Tabor for them, as a favor. Tabor thought Tony was going to keep them. He didn't know they were for me." Monroe's tone was smug. Clearly Tony had done no such favor for me. "I like sketches. I like to see where the artist started. Even Tony—he sometimes lets me have a raw shot he took, before he worked on it. If I buy the final, too."

Gazing at Sam's sketches, I sipped my drink. Scotch, complex, high proof, well balanced. Whatever was in the decanter was damn good.

Monroe followed my eyes. "You know they're close, Tony and Tabor? I think Tony's limited-edition work has gotten even edgier since they met. I'm sure you've noticed that?" His smile said he was pretty sure I didn't know, and hadn't noticed.

"Hmm. I hadn't thought about it. In what way?"

"In a pissing contest way."

If that was right I'd have to tell Lydia; maybe she'd want to catch another one.

"Not that Tabor would care," Monroe went on. "Probably has no idea there is a contest, he's in such a goddamn fog. Amusing to watch, isn't he, the way he blinks and stumbles around? Impressive that a dolt like that can turn out such great work. But with Tony, it's like Tabor's work lit some kind of fire under him. Maybe because Tabor doesn't know what he's doing, and Tony does. I think Tony hates to lose to a guy who doesn't even know what he's doing."

Interesting. In an odd way that aligned with what Oakhurst had said about Sam creating what he, Tony, could only see.

I asked, "Is that what's behind the newest work, do you think? A darkness contest, him and Tabor?"

"What else?" Monroe swept his legs off the hassock and leaned forward. Although no one else was in the room, he lowered his voice. "So what did you think of it? Last night's?"

I looked into my drink. "Like I said, I'm not sure."

"Oh, come on. You're telling me you have a line you won't cross?" I guessed the smirk in his voice was telling me he had no line.

Last night's. I took a chance. "It didn't look . . . staged, to you?"

"No, it didn't fucking look staged. Those eyes? As soon as he sent me the raw photo, I knew. Staged. Are you kidding? Tony wouldn't do that. He never has. That misses the whole goddamn point." Monroe threw himself back in his chair. "How long have you been collecting him? You don't trust him? Why do you bother?"

"I've always trusted him up to now. It never even occurred to me something might not be real." I gestured at the bound young woman, hoped that was the right answer. "But last night's . . ."

"Oh, come on! You know he was there. I saw you with him, for Christ's sake, at his and Tabor's wall. And you have to know she's dead, it's been all over the news. What do you think, that's not really her?" He gave me a hard stare. "No. You don't think it. You hope it. You're not afraid it was staged. You're hoping it was." He finished his drink. "When it comes right down to it, you don't have the balls for this, do you? You're just another candy-ass. I misjudged you. I'd invite you to see more of my collection, but to hell with you. Finished with your drink?"

The question couldn't have been more pointed. I hadn't been, but in another two seconds I was. Another five after that, and I was up and out the door. I didn't say thanks and Monroe didn't say good-bye.

29

I lit a cigarette as soon as I was on the street. I took a few moments to weigh the relative merits of calling Grimaldi but decided she was less likely than I to get invited to see last night's Tony Oakhurst if, as now seemed probable, it was Kimberly Pike's final portrait. Grimaldi would need a warrant, but she'd never get one based on my reading of what Monroe had said. I'd need to see the photo myself and tell her about it.

I headed for the subway to go down to 39th Street.

Had Oakhurst killed Pike? Unlikely; he'd described himself as an artist who could see the pain but not create it. All right, but that didn't account for Heisenberg's principle: observing a phenomenon inevitably alters the nature of it. Oakhurst might go around telling himself and everyone else that he just shoots what he sees, but his subjects—the pain creators—might be changing their behavior because they know he's photographing them. Did that mean there was a wide, blurred line between Oakhurst seeing and recording, and his subjects performing for the camera? I thought of the huge photo of Rick and Laurel, and whomever else, and imagined them writhing while Oakhurst's flash popped off. What else was happening because Oakhurst was there? Were women being killed so Oakhurst could take pictures?

Or was I getting carried away? Maybe Oakhurst hadn't seen the murder. Maybe he'd just stumbled on Pike's body, and all he was guilty of was not reporting it. If he didn't know who the killer was, that wasn't even a crime in New York State.

Though if he did, it was.

At the door to Oakhurst's studio, Amara peered at me from under sleepy eyelids. "Yes?"

"Tony called me and asked me to come over."

"Oh?" Silver rings lifted as her pierced eyebrows rose. "He didn't tell me. Just a minute." She left me in the vestibule while she wafted away to make sure this was true. It wasn't, but I had faith. "Okay," she breathed when she came back. "Come on in."

Oakhurst was already striding toward the door as I entered. "Hey," he said, reaching out a hand. I shook it and he said, "What's up? Come on." He led me to the leather-benched seating area. Amara floated back to her computer. "Want a drink?" Oakhurst said. "Sit down. I didn't call you, why the bullshit?" He was grinning.

"I just had one, thanks. Coke?"

"Soda? Or blow?"

At my headshake, he leaned toward the drinks cabinet and retrieved the scotch and, from a small fridge, a can of Coke.

"I needed to talk to you," I said, popping the lid. "I didn't want to have a slow-motion fight with your spacey gatekeeper. I figured you'd want to know why the bullshit."

"Goddamn it. I'm that easy?" He poured himself two fingers of scotch.

"Afraid so. I just came from Franklin Monroe's place. We were discussing your newest work."

"Ah, Franklin." Oakhurst smiled, his tone noncommittal. He lifted his glass to me. "He let you up?"

"It seems to be a rare privilege."

"It is. He's proud of that collection. Though he usually has the sense to keep it . . . pretty private." Oakhurst took a swig of his drink.

"I imagine most of them do. Your collectors. In the end, though, he decided I was a candy-ass and threw me out."

"Because?"

"I asked him if he thought last night's work was staged."

"Last night's."

"He thought I'd seen it."

"He did?"

I'd suddenly had it. "You have a death-mask photo of Kimberly Pike," I said. "Were you there when she was killed?"

He took some time over this, sipping scotch. "No," he finally answered, a small smile on his lips. "Just after."

"Who killed her?"

"I don't know."

"Then how do you know it was just after? Not hours later?"

"The body was warm. The truck was cold, but her body was warm."

"What the hell made you look in the truck? Jesus Christ, am I going to have to yank this out of you?"

"Or," he said, still smiling, looking me in the eye, "I could just tell you to leave."

"And I might or might not. I might make such a stink you'd have to call the cops. How would that work out for you?"

He shrugged. "I'd tell them you were a crazy man who lied his way in here."

"I'd tell them you're a crazy man who takes pictures of dead women. Look, if you don't know who killed her, you're a creep but not a criminal. Let's knock off this shit. How did you know? About the truck?"

If it bothered Oakhurst to be called a creep by a candy-ass, he didn't show it. He drank some more scotch, and though I figured he was trying to decide what to tell me, I gave him the time. I was banking on his artist's pride overwhelming his caution. It already had: caution would have told him to take a couple of days between the murder and calling Monroe. Pride had wanted to show off the work right away.

I was half right. "Deal?" he said. "I'll tell you about the truck if you tell me how you knew to go to Franklin in the first place."

"That's it? Hell, I'll even go first. You called Monroe to come over and see new work this morning. But he'd been here seeing new work yesterday. So the newest work had to be from last night. I'm sure you have glamour shots from the party, but Monroe wouldn't give a damn about that. So you must have made something last night that would appeal to your private collectors." I tried to keep my voice neutral so "private collectors" wouldn't come out sounding like "ghouls."

Oakhurst nodded slowly. "It couldn't have been work I just finished from photos I took a while ago?"

"Sure, it could, but then when I called, he wouldn't have bitten. I specifically said 'last night's work' and he invited me right up."

Oakhurst nodded. "Pretty good," he said. "Pretty subtle. I like it."

"I'm thrilled. Now, you."

"Now, me." He poured himself another drink. "What people don't know," he said, "is that the best images at high-stakes events come afterwards. Awards ceremonies, championship games, riots, battlefields. When the adrenaline's gone and people are . . ." He trailed off.

"Naked turtles?" I supplied.

"Yeah." He nodded in appreciation, probably not of my memory but of his own metaphor. "So I always hang around. Last night after the action at the back of the Whitney was over, I went to the front and kept shooting until the cops dispersed what was left of the crowd there. Then I came back to the back. I was shooting shoes, hats, water bottles—the shit people had lost, dropped, left behind. I saw someone leaving the truck."

"Who?"

"I couldn't tell. Just a silhouette in the headlights from the highway."

"Man or woman? Fat or thin? Tall or short?"

"Just a silhouette. Elongated, from the lights. Looked like an alien, you want the truth."

"Did you photograph it?"

"I tried. It made good art and bad journalism. Can't tell a thing about it."

"So then you checked out the truck."

"Oh, come on. You wouldn't have?"

"And you found?"

Again, the tiny smile. "Her body. Warm. Oh, she was dead, I'd have called nine-one-one if she wasn't."

Maybe, maybe not; but what would be gained now if I got in his face about that?

"You shot the photos and closed the truck up again," I said. "Why not call 911 then?"

No answer. I worked it out myself.

"Because you thought it was your buddy Sam. Sam the serial killer. That's why you went looking for him. That's why you didn't answer my texts, my calls."

Oakhurst shrugged. "I'm his friend. The least I could do was wait and ask him."

"Did you?"

"Now *that* is a stupid question. You hauled him out of there before I had the chance." He looked up. "Hey, did *you* ask him?"

"I didn't know until this morning that she'd been killed. I don't think he did, either, but of course he says he killed her. So do the cops. I want to see the photo."

"What?"

"The goddamn photo, of her in the truck. The silhouette, too."

"The hell you do. Can I say fuck off?"

"Say whatever you damn please. I want to see the photo."

He blew out a breath, put down his glass, and stood. "What the hell." Pride for the win, again. He led me to the table in the back. "I haven't printed any of these yet." He gave me some smug side-eye. "Franklin's already reserved one."

"Based on the raw photo. Which he also reserved. He told me."

"God, he's an ass."

I made no argument. Oakhurst flicked on a large monitor that took up the left side of the table. He clicked through a series of lists, found what he was looking for, allowed an image to settle and rest.

There she was. Kimberly Pike, looking both better and worse than in the NYPD photos on Grimaldi's board. Those were lit with a crime scene tech's clinically bright flash. This was much lower light, with planes, shadows, and angles carefully considered, shot with a steady hand. In Grimaldi's she was dead, long cold, everything she had been gone. Here, she still looked scared, and shocked.

I took it in, then said, "Now the silhouette."

After a glance at me, Oakhurst clicked some more. On the monitor the bright glare of headlights swallowed the edges of a person-shaped figure in motion. He'd said it looked like an alien, and he was right. Also, that it was good art and bad journalism.

"You tried working on it, right? To see if you could make out who it was?"

"Oh, for crap's sake, of course I did. I tried every trick I knew. Nada."

Nada, except a murderer leaving the scene. I said, "Show me the others."

"What others?"

"The other silhouettes."

"I only had time for the one." He clicked again and the silhouette shrank into a grid of thumbnails. I couldn't make them out, but there were no others like it.

"All right, now everything else."

"What do you mean?"

"All these. Everything you shot in the truck last night."

"I don't show my outtakes."

"Christ, I'm not asking as a critic! Show me the goddamn photos."

My voice held a note that surprised even me. Oakhurst must have heard it, too. After a long look at me, he started swiping through dozens of images. Different angles, different ranges of focus, different exposures. Details, long shots. Her face, her hands, the stab wounds in her chest. The walls and floor of the truck, shiny with the remains of other, nonhuman carcasses. I looked, absorbed, said nothing. Finally he came to the end.

"The rest are just the party," he said. "And the riot." He clicked the monitor off.

"Jesus," I muttered, stepping back.

Oakhurst regarded me and grinned. "You know what? You *are* a candy-ass."

Maybe, but I had the strength to keep myself from decking him in his own studio. Instead I turned and headed for the door.

30

I lit a cigarette as soon as I hit the fresh midtown air outside Oakhurst's studio. I called Lydia but only got her voice mail. "News," I told it. "Call me."

Next, I called Grimaldi. Oakhurst's photos had bothered me, but not as much as I'd played it. I wanted him to think of me as a wuss, and so not a threat. That, plus the great man's pride in his work, reduced the risk that he'd erase any of those images before Grimaldi saw them. I didn't know if they held any evidence that she didn't already have, but they pinpointed time of death to a good eight hours earlier, and that was something.

"Grimaldi."

"Smith. I've got something for you."

"Tell me it's the other earring."

"No. But you'll like it." I told her where I was and what I'd seen. When I was done, she said slowly, "That son of a bitch."

"I'm betting he won't let you in without a warrant."

"I'm pissed enough to call in a SWAT team."

"You can do that?"

"If the guy's not an immediate threat, my captain would have my head. But a warrant'll take hours. Maybe not until morning."

"Not telling you how to do your job—"

"I'm so glad to hear that."

"—but if it were me, I wouldn't get him nervous by trying to go there until you have one," I said. "If he knows you care, he could erase the photos. If he doesn't, his ego means they'll still be there. And it's not like I saw anything in them that could help."

"In your opinion."

"Yeah, but I'm not neutral. I'd love to be able to nail him for something. I was looking."

"You don't get to nail people, Smith. I do. Remember that."

"Right. I will. And when you do see Oakhurst, tell him I sent you."

I hung up and headed across town. In half a block, the phone rang again. Peter Tabor. "Peter," I said. "What's up? Feeling better?"

"I feel like shit. Les and I are trying to do goddamn damage control here. Susan Tulis said you talked to the detective."

"The one who arrested Sam?"

"Of course, her. Who the hell else?"

Well, Ike Cavanaugh, but I didn't say that. "Yes, I did. Why?"

"We want to know what kind of evidence they have."

"I thought Susan told you. A few hairs, that's all. Even with Sam's constant confessing, it won't amount to anything."

"Why not?"

"There's nothing else, and hairs don't have time stamps. He keeps confessing, but he can't tell them anything about the crime or the victim, and no one can connect him up with her."

In most criminal cases, if that was everything, the defense would get an easy dismissal. Given Sam's tenuous hold on reality and his insistence on his own guilt, though, an ambitious ADA might try this case anyway, and a jury might want to put Sam away just to be on the safe side. I didn't say that to Peter. He'd already said he felt like shit, and he sounded like it.

"You sure that's all they have?" Peter said. "If it is and the case is as tenuous as you say, why did they even charge him? Leslie says they must have something else."

"No, I'm not sure, but Grimaldi was pretty straight with me. Peter, this is standard. They want their suspect off the streets while they look for more evidence. If they don't find it, they'll drop the charges. Also," I added, "it's pretty clear now he wasn't at the scene."

"What the hell do you mean, wasn't at the scene? She was killed at the Whitney. He was there until you lost him. Or if it was later, whatever time it was, Susan said the cops think he might have gone back there when you were asleep." The accusation in his tone was unmistakable.

"He ran like a greyhound when the riot was just getting started. She was alive, screaming, 'It's him,' when he took off, and his movements can be tracked after that. She died while he was going from bar to bar trying to get a drink."

"Susan said they can't nail down the time of death."

"They thought they couldn't. There's a witness now, though. Just after the action outside ended, he saw someone leave the truck. He went inside and found Pike's body."

"Jesus, really? Who's the witness? Who did he see?"

"He says he doesn't know. Just a figure in the oncoming headlights. But Sam's movements from the time he ran to the time I found him can be verified. If the witness's story is true, it can't have been Sam."

"If it's true. What if he's lying? Who's the witness? Why didn't he report it right away? Maybe he's the killer."

"I can't tell you, Peter, I'm sorry." Technically, there was no reason I couldn't, except I was pretty sure that if I outed Oakhurst before Grimaldi got to him, she'd shoot me. "But I don't think he's lying. And I don't think he's the killer. The police will work all that out."

A long pause. "Good God," Peter breathed. "What a nightmare this whole thing is."

"I know," I said. "I'm sorry."

"So now that they have this witness, when will Sam be released?" Peter didn't acknowledge my sympathy, but he also didn't tell me to go to hell.

"I don't know. Has he been arraigned?"

"Tonight, Susan says. Unless they drop the charges."

"If they set bail, can you cover it?"

"How do I know? Depends how much they want."

"Well, once the cops have checked out the witness's account, and if there's no new evidence, it shouldn't be long before the charges are dropped."

"What if there is new evidence?"

"Why would there be? If Sam didn't do it?"

That was that. We promised to keep one another updated, and cut the call. Whether Peter was reassured, I didn't know, but I had nothing else to offer. I lit another cigarette and thought about art.

31

I was sitting over a cup of coffee in a Ninth Avenue diner when Lydia called back. "You have news?" she asked.

"Yes, I do. You?"

"Nothing. I think I'd better come back tomorrow morning. You know, get the dog-walking crowd." That was investigative shorthand for people who go out at the same time every day, people who might have seen something out of the ordinary. Sam's apartment had been broken into in the late morning. The neighborhood streets at that same time tomorrow might offer more than the nothing she'd just found in today's late afternoon.

"Unless," she said, "whatever you have makes me superfluous."

"Bite your tongue."

"Then I'll be superfluous and bleeding."

"And you won't be able to say 'superfluous.' No, I still think we'd better find out who broke into Sam's apartment. There's a lot still up in the air. What I have, though, pretty much proves Sam didn't kill Kimberly Pike. Also, that Tony Oakhurst is a ghoul."

"Did that second part need proving? So tell me."

"How about I tell you over dinner?"

"Are you kidding? It'll take me an hour to get back. You can prove Sam didn't do it and you expect me to wait?"

"I'm thinking it'll raise the anticipation of seeing me to a fever pitch."

"And the danger of my clobbering you when I do. Tell me."

So, from a diner booth, with Johnny Mathis on the jukebox on my end and car horns and conversations on hers, I told her where I'd been and what I'd seen.

"Oh my God," she said when I was through. "Ghoul doesn't begin to cover it. I thought artists . . ." She trailed off.

"What about them?"

"I don't know. I guess I always thought of artists as people with, I don't know, souls. I mean, his work is supposed to be great, isn't it?"

"Oakhurst? It is great. He has a soul. It's just rotten."

"I'm disillusioned."

"Then let me buy you dinner. I know a place where the pasta is no illusion."

"We're done for the day?"

"I think we are. Grimaldi might not get her warrant until morning, or at best later tonight. That would mean Sam won't be out until tomorrow at the earliest, unless he's arraigned tonight and Peter and Leslie make his bail, which I'm not sure they can."

"Or that they'd both be equally excited about doing it."

"You're moving from disillusioned to cynical awfully fast."

"Sorry."

"I'll try to remember you the way you were. Anyway, even if Sam buys Oakhurst's photos as proof he didn't kill Pike, the cases he hired me for are still open. I'd like to talk about how to work them. And there are a lot of loose ends still in this one."

"Oh, so all this about pasta is just to get me to a working dinner?"

"The anticipation of seeing me didn't seem to be enough. I had to resort to food."

"Good choice. Where should I meet you?"

"Morandi. Seventh Avenue South. Can you find it?"

"Siri can. An hour?"

"Sure."

We hung up. I had another cup of coffee and thought about art some more. And about Lydia.

32

I was still thinking about Lydia, or thinking about her again, when I woke up in the morning. She'd come home with me after our pasta dinner, but she hadn't spent the night. I'd had the feeling for a while now we were playing a game of don't-ask-don't-tell with Mama Chin, and Lydia was the only one who knew the rules. I just went along. For now, it was all right; in fact, it was more than I'd once dared hope for.

I showered and made coffee. Lydia by now would be on her way to Brooklyn to do the dog-walking due diligence. After I got caffeinated I was planning to take another run at Cromley. I was positive she hadn't gone to Oakhurst's only to tell him about Sam's arrest.

I'd just poured the coffee when the phone rang.

"Smith."

"It's Grimaldi."

"I see that. Get your warrant?"

"I got more than that. I want you here, now."

"Where's here?"

"Tony Oakhurst's studio. Now."

"My pleasure, but what do you need me for?"

"Should I send a squad car?"

"I'm on my way."

I slugged down some coffee and called Lydia. I got her voice mail, so I told it where I was going. "It wasn't an invitation," I said. "I have a bad feeling about this." I jogged to the subway and popped up at Penn Station. On my way to 39th Street, I picked up two more coffees.

On Oakhurst's block, I had to thread my way through a gathering crowd of people, the ones who are drawn to police lines like crows to cornmeal. No SWAT team was in evidence, but the crime scene van took up the loading zone outside Oakhurst's studio, and I spotted the ME's car, too. A freckled black cop whose nameplate read EPSTEIN was standing guard at the half-open door. He stopped me, listened to me, said, "Don't touch anything," and went inside to check with Grimaldi. I could see the doorknob and bell had been dusted for prints.

A moment later, Epstein was back. "She says go in and wait."

I went in. Amara was hunched on one of the leather benches, wrapped in a blanket and sipping from a paper cup. A female officer sat beside her, a reassuring presence also there, I knew, to keep an eye on what Amara said and did, and to keep her from contacting anyone on the outside until the NYPD was good and ready. Behind the sitting area, at the back of the huge room, NYPD personnel of various kinds swarmed around one of the long tables. As the techs moved back and forth, I could see what the problem was.

Oakhurst lay sprawled on the wide-plank wood floor. A crimson splotch ruined his white T-shirt. I couldn't tell from where I stood whether he was alive or dead, but the Tyvek-suited ME crouched beside him was a hell of a big clue.

Grimaldi crossed the studio wearing blue crime scene booties. With nitrile-gloved hands, she handed a pair to me. "Put these on."

"I'll trade." I offered her one of the coffees, the one with cream and sugar.

"God," she said. She took a long pull on it. "I could learn to like you."

"In spite of the historical animosity between our peoples?"

"I need you to look at something."

"Any chance you'll tell me what the hell happened first?" I sat on the leather bench across from Amara, who seemed not to notice me at all. I put my coffee down, pulled the booties on, picked up the coffee again, and stood.

Grimaldi led me to a long table one over from the one Oakhurst lay beside. Once we were out of Amara's earshot she said, "Someone killed that son of a bitch, what do you think?"

"I don't suppose you know who?"

"I don't suppose you can tell me?"

"I just work here. Speaking of working here, is she any help?" I pointed my coffee cup toward Amara.

"I was on my way here with the warrant when she called nine-one-one. The EMTs pulled up the same time I did. She says she opened up as usual and there he was."

"When?"

"About an hour ago. If you mean when was he killed, one A.M., give or take."

"How?"

"Shot."

"Did you find the gun?"

"We found *a* gun. A .38."

"That's right?"

"Seems right. Two shots fired, two .38 slugs in the floor. It's being tested."

I looked at her over my coffee. "You have the gun, why don't you sound excited?"

"It's his."

"Oh. Crap. But not suicide?"

"Hard to shoot yourself in the gut from six feet away. Also someone shot one of his fingers off. That's actually easier to do to yourself, but I'm thinking he didn't. But I'll tell you something interesting. He's missing an earring." She tilted her head. "Well, look at that. I surprised you."

"You sure did."

"And somehow, call me crazy, I think this is connected to all the shit swirling around your wacko."

"Couldn't be a break-in? Or maybe sex play gone wrong?"

"Could be Santa Claus coming down the chimney armed for bear, for all I know. In case it's not, though, you got any bright ideas?"

"No, but I'll bet he had enemies."

"Oh, no shit, Sherlock."

"At least we know it wasn't Sam."

"How do we know that?"

"Isn't he still locked up?"

Grimaldi gave a grim smile. "He's out. Arraigned in night court about half past ten. Bail set at a quarter mil, brother and sister-in-law there at the ready."

"With the money? The sister-in-law, too?"

"Cashier's check. I guess they really didn't want their wacko to have to spend the night in jail. He was out walking the streets before midnight."

"Oh," I said, noting that at least briefly Sam wasn't my wacko, and wondering where he'd actually spent the night.

"So, we don't know that after all," Grimaldi said.

"Did you talk to Ellissa Cromley yesterday about where she got the box with the earrings?"

"You don't ask for much, do you?"

"You called me. And I brought you coffee."

"Of course I talked to her. Same story you got. She heard Tabor's door shut, thought it was him arriving, but it must have been someone leaving, because no one was in there. She saw the drawer, took the box so Tabor wouldn't run to me and incriminate himself with it."

"She give you any idea who it was who put it there?"

"She give you one?"

"I'm not a cop."

"Oh, really?" She gave me a silent stare, then turned. "Hirahara." She raised her voice. "You guys done with this?"

An Asian woman in a CSU jacket, dusting for prints over by Amara's desk, gave Grimaldi a thumbs-up. Grimaldi kept her nitrile gloves on anyway and clicked on the monitor, smearing the remaining traces of print-lifting powder.

"These are what you saw yesterday, right?" she asked. "I need you to tell me if they're all here."

"I'm not sure I can do that. There were dozens."

"Try."

"Amara might know more than I do."

"She turned it on for me. Then she fell apart. Look at her."

I did, then glanced at Grimaldi. Lydia had said yesterday that I was showing unaccustomed consideration for the sensitivities of a cop. Now that cop was showing surprising concern for the emotional state of a witness. "Well," I said. "Okay, then."

Before we could get started, my phone rang. Lydia. Grimaldi said, "Let it go to voice mail," but I'd anticipated that and answered fast.

"Smith. Thanks for calling, Paul. I'm hoping you found that witness. They're going to court this afternoon."

"Someone's listening," Lydia said. "Grimaldi?"

"Right. Is he there?"

"He, who? There, where?"

"Well, try Victor. See if he knows."

"Victor, Victor . . . Sam's bar. You're looking for Sam. I thought he was in jail."

"Yes, and no. Thanks."

"On it. Can you tell me what happened at Oakhurst's?"

"No, that's over."

"He's dead."

"Right. Thanks, talk to you later."

I said sorry to Grimaldi as I put the phone back in my pocket. "I have this guy hunting down a witness who got cold feet on another case."

"Keeping your wacko out of jail isn't full-time work for you?"

It seemed like a bad time to remind her that that wasn't actually what I'd been hired to do. I settled for, "And I don't get paid overtime like you do, either."

"Oh, screw you. Look here."

We both drank coffee as Grimaldi flipped through Oakhurst's photo file. I was struck, as I had been yesterday, by the way some of these images were abstractly, aesthetically beautiful if you didn't mind the subject matter. Most of what went by, though, were almost-identical shots, where Oakhurst hadn't quite gotten the angle or the focus or the light the way he wanted it; and many were blurry or shadowy blunders. Oakhurst, I thought, would have hated the attention we were paying to his outtakes.

After a while, something occurred to me. "Did you check his camera?" I asked Grimaldi. "He might have taken shots of his visitor last night."

She rolled her eyes above her tilted-back coffee cup. "I'm starting to remember why my people don't like yours. Of course we did. Memory card's gone. Also his cell phone, because I know you were about to ask. Just look at the pictures, please."

Watch the birdie. We continued going through the photos I'd seen yesterday. I didn't like them any better than I had then, but nothing stood out as missing. Until we came to the end.

"Where's the silhouette?" I said. "It's not here."

"What silhouette?"

"It's why he checked the truck. He saw someone leaving it, just a silhouette, he said. He showed it to me. It's true, you can't tell anything by it. But where is it?"

"If you can't tell anything by it, maybe he erased it."

"You can't tell anything, but it's beautiful. As art, as a photograph. And look at this." I waved at the monitor. "Half of these aren't any good, not useful *or* beautiful, but he hasn't erased them. I bet he never erased anything, given the size of his ego. If he keeps all his outtakes, where's the silhouette?"

Grimaldi tapped her empty coffee cup on her lip, looking at the screen. She put the cup down and clicked again, opening the Whitney Riot file, and scrolled through to the end. "Nothing." She looked across the room. "Stay here."

She walked over, leaned down and spoke to Amara. Amara paled, then rose unsteadily, huddled into the blanket. Steadfastly not looking to either side, she followed Grimaldi back to the table.

"It's okay," Grimaldi said. "Take your time."

Amara rolled over a stool, sat, bit her lip, and started clicking. A panel of data appeared at the side of the final photo in the Riot folder. "Is that what you wanted to see?" Amara spoke in a soft monotone. Pointing to a set of numbers in 24-hour format, she said, "That's the time he took it."

"What about the first one in the Truck folder?"

Amara opened that folder and called up the data on the photo.

"Damn it," Grimaldi said. "Almost fifteen minutes later."

"Isn't that unlike Tony?" I asked Amara. "When he's found something worth shooting, to go that long without a shot?"

Amara looked up at me and suddenly giggled. "Tony called you a candy-ass." The giggling wasn't a good sign; she could lose it any minute.

"He is," Grimaldi said, putting a hand on Amara's shoulder. "But this is important. Try to hold it together, okay? Assuming Oakhurst—Tony—took photos in that fifteen minutes, where would they be?"

Amara looked from me to Grimaldi. She took a deep breath, nodded, and squinted at the screen. After some more clicking and mouse-moving, she came up with a long list of names and numbers, which reorganized itself as she sorted it.

"There," she finally said, sounding a little surprised. "He hid a folder. He never does that. But see, the time? It's from between the Truck folder and the Riot one."

"Can you open it?" Grimaldi leaned forward.

Amara clicked some more. She frowned, moved the mouse, clicked again. Finally she sat back, looked at Grimaldi. "It's empty."

Grimaldi said, "You sure?"

Amara nodded. "It's hidden, but it's empty. I don't know why he'd do that."

"I'm betting he didn't. I think the killer erased what was in it."

Amara jerked her hand from the mouse as though it were on fire.

"All right," Grimaldi said. "Just one more thing. Are there any more hidden folders here?"

Pale as a sheet, Amara stared at the mouse. She reached out for it tentatively, this thing the killer had touched. Swallowing, she clicked some more, ran through a few screens. "No," she finally said. "Just that one."

"Okay. Good. Thanks. You can go home. Is there someone you can call?"

"I'm okay." Amara stepped off the stool. If being pale, shaky, and borderline hysterical was okay, she was fine.

"Leopold!" Grimaldi called across the room to the cop who'd been sitting with Amara. "Amara here can leave. Find someone to take her home."

As Amara drifted across the room, Grimaldi turned back to me and said, "So, shit. The killer took the damn camera card and erased the damn photos. And took an earring. Like flipping us the bird. I hate wiseasses."

"Good thing I'm just a candy-ass," I said. And then I had an inspiration. Because the first guy who'd called me that was Franklin Monroe.

33

I didn't share my lightbulb moment with Grimaldi, just waited for her to dismiss me.

"Okay," she said as the ME's techs zipped Tony Oakhurst into a thick black bag. "I've got work to do. Unless you have something else brilliant to add, you can go."

I shook my head. "I got nuthin."

"Yeah, well, don't disappear on me, in case I need you again. And I hope you don't feel like you've just got to tell people about this? Because I can put you on ice as a material witness if you think the urge is gonna be irresistible."

"About the photos? Or that Tony's dead?"

"The photos and the earring, for Christ's sake. He's probably on the news already."

That might've been true. The CSU and ME's vans plus the NYPD radio would make Oakhurst's death hard to keep secret. I wondered what he'd think of the crime scene photos of him lying dead on his studio floor.

"I won't mention them," I said.

"I might have to arrest your wacko again."

"Why?"

"Because I might finally think he killed somebody!"

"Yeah, okay," I said. "I understand."

Grimaldi nodded. "Epstein! Let this guy out."

The crowd outside had grown, and Grimaldi was right: the news vans had arrived to join the NYPD in filling loading zones all up the block. I pushed my way through and east, ignoring the shouts of "What's going on?" "Who're you?" "Who's dead?" One imaginative soul shouted, "How many?"

I cut and ran east; after a couple of blocks, when even the reporters had given up, I took out my phone.

Monroe wasn't happy to hear from me. "Oh, what the hell do you want? Can I be blunt? You're not my kind of guy, Smith."

"You're not mine, either, Franklin, but right now, you need me. I'm not a collector. I'm a private investigator and I want to talk to you. So do the police, but they don't know that yet. Are you home?"

"A private investigator? What the hell did you mean by telling me you were a collector, then?"

"Tony told you that for his own reasons. I went along with it for mine. Are you home? I'm coming up there now, and you'd be stupid not to let me in."

I hung up, jumped in the subway, and walked into Monroe's building twenty minutes later. I hoped, in that time, he hadn't figured out what I was coming for.

In the lobby, I went through the announcing-calling rigmarole with the doorman, who finally sent me up. Monroe was waiting in his open doorway, this time without the bright, toothy smile.

"What?" he demanded.

"Let's go in."

"Why?"

"So I don't decide to yell your name while I bang on all the other doors in your hallway."

"Are you insane?"

"Who knows?"

Monroe blew out an aggravated breath and stepped aside.

I waited for him to close the door. "The raw photo from the night before last that Tony sent you. I need to see it."

"Ask Tony."

"Someone shot him early this morning. Probably over that photo." I didn't know that, but that was why I wanted to see it.

"What?" Blood drained from his face. "Shot him? Who? Is he—dead?"

"Yes, he's dead. If I knew who, I wouldn't be here. But hey, there's an upside. You'll love the crime scene photos from his studio." I gave him a few seconds to absorb the news. "Whoever killed him erased some of the photos he had from the night at the Whitney. That makes you the only person known to have a copy of what he sent you."

I was following a gut feeling that what Oakhurst had sent Monroe was not one of the images I'd seen but something else, something he was particularly—and privately—proud of.

Monroe had caught the most important word. "Known?" he said.

"So far, only to me. That could change. I could tell the police, which I'll probably do. I could also make sure everyone and his monkey knows you have it and wait and see what happens. We know what happened to Tony."

"You're a fucking SOB."

"I'm guessing from you that's a compliment. Show me the goddamn photo."

Scowling, Monroe took his cell phone from his back pocket. I was aware of a slight tremble in his hands as he swiped through photographs. Apparently his private collection hadn't prepared him for an encounter with the real thing. He turned the phone to me.

What was on his screen looked disappointingly like the photos I'd already seen of Kimberly Pike dead on the floor of the truck.

Maybe that's all it was; maybe Oakhurst hadn't sent Monroe anything from the hidden folder. It's not like the ones I'd seen already weren't plenty dark: dark enough for Monroe, too dark for Konecki.

But I had that gut feeling. "Send it to me."

"Not on your life."

"My life's not the issue here."

"Is that a threat?"

"Not from me, but probably, yes."

"No. Get out."

"You know withholding evidence in a murder investigation is a crime?" I smiled. "Actually, now that I think about it, you might have killed Tony yourself, to raise the value of your collection. Sure. And especially the price of his final work, which now only you have, since you erased the files on his studio computer."

"You can't be serious."

"Well, no. You don't have the balls for that. But just think what a pain in the ass it's going to be for you once I lay that theory on the NYPD detective on the case. They're dying to make an arrest. Sorry, bad choice of words."

After a long glare, Monroe punched some numbers on his phone. I took my phone out and waited. When his text arrived, I opened it. "It's full-size?" I said. "I want all the detail."

"Yes. Now, get out."

"I wouldn't erase that," I said as I pulled the door open. "The NYPD will want to see it."

He slammed the door behind me as, a little anticlimactically, I walked down the carpeted hall to the elevator.

34

I took the subway heading downtown. Leaning against the door at the end of the car, I stared at the photo I'd gotten from Franklin Monroe. If my gut was right, something about it was worth erasing, maybe worth killing for.

I enlarged the photo, spreading its pixels apart as though the answer might be imprisoned between them. The image grew abstract. Shapes, tones, and lines replaced flesh and frightened eyes. The colors were soupier than I was used to seeing in Oakhurst's images, and I began to develop a new respect for how much work he did to make a raw photo into art. I wondered if he knew from the moment he saw an image how he wanted it to turn out, or if he played with it until he discovered its potential. Or, he would have said, its naked-turtle truth.

I was no nearer understanding what was important about this photo when the train got to Grand Central. I decided to skip the shuttle and walk across to the West Side. Maybe the fresh air of Times Square would clear my head. I threaded the crowded blocks to Fifth Ave., then along 42nd Street past the library. I took a detour into Bryant Park to see if the bees in the hives at the Sixth Avenue end were working as hard as I was. I watched two guys playing pétanque in hopes that the clanking of metal balls would jar something loose in my head. It wasn't until I got to Broadway, though, that anything clicked. It was Batman who did it.

It gets harder all the time for the Times Square costumed characters to make a living taking photos with tourists. It used to be all they had to do was stand there and wait. Now, there are so many of them that some have developed acts to attract attention. They juggle, they tap dance. I saw Spider-Man swinging on a streetlight. Superman was taking a breather outside the chalk-drawn ring where his tag-team partner, Batman, was wrestling with a New York icon: an alligator from the sewers.

I stared. An alligator. Damn.

I whipped out the phone and found the photo. I enlarged it, and there it was, the thing I'd seen—though not noticed—in this one and not the others, the thing that earmarked this image for the most private of Oakhurst's private collectors, the thing that made it worth erasing, worth killing for.

On the truck floor under Kimberly Pike's right shoulder, a blue blob. When I enlarged it, I could see, even in its unretouched, soupy-color state, spots of yellow patterning the blue.

Alligators.

It was Sam's tie.

I slid the phone into my pocket and quick-walked the few remaining blocks from Times Square to Sam's studio. The ME's car was gone from Oakhurst's building, but the CSU and news vans were still in place. The gawker crowd had thinned, and no one paid any attention to me coming up the other side of the street.

I buzzed Sam and got no answer. I hit half a dozen other buzzers, not including Cromley's. When I finally got a "Who's there?" I answered, "FedEx," got buzzed in, and took the stairs so I wouldn't run into the expectant package recipient. On Sam's floor the stair door opened onto an empty hallway. I knocked briefly at his studio and again got nothing, so I let myself in, to that squared-off orderliness of all the spaces Sam inhabited except his head. I was prepared to calm Sam down if he was there and my entrance scared him—though if he was working he might not even notice me—but I was hoping I hadn't knocked loud enough that Cromley next door would be alerted to my presence. But Sam wasn't there, and my strategy didn't work. I had just closed the door behind me and pressed the speed dial for Lydia when the pounding started.

"Who's in there? Let me in!"

"What's up?" Lydia said in my ear. "Can you talk? What's all that noise?"

"I can talk, I'm in Sam's studio, and that's Ellissa Cromley."

"I heard you!" Cromley yelled. "Someone's there!"

"What's her problem?"

"I don't know. But Tony Oakhurst's is, he's dead."

"So you said. In his studio?"

"Yes."

"Any idea who?"

"No. You still in Brooklyn?"

"Yes."

Through the door came "Open up!"

"Did you find Sam?" I asked Lydia.

"No. Not at home—at least, no one answered when I rang and knocked and said it was me—and not at the bar. Victor hasn't seen him. When did he get out?"

Pound, pound. "Goddamn it! I'm calling the cops!"

"Bailed out at midnight by Peter and Leslie. Okay, if you don't find him, keep on that break-in thing. Let me go head off Cassandra here."

I thumbed the phone off and went to the door, to face Ellissa Cromley. I found myself facing her gun.

"Shit," I said. "Put that thing down."

"Oh, yeah, big man?" Cromley gave me a nasty grin. "What the hell are you doing here?"

"Looking for Sam."

"Sam doesn't want to see you."

"How do you know?"

"He doesn't want to see anyone."

"Ah. He's in your studio."

"Oh, the detective makes a deduction."

"Move aside."

"Hold it!" She waved the gun. "You broke in here. He doesn't want to see you. Go away or I'm calling the cops."

"I didn't break in. I have Sam's door code." Which he'd given Lydia, not me, but still. "And I'm going to your studio to talk to him, so either put that thing down, or shoot me with it." That might not have been the smartest thing to say under the circumstances, but I don't like having guns waved at me, and this was the second time for this one.

Cromley didn't move.

I snapped my right arm out and a can of pencils clattered to the floor. When Cromley's eyes flew to the sound I lunged left and brought my fist down on her gun arm.

"Ow!"

The gun hit the floor, but it didn't discharge. I pulled my own gun out, leveled it at Cromley. She looked up from her bruised wrist. Her eyes grew wide.

"No! No."

I held steady another moment and then slipped my gun back in its rig. "No. But you need to think a little harder before you start throwing threats around and backing them up with guns. People take that stuff seriously."

Not surprisingly, Sam's studio didn't have a pile of rags lying around. I ripped a piece of paper off a drawing pad and used it to pick up Cromley's gun. I checked the load. It was empty. I sniffed it, wrapped the paper around it, and put it in my pocket.

"Give that back!"

"It's been fired recently."

"So that means you can steal it?" She rubbed her wrist. "Target practice. I'm a responsible gun owner. You shouldn't own a gun if you don't know how to use it."

"You also shouldn't wave one around if it's empty. And if you were a responsible gun owner, you'd have cleaned it after target practice."

I pushed past her, out of Sam's studio, and through the open door into hers.

I found Sam on the couch in the clearing, stubble on his face, empty beer bottles on the floor by his stockinged feet. "Hey," he said. "Where've you been?"

"Have you been looking for me?"

Sam looked confused. "No, I just wondered where you've been."

Cromley was right on my heels, cradling her wrist. "You hurt me!"

"I'm sorry," I said. "I hope that's not your painting hand."

"You hurt her?" Sam said.

"She pulled a goddamn gun on me."

"Ellissa's gun? It wasn't loaded," Sam said. "She just wanted to scare away whoever was in my studio. In case it was the same person who messed up my drawer."

"Brilliant. And what if he'd had a gun?"

"You did have a fucking gun!" Cromley answered.

I said to Sam, "I need to talk to you."

"You don't have to, Sam," Cromley said, rubbing her wrist.

"Don't have to talk to him? Why wouldn't I? I like him. Not like that lawyer. Lupe. Where's my other lawyer? Susan. I liked her. Lupe was mean."

"She was trying to protect you, Sam. It's her job." I dropped onto the couch beside him. Snarling, Cromley swept a stack of papers off a milk crate and settled on it.

"She told me to shut up," Sam complained. "She said she'd get me drawing paper, but she didn't."

"She would've if you hadn't been bailed out."

"Why did they do that, Peter and Leslie?"

"Because you're not guilty," said Cromley.

"I wanted to stay. Everyone's safer if I'm in jail."

"I don't think so," I said. "But tell me. Where did you go last night after you got bailed out?"

"Peter wanted me to go home with them."

"Did you?"

"I said I wanted to come here. Peter said no but Leslie told him she was too tired to fight about it. That was kind of funny, because the way she said it was like they were fighting about it already. She told the Uber guy to bring me here. Peter flopped back on the seat like he really *was* tired and told me he was sorry. I don't know what for; they were doing what I wanted. They dropped me here and they went home."

"You came up to your studio?"

"I tried to work. I got some ideas in jail. But every time I heard footsteps, I got nervous. So I came over here and had a drink. I got tired and took a nap on the couch."

I turned to Cromley. "Were you here?"

"In the middle of the night? You think I have no life?"

"When did you get here?"

"Early this morning."

"Where were you last night? When you were having your life?"

"Who the hell are you to ask me that?"

"Never mind." I was pretty sure Grimaldi would get around to asking these same questions eventually. I had other things I wanted to ask these two. "I want to talk to each of you, and I want to do it separately."

"Who cares?" Cromley said.

"Wait." Sam looked at me. "This is really important, right? You said it like it was."

"Yes."

"Okay."

"Sam—" Cromley began.

"No." He stood up. "It's okay. Come on," he said to me. "We can go to my studio."

"If you leave before you talk to me," I said to Cromley as I followed Sam out, "you'll be making a big mistake."

"Sam didn't kill anybody," Cromley said.

In a voice more kind than I expected to hear from myself, I said, "I know."

35

Sam pressed the code on his studio door. We walked in, and he turned to face me.

"Sit down, Sam."

"No. That means bad news."

"It's bad news whether you sit or stand."

He didn't move.

"All right," I said, "I wanted to be the one to tell you this. Sam, Tony's dead."

"What?" Sam tilted his head, as though I'd suddenly started speaking a foreign language. "No, he's not. Tony? He's right down there." He turned and walked to the window. I followed, and we gazed across the street to the now-sparse crowd, the NYPD vans, Epstein still at his post at Oakhurst's door. Sam grew very still. He stared, without moving, for a long time. "Oh," he said. "Oh. Oh, shit. Smith, why are the police down there?"

"I told you, Sam. Tony's dead."

"No. No, no. Oh my God, are you right? Tony's dead? What happened? Oh, shit, Smith, did I kill him? *Did I kill Tony, too?*" By the end he was yelling, staring wide-eyed at me.

"You didn't kill anyone," I said. "Except Amy, years ago. Okay? Someone killed Tony. But it wasn't you."

"How do you know? How do you *know*?"

I didn't know. But I was getting more and more sure.

I told him, "I need to ask you something important. From the night of the opening."

"Tony was there. Tony was there, and now he's dead?"

"Sam. I know it's hard. But I need you to answer this, okay?"

"Answer what?" He scrunched his forehead, as though I'd already asked him something and he couldn't remember what it was.

"At the Whitney, when we were leaving. What happened to your tie? The blue one with the alligators."

"My tie?" He frowned.

I thought back to the cab ride, the drinking he did in his apartment. "You didn't have it on when we got home. It wasn't in the pile of clothes you left by your bed. You took it off at the Whitney and waved it around. Then what happened to it?"

"Oh. Right. That made Leslie mad." He grinned, then the grin faded. "She took it away and stuffed it in the trash can. I didn't like that because it was mine, but I didn't really care because I hate ties."

"So you didn't have it when Tony found you at the bar? You didn't give it to him?"

"Why would I give it to Tony? He never wears ties, just T-shirts. Anyway, I think he's dead."

"So, by the time we all got downstairs and left by that rear door, you didn't have it?"

"Well," he said, "well, actually, *I have no fucking idea!* Who cares about a fucking tie?"

That was it; he was gone. He dropped onto the folding chair by his drawing table, and he started to cry. "Go away," he said. "Get the hell out of here. Leave me alone."

"All right. But, Sam? Don't leave. Promise me you won't leave."

"Oh, sure. Why not? I'll stay here forever. Maybe Tony's ghost will come visit me. Just *go away!*"

I walked out into the hallway. Before I went to Cromley's studio I called Lydia.

"I was just about to call you," she said. "Two things. One, Sam's not around here anywhere."

"I know that. I was just with him in his studio. I told him the news about Oakhurst and he fell apart."

"Oh. Poor Sam. Will he be okay?"

"I don't know. He threw me out. I made him promise to stay there, but I don't know if he will."

"Should I call him?"

"I'm not sure he'll answer the phone, but you can try."

"Okay. Meanwhile, I found a witness who saw someone at Sam's building when Sam was in Victor's."

I'd almost forgotten that that was the point of Lydia's going to Brooklyn this morning. "Great. Who?"

"All I have is the description she gave me. I didn't have a photo to show her. But from what she said, I'm ready to put money it was Ike Cavanaugh."

36

Yet again, the angel on my right shoulder told me to call Grimaldi, and the guy on the other side said I'd get more accomplished on my own. The right-side guy wanted to know if this was about getting things accomplished, or if it was personal. The left-side guy told him to guess.

I called Queens North Homicide, asked for Cavanaugh, was instructed to leave my phone number, which I did. Then I went down the hall and knocked on Cromley's door. Nothing, so I pounded, and still nothing, so I pounded and yelled, until a dreadlocked black guy with white smears on his arms stuck his head out of a door farther down the hall and said in a heavy Jamaican accent, "Yo! Ellissa not here. She leave as I come. Now shut all de noise, leave people to work."

"Sorry." I lifted my hands and retreated to the elevator. On the sidewalk, I lit a cigarette and waited for my phone to ring, for Lydia to show up, or for a cup of coffee to come skateboarding down the street. None of those things happened, so, still waiting for the first two, I headed for the diner on the corner to see what I could do about the third.

The place smelled of toast and sizzling grease and the coffee was delivered on a tray, not a skateboard, by a young Latino guy who took my order for eggs and bacon and had just come by to refill my cup when my phone finally rang. It was a number I didn't recognize and a voice I did.

"You fuckin' called me, Smith? What the hell is your problem?"

"Jesus. Is that your version of 'good morning'?"

"Only to assholes," Cavanaugh said. "What do you want?"

"To talk to you. In person."

"I'm busy."

"So am I."

"Whoop-de-doop. Is this where you tell me I'll be happy if I hear what you have to say?"

"No. It's where I tell you you'll be unhappy if you don't."

"What's the difference?"

"None, to me. I can call Grimaldi. She'll talk to me. And she'll listen."

"Oh, fuck her. And you."

"And the horse I rode in on, but I think you should come talk to me, Cavanaugh. I'm at a greasy spoon called All Day Coffee." I gave him the street corner. "I'm about to have breakfast. I'll be here until I'm done." I hung up. Then, because I hadn't actually said I wouldn't, I called Grimaldi.

"Where are you?" I asked when she picked up.

"Fine, where are you?"

"I'm in a diner around the corner from Oakhurst's studio and I'm about to have some interesting company. Come join the party."

"I'm not there anymore, I'm back at the precinct. I went oh for two looking for your wacko and his next-door friend across the street."

That must have been while I was at Monroe's, Sam was snoozing at Cromley's, and Cromley was having her life.

"Plus," Grimaldi said, "some plaster-covered Rastafarian told me to put a sock in it."

"I'm buying him earplugs. I have something you might want."

"You say that to all the girls."

"Last time I said it to you, it was true."

"Jesus, Smith. I'm supposed to go all the way the hell back down there because you're being cute with me? Just tell me what you have."

"A couple of fascinating facts, and a gun."

"Whose?"

"Come on, Detective, put on the siren and do some aggressive driving. It'll make you feel better."

"If I get there and nothing you have is useful, I guarantee I'll feel better than you will."

"You say that to all the boys."

I hung up, called Lydia, told her voice mail where I was, and settled into my eggs. Lydia walked in not five minutes later.

"Hat trick," I said.

"Excuse me?" She kissed my cheek and pulled out a chair across the table.

"Never mind. How are you?"

"Used to this hour of the day. You?"

"Beginning to see its glories. You want some tea?"

"Are we staying?"

"We're having company."

"Then, yes." I waved the waiter over. Lydia ordered tea and an English muffin. "Who's coming?" she asked.

"Ike Cavanaugh. And Angela Grimaldi."

"Sounds like a party. Or an explosion."

"Tell me about it. The description you got—you're pretty sure it's Cavanaugh?"

She nodded. "An actual professional dog walker. She noticed this chubby guy in a car—a blue Regal, not in great shape—"

"The guy or the car?"

"Both. He was parked two blocks down, just sitting there the way people do when they're waiting for the parking to get to be legal, but it was already legal. When she came back the other way with the dogs, she saw the guy get out of the car and head down the street."

"In the direction of Sam's place?"

"Yes. He even crossed to Sam's side when he got near there."

"She noticed that?"

"She's a writer. He intrigued her."

"I thought she was a professional dog walker."

"It's her day job. Who makes a living as a writer?"

"Good point. Did she see anything else?"

Lydia shook her head. "She went the other way. Had to drop off the dogs." Lydia's tea and English muffin arrived. "Tell me about Tony Oakhurst," she said, squeezing lemon into her tea. "I called Sam. He did answer, and he's a mess. He's afraid he did it. Any chance of that?"

"Highly unlikely."

"I asked him to promise to stay in the studio, too."

"Good. I may want to stash him somewhere later. Oakhurst, someone shot him about one A.M. And they took an earring."

"Wow. A serial killer who swings both ways. That's new."

"And that's not the most interesting thing I found this morning." While we ate, I filled her in: Oakhurst's death, his empty and presumably erased hidden photo folder, the raw photo he'd sent to Monroe, which I showed her. Cromley's gun and Sam's tie.

"See how productive mornings can be?" she said, putting down her cup. "But, Bill, there's no way Cromley's is the gun that killed Oakhurst, is there?"

"No. It's a .25 and he was shot with a .38. They're pretty sure it was the one they found, his own. Still, it's interesting that hers has been fired."

"It's also interesting about the tie." She stared at the tabletop. "I don't think Sam had his tie when we found him. Or even when the riot started."

"He didn't. I asked him. Leslie threw it in the trash can by the elevator."

"So someone took it out again."

That promising line of inquiry was brought to a temporary halt by the entry of the bull into the coffee shop. Ike Cavanaugh stopped just inside the door.

I gave him a genial wave. He saw my sarcasm for what it was, scowled, and marched over.

"What the fuck?" was his greeting when he reached the table.

"Have a seat, Detective."

"Who's she?"

I resisted the urge to say, *Your doom.* "My partner, Lydia Chin. Lydia, Detective Ike Cavanaugh."

"Yeah, great," said Cavanaugh. "Talk fast. I'm not staying."

"Sure you are. Sit down." I waved for the waiter again. "Coffee?" I asked Cavanaugh. "I'm buying. Go on, sit down. You came all this way to hear what we have to say. You won't hear it standing."

Cavanaugh's jaw tightened. "Coffee," he told the waiter. "And a goddamn jelly doughnut." I caught Lydia suppressing a smile: cops and doughnuts. Cavanaugh dropped his bulk onto a chair between Lydia and me. "Okay," he said. "This better be good."

"Just what I was thinking," came another voice. All three of us looked up, and there was Grimaldi.

37

At our table in the diner, Cavanaugh seared me with a murderous glare. "You son of—"

"Yeah, I know. Sit down, Detectives." That was for both of them; she was still standing, and he was standing again.

"This," Grimaldi said as she pulled a chair out, "is something I never thought I'd see. I'm not even sure what I'm seeing. Hi, Lydia. Ike, sit your ass down. I don't know what this is about, but I came all the way down here for it, so let's get it done. Coffee," she told the waiter, who was back with Cavanaugh's order. "And one of those." She pointed to the powdered-sugar-covered, jelly-oozing pastry on the plate.

"Oh, hell," I said to the waiter. "I'll have one, too."

"Señorita?" the waiter said to Lydia, but she shook her head. He left and I joined Grimaldi and Lydia in staring up at Cavanaugh until he slammed himself back onto his chair.

"So," I said, "it's been a hell of a morning. First." I took the paper-wrapped pistol from my pocket and put it on the table by Grimaldi. "It's Ellissa Cromley's." I said. "It's empty. But it's been fired recently."

Grimaldi lifted a corner of the paper. The waiter, returning with the doughnuts and the coffeepot, stopped, eyes wide, a foot away from our table.

"It's okay," Grimaldi said, baring the shield clipped to her waistband. "We're cops." If that "we" implied more than the absolute truth, what harm?

She slipped Cromley's wrapped gun into her own jacket pocket. The waiter slid the doughnuts onto the table, splashed coffee into cups, and beat it.

Grimaldi bit into her doughnut, napkined her mouth, and said, "All right, give. Who fired it, Smith? At who? How did you get it? Where's Cromley now?"

"The only one of those questions I know the answer to is how I got it. She pointed it at me so I took it away."

"Where?"

"In Sam's studio."

"She there now?"

"She wasn't when I left, or in her own, either. Your other questions, I don't know. She said she fired it at target practice, for what that's worth. But that's not the main reason I called."

Grimaldi looked at Cavanaugh and Lydia over her coffee. "The guy has a recently fired gun in the middle of a homicide investigation and he has a better reason for calling?"

"I think it's this," Lydia said. "I've been out in Greenpoint trying to see what I could find out about the break-in at Sam's apartment."

Grimaldi narrowed her eyes, but I was more interested in watching Cavanaugh. His doughnut stopped halfway to his mouth, then continued into the savage clamp of his jaws.

Lydia looked at me to see how I wanted to play it. I decided not to beat around the bush. "It was you, Cavanaugh," I said. "We have a witness. A dog walker saw you stroll up the street and end up at Sam's door. He was surprised, he said, because the only person he'd ever seen going in or out from there was a little skinny guy, and now there was you."

The "he," of course, was just a little insurance to protect the professional-dog-walker-writer, in case Cavanaugh had noticed her. I met Lydia's gaze, gave the tiniest nod. Without missing a beat, she took the story up.

"He saw you go in," she said. "He gave a pretty complete description."

Just to be uncalled for, I added, "Of you and your car both."

The guy on my left shoulder slapped my back for the brazenness of the lie, then flew over and slapped Lydia's. Lydia took a bite of her English muffin.

Grimaldi's glare bayonetted Cavanaugh to his seat. "Ike, you stupid son of a bitch, what the—"

"Yeah, yeah, okay," Cavanaugh said. "Somebody needed to be looking for evidence. You were in and out of there in five minutes. You think that creep is just some poor mistreated genius—yeah, like you—so you don't fucking even try! Someone had to at least look."

Grimaldi was scarlet. "I'll have your ass in a sling, Ike. A fucking illegal search? What the hell were you going to do with anything you found?"

"Doesn't matter," I said. "He wasn't planning to find anything, not like you mean. That's not why he went." I looked at Cavanaugh and said, "You went into the medicine cabinet. Sam said someone had put the toothbrush back the wrong way."

"What the hell does that mean, toothbrush the wrong way?" Cavanaugh looked around the table. I don't know what we looked like to him, but to me he looked like cornered prey. "You're gonna listen to a damn crazy madman about which way his toothbrush was?"

"You went into the medicine cabinet," I said, "found his comb, took hairs from it—"

"Jesus Christ in a cathouse, Ike," Grimaldi breathed, "tell me that's not true. Tell me you did not plant evidence."

Grimaldi stared waves of fury at Cavanaugh. He glared back, but behind his belligerence was a wall of defensive anger. If we weren't in public, I thought, there'd be a fistfight right now.

Or maybe there was going to be one anyway: Grimaldi jumped to her feet. I grabbed her arm, but she shook me off with a snarl and stalked out the door. I watched through the window while she took out her phone and made a call. No one at the table spoke until she came back in.

She sat again. "You signed out the evidence box," she said to Cavanaugh. "In the Pike killing. You goddamn signed out the box."

Cavanaugh's thick hands gripped the edge of the table. "I just wanted to look. See if I could find anything you—"

"Horseshit," said Grimaldi. "You put the hairs in. On her sweater. You stupid—"

"He killed her!" Cavanaugh's gaze swept around the table, pleading for us to understand. "And those other girls. Don't you get it? I didn't want him to kill anyone else."

In my head I heard Sam, sitting in my living room the night this started. *Smith? I don't want to kill anyone else.*

"Shit." Grimaldi held Cavanaugh's eyes until he finally looked away. Then she turned to me. "And you. Why the hell did you feel like you had to do it this way? Why not just tell me what you had? Let me take him up without all this drama?"

"Because there's something else. Another piece of evidence that was planted. And then unplanted." I took out my phone. "This is a photo Tony Oakhurst sent to one of his private collectors."

Cavanaugh said, "Oakhurst? That asshole who was taking pictures at that swanky museum party?"

Grimaldi looked at him sharply. "The Whitney? How do you know who was doing what at that party?"

I said, "Didn't he tell you he was there?"

"I don't need sarcasm from you, Smith. Ike?"

"Yeah, I was there. Because I knew you wouldn't be."

The look on Grimaldi's face made me think about fistfights again.

"Cavanaugh," I said, "Oakhurst's dead. Someone shot him last night."

"The fuck?"

"And I think this photo might have had something to do with it." I turned the phone to face them all.

All three of them leaned forward to look at it, though Lydia had seen it already.

It took Cavanaugh a moment. "Oakhurst was in the truck? With the dead girl?"

"Yeah, Ike, and we already knew that, so maybe you better just shut up," said Grimaldi. "Smith, we've seen these, what's the big deal?"

"Not this one. Look closer. I think this is one of the erased ones. See that blue blob by her shoulder? It's the tie Sam was wearing that night."

Grimaldi grabbed my phone, spread the photo, and peered at it. "Where the hell did you get this?"

"I was following a hunch." More than a hunch, but Grimaldi's pissed-off needle was up in the red zone already. "I thought Oakhurst might have sent it to a guy named Franklin Monroe, so I went up to see him. I can give you his info."

"You goddamn better give me his info. And send me that." She handed me back the phone and watched me do it, then sat back in her chair and stared into space. When she spoke, it was quietly, deliberately. "The tie wasn't in the truck when we found her."

"Oakhurst has photos with and without. He must have taken it. But here's the thing. Sam didn't have it when we left the Whitney. Leslie—his sister-in-law—had thrown it away."

"Why would she do that?"

"He was making a scene with it."

"I see." She bit her lip. "And you think Ike here took the tie out of the garbage to the truck and planted it. Like he did with the other goddamn evidence. Meaning, he at least knew the girl was dead and maybe even saw the killer, and never said anything." She regarded me. "Now, normally, I would say you can take a bullshit theory like that about a cop and shove it, but as it happens, Ike"—she turned to Cavanaugh—"you *were* at the party and you *have* planted evidence." She slapped her hands on the table and stood. "So give me one good reason I shouldn't arrest your sorry ass right now!"

The waiter and the other two tables of diners looked over in alarm. It occurred to me I was going to have to leave a really big tip.

Cavanaugh stared up at Grimaldi, and she down at him. Again I wondered if I'd have to stop a fight. Then Cavanaugh started to laugh. "Oh, my fucking God!" he hooted. "Oh, my fucking Aunt Fanny! The tie? The goddamn tie?" He wiped his eyes.

"If you think any of this is funny, Ike, I'd sure as hell like to know why," Grimaldi said.

Cavanaugh's hilarity abruptly cleared. He pushed back his chair and stood, too. "No, it's not funny, Girl Genius." His voice was harsh. "Maybe some cop planted hairs because they thought that little creep deserved to have his ass handed to him on a platter and you weren't doing it. Maybe some cop's going to put in his papers soon because if the way this shit is going down is police work now, the hell with it. But if you think there's any way I found that girl's body and didn't call it in, if you think there's any way I stuck that tie under her in a fucking freezing meat truck and left her there . . . Fuck your mother, Grimaldi."

Lydia had said this meeting sounded like a party or an explosion. The party was clearly over. I stood, too, wondering if between Lydia and myself we would be able to find a way to stop the explosion.

Still seated, Lydia glanced at me. She said, "Detective Cavanaugh? What about the tie?"

Everyone looked at her. "The tie made you laugh," she said. "Why?" She took a sip of tea and waited.

A tight grin strained Cavanaugh's lips. "The fucking tie," he said. "The fucking tie Girl Genius here was ready to bust my ass over. I never touched the goddamn thing. I didn't take it out of the trash."

"And that's funny?"

"No. This is. I saw who did."

"The hell you say," Grimaldi snapped. "Who? Oakhurst?"

"Oh. Oh, now it's useful that I went to that party, missy? Now you want me as a witness?"

"That's it. Ike Cavanaugh, I'm arresting you for tampering with evidence and—"

"Oh, shut it, Grimaldi. It wasn't me and it wasn't Oakhurst. It was that stone bitch who threw it out. It was the sister-in-law."

38

Good work, partner, I thought. Party canceled, but explosion averted.

With an obvious effort to stay under control, Grimaldi said to Cavanaugh, "The sister-in-law—Leslie Tabor? She came back for the tie?"

The two cops and I were standing, and Lydia sitting, around the table.

Grimaldi went on, "Or she took it out again right after she threw it away?"

"She came back. Ten, fifteen minutes later."

"She went back into the Whitney? After they all left?"

"To talk to a client," I said. "To calm him down. That's what she told me, anyway. One of Sam's collectors is a client of their architecture office. She wanted to make nice."

"Who's this client?"

I gave Grimaldi Sanger's name and number. She took a deep breath and looked around at all of us.

"All right." Grimaldi spoke to Cavanaugh. "Go back to your precinct, Ike. Keep your head down. Start working on those retirement papers. I swear if you're still on the Job when this case is closed, your ass is mine. Smith, where am I likely to find Leslie Tabor this time of day?"

"Their office, I'd think. Can I come?"

"Are you fucking kidding?"

"Yes. Go with God, Detective."

"Stay out of my way." Grimaldi spun and left.

Cavanaugh curled his lip at me. "Go with God? Go to hell!" He stomped out of the diner, bequeathing me and Lydia all the stares from customers and staff. It seemed like a good time to leave that big tip and clear out. I dropped two twenties on the table amid the coffee and doughnut debris.

"Where are we going?" Lydia asked as we swung out the door.

"To find Sam. I get the feeling a lot of shit's about to hit the fan, and I don't want him running around loose."

"Do you have a plan?"

"Not yet. I'm sure he won't go to Peter's. But let's at least find him."

We headed up the block to the studio building. The news and NYPD vans were gone. So was Epstein; yellow crime scene tape had taken his place at Oakhurst's door.

"Are you thinking Leslie Tabor found Kimberly Pike's body and left Sam's tie there to implicate Sam?" Lydia asked.

"At best," I said. "Or she killed Kimberly Pike and left Sam's tie there to implicate Sam."

"Why Pike?" Lydia asked. "Why then?"

"Because she could?" I said. "Or because she cracked?"

"Or because it's been her all along?"

"According to Cromley, unlikely."

"That's not exactly right, I don't think," Lydia said. "Unlikely if these are actual serial killings. But what if they're something else? Something—what did you say Cromley's word was—opportunistic?"

"Like what?"

"I don't know."

"Well, keep thinking."

"As if I wouldn't."

Sam didn't answer when we knocked at his door, so Lydia used his code. We found him sitting in front of the window, staring down.

Lydia walked forward and said gently, "Sam."

"I killed him." Sam spoke without turning. "My friend Tony. I killed him, Lydia. Why did I do that?"

"You didn't, Sam. Someone else did."

"Who? Why would anyone else?"

"We don't know yet. But it wasn't you."

From the doorway, I gestured to Lydia that I was going next door, and she nodded. I wasn't gone long, though. Cromley didn't answer my knock, my thumping, or my yelling. Neither did her Jamaican neighbor; he'd probably given up and gone someplace quieter, like Grand Central Station. I tried the combination that had worked before, but Cromley must have caught on and changed it.

I gave up and walked back to Sam's studio. I found him slipping drawing pads and pencils into a canvas carryall. He smiled at me. Sam, apparently, had had another mood swing. And Lydia had had a brainstorm.

Sam said, "I'm going to go meet Lydia's mother."

When we hit the ground floor, Sam was out the elevator door first, which gave me just enough time to grab Lydia, kiss her, and say, "What did I ever do to deserve such a brilliant partner?"

"Nothing. You don't."

We hailed a cab to Chinatown, and Lydia called home. She spoke in Chinese, clicked off, and said, "She can't wait."

"I'm sure," I said.

"No, for real. She's thrilled I'm asking for her help."

"Come on, I could hear her yelling at you through the phone."

"You need to translate."

"I don't speak Chinese."

"The language," Lydia said, "isn't what you need to translate."

The cab left us north of Canal. Sam stared around in wonder as we made our way to the single block of Mosco Street. "Everyone here is Chinese," he said to Lydia.

"My mother's Chinese, too. Just so you know."

We climbed the four flights to the Chin family apartment, me in the rear. "Take your shoes off," Lydia said to Sam as she turned the locks. He did immediately, with the result that when the door opened and Sam went to shake hands with Lydia's mother, he offered her his shoes. She stared, broke into laughter, and pointed at the entryway floor. Sam put his shoes down, precisely lined up with the pair beside them.

Still smiling and shaking her head, Lydia's mother said in English, "You come in." She did shoot me the usual suspicious glare, but that seemed pro forma.

Sam peered around in frank fascination. He spotted Lydia's father's collection of mud figures—small, delicate brown clay sculptures of peasants, fishermen, and monks—and marched across the room. He stood at the cabinet, drinking them in.

Lydia's mother said, "We have tea now." The English must have been for Sam's benefit; I never got that many words in a row.

Sam turned, a delighted smile transforming his face. "These are great, these statues! Oh, look at the ducks!" He pointed to a brushwork scroll that hung over the couch.

Lydia's mother brought out a pot of tea and four tiny cups. We all sat and Lydia poured, first for her mother, then for Sam, then me, herself last. Sam watched carefully to see how Lydia held the delicate little cup and followed exactly. He sipped just as she did, then put his cup down and pointed at the old worn chair that none of us had sat in. "That's important, right?" he said.

Lydia nodded. "It was my father's."

"He's dead?"

"Yes."

"So's mine. All I have now is my brother. You have your mom, that's nice."

"Yes, it is. I also have brothers. Four of them."

"Do they take care of you?"

"They try."

Lydia's mother had been following this conversation as though it were a ping-pong game. Now she said, "Ling Wan-Ju brother, all very smart, very good son. Like Ling Wan-Ju, all same. My children, all same." She sat back and sipped her tea with a self-satisfied smile.

Lydia said to Sam, "Ling Wan-Ju is my Chinese name."

I said, "Holy—" I stopped myself before a word got out that I was sure was in Lydia's mother's limited vocabulary. I stood. "Thank you, Mrs. Chin. The tea was delicious. Thank you for looking after my friend." I bowed.

Lydia shot me a quizzical look and also stood. She spoke in Chinese to her mother, who answered. They went back and forth, seemed to reach the end, and Lydia said to Sam, "She says to make yourself at home. You can sketch anything you want."

"Will she sit for me?"

Sam, not just working with someone else in the room, but drawing from a live model? When I had time, I'd consider this astonishing turn of events. Right now I was tying my shoes.

Lydia spoke to her mother, her mother laughed and swatted the air, and Lydia told Sam, "She says no one wants a picture of an old lady."

"I do."

Lydia and her mother exchanged words again. Lydia said to Sam, "She thinks you're ridiculous, but she'll try to be a good host."

"So, yes?"

"Yes. See you later."

Lydia slipped her shoes on and we left. "*What?*" she said as soon as we were out the door.

"Your mother. She's a genius, like you."

"That word's being thrown around too much today. What are you talking about?"

We double-timed down the stairs and headed for the subway. I pulled out my phone and called The Tabor Group, only to be told Peter was still home sick and Leslie was out at a meeting. I wondered if the meeting was with Grimaldi, who'd hauled her down to the precinct, or if the detective was cooling her heels in some client's waiting area while Leslie finished up. Grimaldi cooling her heels was a concept I wasn't sure I could wrap my head around, though if anyone could make it happen, my money was on Leslie.

I called Grimaldi and got voice mail. "I'm on my way to Brooklyn, to Peter Tabor's," I said. "Call me." I wasn't sure what my inspiration would be worth to her, but I also didn't want her to get on my case for freelancing.

"So?" Lydia demanded as I put the phone away. "What about my genius mother?"

"Your genius mother said all her children are the same." We reached the entrance to the subway.

"You think she's going to admit to an outsider that her daughter's a black sheep?"

"What if all the sheep are black?"

"Explain, please," Lydia said as we slipped through the turnstiles. The R to Brooklyn pulled in and we got on.

"I told you Peter tried to get Sam to draw flowers and stick figures when they were kids?"

"I remember. But Sam never did."

"He wouldn't fake it. Probably less 'wouldn't' than 'couldn't.' Peter could. He told me he didn't care any more about flowers than Sam did, it was just to keep the grown-ups happy. He said the drawings he made that he liked were the ones that only he understood. He once told his mother a drawing was camels when it was people and dogs."

"Hidden meaning in the drawings. Like Sam's, but not like Sam's."

"Not like Sam's. But like *Sam*."

Lydia's eyes went wide. She grabbed my arm. "Oh my God."

"Peter Tabor's a space cadet. Not like Sam, but like Sam. A genius who never really bloomed until Sam was locked up."

She stared at me. "And the first of these killings . . ."

"If the one in Hoboken actually was one of these, if it was the first, it was just about when Peter learned Sam would be getting out."

"A stress event. The stress event triggers are real."

I nodded. "They're just not Sam's."

39

Peter and Leslie lived on a tree-arched block of brownstones in Cobble Hill. The neighborhood was quiet, the afternoon sun glowing through the fresh green of spring in the branches, when Lydia and I made our way from the subway stop to the Tabors' house and up the tall front stoop. Nothing happened when I rang the bell. We waited. I considered yelling through the door that Peter had better let us in or I'd go howling up and down the block pissing off the neighbors. I was disappointed in myself for the lack of imagination demonstrated by my willingness to use the same threat twice in one day, but I was about to do it anyway when the door cracked open.

"What the—Oh, for shit's sake." Peter paused. "I thought you were the pizza guy. Get out of here." He looked the way he'd sounded yesterday on the phone: like hell. His red-rimmed eyes were sunken, his face unshaved. Worst was the defeated slump of his shoulders. Hunched and drooping, he looked more than ever like Sam.

"No." I pushed past him—an easy task—and Lydia followed me in, shutting the door. We stood in the parquet-floored entry, before a curved staircase. "Peter." I said. "We know."

"You know what?"

Nothing, really, but while I was thinking how to phrase my suspicions, Lydia spoke.

"We know you didn't mean it."

"Didn't mean what?" Peter asked.

"At least, not the first time," Lydia said. "The time in Hoboken."

Peter's features, his body language, nothing changed. He kept his eyes on Lydia, but I wasn't sure he was seeing her.

"You were just—what was it Leslie called it? Tomcatting. You just wanted a good roll in the hay. That's what you told yourself. Though you like your rolls in the hay a little rough, don't you, Peter? Isn't that why Leslie stopped sleeping with you? That's what she told Bill."

That wasn't exactly what Leslie had told me. But I could see what Lydia was doing. She was letting Peter think we knew more, and on a more intimate plane, than we did. Softening him up. Breaking him down.

She continued, "Though you probably didn't consider that any more of a loss than Leslie did."

At that, Peter flinched.

"But that night in Hoboken," she said, "you'd just learned Sam would be getting out. That he was going to be your problem again. You picked up a girl, took her to the park, and that night's roll was a little rougher than usual. Maybe she didn't like it, maybe she screamed, maybe she hit you. Maybe you only took out your pocketknife to make her shut up, but she didn't stop, so you stabbed her. You stabbed her like Sam had when he killed Amy Evans. And you felt a thrill. Sam never felt it. But you did."

As Lydia spoke, Peter's expression changed bit by bit. Looking at her now, he wore the face Sam had worn as we'd driven over the bridge—absorbed, attentive, fascinated.

"You took one of her earrings," Lydia went on. "You wanted to remember how it felt. You wanted to remember, because as great as it was, that feeling while it was happening, it was also horrifying once it was over, to think you'd done it. You wanted to remember because you weren't ever going to do it again.

"But the night after Sam got out of prison, you went out. You said you were with clients, but no, you were picking up Tiffany Traynor. And the night after Sam's show opened, when you found Annika Hausman. Those were big stress events for Sam. He drank himself into a blackout. But they were also big for you, and you dealt with them differently.

"You took earrings those nights, too. And two nights ago, at the Whitney. Kimberly Pike's earring. But that one you took from the other ear. Tell me why."

"No," Peter said, in a calm, reasonable way. "I didn't."

"There's no point in this, Peter," I said.

He turned the interested face, Sam's face, to me.

"Now that we know it was you," I said, "the cops can show your picture around. Trace your movements. Talk to your clients. It'll be over soon anyway. But right now, the cops are focusing on Sam, and he's starting to crack." Actually, Sam was probably focusing on his sketch pad, shading Lydia's mother's features while the two of them laughed and talked incomprehensibly to each other. "You've spent so much of your life helping Sam keep it together. You've been a great brother to him. You have no way out of this. But you can still help Sam."

"Fantastic! Just fantastic." A new voice: Leslie, coming around the staircase from some room in the back. She spoke to Peter. "You let them in? What the hell is wrong with you?"

"Leslie," I said.

"Oh, I heard you." She fixed an angry glare on me. "The 'you're such a great brother' speech. The 'save Sam' speech. I've heard it before, heard it for years in all kinds of different ways from Sam. 'You're my brother, save me, save me!' Even from Peter, about himself. The '*I'm* such a great brother' speech. The 'the hell with my career and my marriage, look, I'm saving Sam again!' speech."

Peter tried to answer. "Les, I—"

"Oh, shut up, Peter! Bastards, both of you. Goddamn geniuses, the rest of the world has to step aside, stand on our heads, do whatever has to be done so the Tabor Brothers can express their brilliance. All my life, Peter, all my goddamn life, that's what I've been doing for you, and now you and your crazy brother ruined everything!"

I suddenly thought of Sam's answer when I'd asked the other day if he wanted to go to Peter's. *You're as crazy as I am*, he'd said. *The Crazy Brothers*.

With a change of tone, Leslie turned to me. "If the cops are focusing on Sam, fine. Because Sam's a killer. He's guilty. All Peter's guilty of is being a flaming jackass and doing everything he could think of to throw his life away—and mine with it. They arrested Sam because they have evidence. They'll find more."

"Peter's guilty of a lot more than that," I said. "And so are you. The evidence they have—Sam's hairs on Kimberly Pike's sweater—was planted by that cop Ike Cavanaugh. The one who worked the Amy Evans killing."

Leslie narrowed her eyes. "What are you talking about?"

"He was sure Sam was guilty, too, and sure he was going to get off. So Cavanaugh did what he could."

"I don't understand."

"Figure it out. I don't care. That's not why we're here. From the moment I told you the cops had been to Sam's yesterday, you said they must have evidence and they'd have more. You didn't know about the hairs, but you knew about the 'more.' You knew all about the box and the tie."

Leslie's face flashed crimson.

Peter, looking from me to Leslie, said, "What tie?" His voice now also sounded like Sam's, that perennial confusion: *There are so many things I don't get.*

"Sam's tie from the Whitney was in the truck with Kimberly Pike's body," I told him. "Tony Oakhurst took it, though. Oh, you didn't know that?" I said to Leslie as her lips parted soundlessly. "The cops never found it. They didn't find the box, either, but they have it now. Peter, you asked, 'What tie?' but you didn't ask about the box. You know what box."

He swallowed and nodded. "The one with the earrings."

"Shut up, you idiot!" Leslie roared.

He looked at her. "You took it. You said you were going to hide it or throw it away or something." Any difference between the sound of Peter and the sound of Sam was now gone. "What did you do with it?"

"Christ!"

"She put it in Sam's studio, Peter," I said. "The same way she put the tie in the truck with Kimberly Pike. So the cops would be sure to find it. To implicate Sam. But they didn't find it. Ellissa Cromley took it, like Tony Oakhurst took the tie."

Peter said, "No, Les, you didn't do that. So Sam would look guilty? No, you didn't."

"Yes, she did," I said. "She took the Hoboken earring out, because that was while Sam was still inside, and then she put the box in Sam's studio. Ellissa Cromley is Sam's friend, though. She's nuts, but she's trying to be as good a friend as she can. I think she half-believes he *is* a serial killer, but she still doesn't want him caught. She heard someone in his studio. She thought it was Sam. But it was Leslie." I said that as though it were proven fact. "Cromley found the box and took it. I found it in her studio and *I* took it. Now the police have it. I'm curious, though, like Lydia is, why you took Kimberly Pike's earring from the wrong ear?"

I was also curious where the hell Grimaldi was, but maybe it was okay she hadn't called yet. The more Lydia and I could get out of these two before they were arrested and got lawyered up, the better. It was all hearsay, none of it usable in court, but it would give Grimaldi a place to begin.

Peter stared calmly at me. "I didn't."

"Peter, come on, there's no point anymore—"

"No," Lydia interrupted me. "He didn't. He didn't kill Kimberly. Leslie did."

"You bitch!" Leslie took a step forward.

Lydia ignored her and went on. "I don't know why it took me this long. I must be losing it. That's why the earring was from the wrong ear. You didn't know. Outside the Whitney, when Kimberly was screaming, 'It's him, it's him'? She didn't mean Sam. She meant Peter."

"Jesus," I breathed. "We're both losing it. Maybe we should retire. She recognized you as the dark-haired white guy who'd hit on Annika, didn't she, Peter? And you realized that, Leslie. That's why you had to kill her."

Leslie's breath was starting to come hard, as though she'd been in a fight.

"Here's how I think it went down," I said. "Leslie, you found the box in one of those organizing whirlwinds you were having because Peter was letting everything go to hell. You confronted Peter and he spilled. That's why you were so testy when we spoke, Peter. And then, when Leslie killed Kimberly Pike—for *you*, to hide your crimes—that knocked you down. You felt like hell. You couldn't go to work. You couldn't think. But Leslie could, as usual. She planted evidence. She took care of things."

"And I'm going to take care of them now." Leslie spoke in a steel-hard voice. In her hand was an automatic, small, but not a .25 like the one Cromley had been waving around. This looked like one of the new smaller 9 mms, and Leslie looked like she knew what to do with it. Proof of that was that she was pointing it at Lydia, not at me. She might not have known Lydia shoots better than I do, but she'd clearly calculated the difference between my reaction to being threatened and my reaction to Lydia being threatened.

"I know you both have guns," Leslie said. "Put your hands on your heads. Very slowly."

Lydia and I did what she said.

"Les!" said Peter. "What are you doing?"

"Saving my own ass and, as usual, yours with it. You should never have let them in. This is on you."

"No," said Peter. "No, don't." He sounded about as effectual as Sam ever had, and Leslie paid him about as much attention.

"Now take your guns out and put them on the floor one at a time," Leslie said. "You first, Smith."

I did, and after me, Lydia did the same.

"Pick them up, Peter. Peter! The damn guns!"

Peter bent in slow motion and collected our weapons.

"Get in the basement," Leslie said, moving the gun just once between me and Lydia. "Peter, you come, too. You're going to help me do this."

"No," he said again, but he started to trudge toward a door under the curving stair.

"The police know we're here," I said. "I called them before we left."

"Yeah, sure. The cavalry's on the way. Though if that's true, it's just more reason to do this fast. So, move or I'll shoot her right here, and then you, and then Peter will drag you downstairs." Leslie leveled the gun at Lydia's head.

The doorbell rang.

Both Leslie and Peter snapped their heads to the door. Lydia dove under the gun, shouldering into Leslie's knees. They fell together. The gun discharged. Glass rained down as the bullet broke the hanging lamp. Lydia wrestled the gun from Leslie and flung it away. I snatched it up, pointed it at Peter in case he was thinking of using one of the two he was holding. He just stared at me.

Lydia was trying to pin Leslie down, but Leslie kept struggling, so Lydia hauled back and clocked her one. It slowed Leslie but didn't stop her. Lydia slugged her in the gut. Leslie moaned and curled around herself, like a centipede when you touch it.

Panting, Lydia stood. Peter kept staring. I went to open the door for Grimaldi. "What the hell took you so long?"

A confused look. "We told you half an hour."

It was the pizza guy.

40

Eventually, it was Grimaldi.

Before that, I'd grabbed the pizza, given the guy a twenty, and shut the door in his drop-jawed face. I wasn't sure what he'd seen or heard, but the worst that could happen was he'd call the police. I dumped the pizza on the hallway table and told Peter, who was still just standing there, to put the guns on the floor. He did. I told him to go sit in the living room. Face pale and flat, he did that, too. While I collected the guns, Lydia hauled Leslie up, dragged her into the living room, and dumped her on the couch. Leslie started to stand, but she snarled and dropped down again when Lydia raised her fist.

"You're wrong, you know," Leslie said, rubbing her jaw where Lydia had hit her. "It was Sam. He killed them all. Yes, sure, I put the tie under the body in the truck. And when I found the box in his apartment—God, yes, all right, I went there looking for something, any kind of evidence. When I found that goddamn box, I knew exactly what it was. I was disgusted, oh my God. I put it in the studio to be sure the police saw it. Don't you see? We had to get rid of him, had to stop him before he just kept killing people—"

"Stop it, Les." That was Peter. His head was turned toward her, and though his voice was dull, his stare was fierce. "Stop it. You're lying. You got that box from me, not Sam. I killed three women. You killed another and, God help me, that's my fault, too, and I'll never stop being sorry. About all of them. I couldn't . . . I'm not . . . I don't . . . Oh, God." He rubbed his hand down his face. It came away damp with tears.

The doorbell rang again.

Lydia, gun out while she kept an eye on the Tabors, stepped out of the doorway's line of sight. I put my gun away in case it was Grimaldi and she decided to shoot me. I opened the door and said, "You forgot the anchovies."

"What the hell are you talking about?" It was, in fact, Grimaldi, and she frowned.

"The extra pepperoni was pretty cool, though," I said. "Come on in."

She did. "What the holy hell is this?"

I explained the situation. Grimaldi listened without interruption. When I was done, she called for backup. She Mirandized both Tabors and, Leslie red with fury and Peter damp with weeping, sent them off in separate squad cars.

"Which one of them killed Oakhurst?" Grimaldi asked. We were standing on the stoop watching the cars drive off. "And why?"

"Ask them. Though my money's on Leslie. Probably because once she saw the photo with the tie, she was afraid he'd identify her as Pike's killer."

"When did she see the photo?"

"After he identified her as Pike's killer and invited her to come see it?"

"Why would he do that?"

"He was interested in what turtles look like without their shells."

"I'd like you better if everything you said made sense. Get in."

Lydia and I rode to the precinct with Grimaldi. While the Tabors were booked, we followed her up to the squad room. The big detective, Iglesias, looked up from his desk when we came in.

"Closed it?" he asked.

Grimaldi nodded. "Unless the DA says otherwise. Thanks for the moral support, Gabi."

"What I'm here for." He went back to his typing.

Grimaldi deposited me and Lydia into separate interrogation rooms to take our statements. She started with me.

"I recommend you be plain and fast—none of those metaphors and whatever," she said. "Because as soon as those sons of bitches are lawyered up, I'm going to go at them, and if I'm not finished with you guys by then, you'll be here for a while."

I was straightforward in my recital and apparently so was Lydia, because by the time we were sent away with instructions to remain available, the Tabors' lawyers had not yet arrived. Two attorneys had been called, one for her, one for him.

"You think they'll try to sell each other out?" Lydia asked as we left the precinct and headed for the subway.

"She will. She'll try to pin Kimberly Pike and Tony Oakhurst on him, in addition to the ones he did. He won't. He'll take the rap for what he did. He might even try to cop to what she did. I don't think he's together enough to make that work, though."

"For better or worse, for richer or poorer."

"In sanity, in lunacy. Do I hear you knocking marriage?"

"Not really. Only, how do you know if you're married to a crazy person?"

"By definition," I said, "I would be."

As we walked, Lydia called her mother. She spoke in Chinese, then she pulled me over to the shelter of a building wall and switched the phone to speaker.

I heard: "Hi, Lydia. It's Sam."

"I know, Sam. We'll be back soon. We can talk then."

"Did you do it?"

"Do what?"

"Solve everything."

Lydia and I met each other's eyes. "Yes," she said. "We did."

"Did I kill Tony? All those women, and Tony?"

"You didn't kill anybody."

"I killed Amy."

"But nobody else."

"How do you know? Because you know who did?"

"We'll talk about it when we get there. It'll be soon."

"Okay."

The phone was quiet for a moment and then Lydia's mother's rapid-fire Chinese came streaming out. Lydia answered, and that conversation was short.

"How's it going there?" I asked when she switched off.

"I think she's ready to adopt him. Though he won't let her look at the drawing."

"She might change her mind when she sees it, then."

In Chinatown, we stopped for red bean cakes and made our way to the Chin apartment. We'd agreed I would be the one to tell Sam, but we hadn't figured out how. Lydia unlocked the door and we stepped into the tiny entryway to take off our shoes. I could see Sam in the living room, drawing pad in his lap.

"Hi!" he called. "Oh, it's you. I thought it was Ellissa."

Lydia stepped into the living room. "Why would it be Ellissa?"

"I called her to come here. I told her that it was all okay, you knew who it was and it wasn't me, and you'd tell us all about it, but meanwhile I wanted her to see all these wonderful things your mom has. The tiny statues, and the ducks, and the cabinet with the little people inlaid on it."

So much for Sam's being stashed away. Well, it wasn't necessary anymore.

"She'll have to buzz from downstairs," Lydia pointed out.

"Oh, right. I guess she will. Hey, look where I'm allowed to sit."

It must have been true that Mrs. Chin had grown fond of Sam. He was in Lydia's father's chair.

"Wait, just a second." Looking from his model to his pad, Sam added a few lines and said, "Okay, time for a break." He put the pad aside and jumped to his feet. He wiggled a come-on-get-up hand to Mrs. Chin, who stood from the couch and stretched, then walked across the room to look at what he'd done. Smiling, she blushed, waved at the air in front of her face, and spoke to Lydia.

"She says you're a very bad artist because you're making her look too pretty," Lydia told Sam.

"What do you mean? She's beautiful. You're beautiful!" he called to Mrs. Chin, who'd taken the red bean cakes and disappeared into the kitchen, where she was bustling with the plug-in tea kettle. "Does she really think I'm a bad artist?"

"No more than she thinks she's a bad cook when she apologizes for dinner. Can we see?"

Sam turned the sketch pad to face us.

"Oh, Sam," Lydia breathed. "That's gorgeous."

It was. No mistaking it was Lydia's mother, every wrinkle and gray hair shown; but also a glow of energy, kindness, humor. She didn't just look pretty. She looked absolutely captivating.

I peered more closely. The drawing was exactly what it looked like; nothing violent or ugly hid in its shadows. "Sam," I said. "That's terrific. I didn't know you did this kind of thing."

"What kind of thing? I told you I did portraits inside, of the other cons."

"Yes, you did. I just—"

The doorbell buzzed before I could get my foot too far into my mouth. Lydia went to ask who it was, and to no one's surprise the answer was, "Ellissa Cromley, who's this?" Lydia didn't answer, but she did buzz Cromley in.

Cromley's arrival would complicate the issue of how to tell Sam about Peter and Leslie, but he seemed to have forgotten his questions for now in his excitement about his drawing and the things he wanted to show Ellissa. I relaxed, thinking maybe now I'd have more time to figure out how to break it to him. I wasn't prepared, therefore, when Lydia, having gone to the door to open it for Cromley, backed into the room with her hands up, keeping a distance from Cromley's gun.

41

"Hi, Ellissa! Come see this—Wait. Ellissa? What are you doing? You don't need that here, it's not like at the studio."

"Oh, Jesus," I said. "I'm getting tired of this shit."

"What shit? Get your hands up!" Ellissa barked.

"It's amazing. Even when you're desperate you're unoriginal."

"What are you talking about?"

"That's the third time today someone's stood behind a gun she wasn't going to use. And twice it was you." Actually, I wasn't sure Cromley wasn't planning to use this one, and I was certain Leslie had had every intention of using hers. But planting the thought that it wasn't going to happen seemed like a good idea.

"Ellissa?" said Sam. "Come on, I want to show you some things."

"We have to go, Sam. You wait outside, and then I'll come down soon and we'll go."

"Go where?"

"Far away. Where you can paint anything you want and no one can bother you. I'll take care of you."

"We can do that here. I can be in my studio and you can be in yours and we can visit and drink beer. That's what artists do."

"No, we can't. How can we? Now that they know. We have to go away."

"You mean Lydia and Smith, and they know who killed everyone? That's right." Sam turned to me. "You said you did and you said it wasn't me. Who was it?"

Both Sam and Cromley looked at me, he with absorbed interest, she with wide-eyed fear.

I saw the light dawn in Lydia's eyes the same moment I felt it dawn in mine.

"It was three different people, Sam," I said. "One of them was Ellissa. She's the one who killed Tony."

Sam looked at Cromley. "Tony was my friend. Why would you kill him?"

"Because Tony told her *you'd* killed Kimberly Pike," I said. "He thought he had proof."

"He thought I killed her? So do I."

"You didn't. Leslie did."

Cromley shook her head. "Sam killed her. I saw the photos."

"Wrong. Your Bonnie-and-Clyde fantasies aside, Sam's not a serial killer."

"Neither were Bonnie and Clyde, dumbass! Tony's photos—"

"A frame. Leslie killed Pike and left Sam's tie with her body. Tony photographed the scene and then took the tie. He fell for the frame, and so did you. He showed you those photos to torture you, didn't he? Just to see what would happen."

"And he saw! He saw!" She looked at Sam. "He wasn't your friend."

Sam said, "You killed him?"

"He said, 'Sam's a killer! Look, see! They're going to take him back to jail!' He thought I'd fall apart. Idiot. I had my gun with me. You thought I was stupid for having two guns." She sneered at me.

"Of all the things I ever thought you were, I never thought you were stupid."

"I had the second one for insurance," Ellissa continued. "In case some shit like you stole the other one. And I took it to Tony's for insurance, too. But he had one, too! In the back of his jeans, like he was scared of me. Asshole!"

"You had a gun," Sam said. "Why shouldn't he be scared of you?"

Cromley didn't react to the Sam-logic question. This was her moment in the sun. She'd done something that mattered, something that had a big impact, and she wasn't going to let it go unnoticed.

"As soon as I saw his gun," she said, "I shot it out of his hand. I'm pretty good, you know. With all kinds of guns." She waved her pistol to encompass Lydia, Sam, and me, as if daring us to test her. "He screamed! Big macho man! When he dropped the gun, I grabbed it and shot him with it. Right in the gut. The bastard. Then I thought for a minute, and shot his hand, too. And I dug my gun's bullet out of the floor and picked up my shell casing. That's called 'policing your brass.'" She directed that, with a smirk, at me. "Then I erased the photos and took the memory card out of the camera. You see, Sam? I can take care of you. But we have to go away."

Sam stared at the carpet, his brow furrowed. Lifting a finger, he said, "Leslie killed that woman in the truck. But she wanted people to think it was me, so she put the tie there. Tony believed it, but he took the tie out. But he showed you the pictures with it. You got mad at him and killed him. Is that right?" Sam turned to me. "Smith, is that right?"

"It's right, Sam. Ellissa, put the gun down."

"No! Stay there!"

"Smith," said Sam, ignoring Cromley, "did Leslie kill those other women, too? You said it was three people."

"She didn't. But we don't know who did." This seemed like the wrong time to shake up his world any further.

"That's not true. You do know." He looked at Lydia. "When you called, you said you knew. But now Smith doesn't want to tell. Why?" He frowned in thought. "Because you think I'd be upset. So it must have been someone I like. It wasn't Ellissa, because she would have said so. It wasn't Tony, because he thought it was me." His logic was unconvincing, but his conclusions were correct. "It wasn't Peter, because I'm the crazy one."

Sam stared at the floor another few moments, then turned to me. With that rare, unnerving clarity, he met my eyes. "It *was* Peter, wasn't it?"

"Yes," I said.

"Why?"

"He lost it, Sam. Like you thought you did."

"He doesn't even drink."

"No."

"He's just crazy?"

"Yes."

"Peter?"

"Yes."

"Sam!" Cromley barked as the situation started to escape her control. "Go downstairs and wait."

Sam turned to her. "But you killed Tony," he said. "So you're crazy, too. And you want me to go downstairs so you can kill Smith and Lydia and her mother." He stepped forward, arms out, as if to hide Lydia and me behind him. "But I won't."

Cromley said, "Her mother? Where's her mother?"

And Lydia's mother came out of the kitchen carrying a tray with a teapot and little cups, took in the situation, stopped, and hefted the tray, with pot, cups and all, across the room and into Cromley's face.

42

I expected it would take a lot of time and effort to get and keep Sam under control, but I was wrong. While Lydia tied Cromley's hands and, as she had with Leslie, hauled her up and into a chair, and I called Grimaldi to tell her the case wasn't as closed as she'd thought, Sam methodically went through the room, picking up every scrap of porcelain. He piled them piece by piece on the lacquer tray, Mrs. Chin following behind him, wiping the floor with paper towels. She kept up a stream of talk with Lydia, and when Sam lifted the fragment-laden tray and started to tell her how sorry he was, she took the tray from him and laughed. I didn't know what she said to him in Chinese, and neither did he, but he laughed, too.

Then, sobering, Sam crossed the room to Lydia's father's chair, where he sat and stared at the floor.

Grimaldi arrived with Epstein, asked if we were really done now and, if not, could I give her more warning next time. She heard me out, and demanded that everyone—including Lydia's mother—be at the precinct in an hour to give statements. She took Cromley's gun, Epstein took Cromley, and they left. Sam didn't look up, even when Cromley called his name, until the door shut behind them.

"She wasn't my friend," he said.

"No," I answered.

"Tony, either. Or Leslie. Or even Peter."

"No."

"So," he said slowly, "that means I don't have to listen to any of them. I mean, I never listened to Leslie. But Ellissa, and Peter. They're as crazy as I am."

"Crazier," said Lydia.

"So no one's going to tell me what to do anymore. I can do what I want."

"Pretty much."

He nodded thoughtfully. "So, for one thing, I don't have to stay with Sherron."

I glanced at Lydia. "No," I said, "you don't."

"Other galleries wanted me. Maybe I can find someone I actually like. And a new studio in a different place. Smith, you know about art. Will you help?"

"Yes."

"Okay," he said. "Thanks."

Mrs. Chin said something to Lydia and vanished into the kitchen once more, where I heard her running water into the plug-in kettle.

Sam spoke to Lydia. "Your mom's making tea? What's she going to put it in?"

"We have lots of teapots."

"And cups?"

"And cups."

"Okay," he said again, and we all settled back to wait.

ACKNOWLEDGMENTS

My agent, Josh Getzler
#TeamGetzler!

My publisher, Claiborne Hancock
My editor, Katie McGuire
All the fine people at Pegasus Books, such a pleasure to work with!

Charlotte Dobbs

Elisabeth Avery, Jackie Freimor, Sharyn Kolberg, Margaret Ryan,
Carrie Smith, Cynthia Swain, Lorena Vivas, Jane Young

Steven Blier, Hillary Brown, Susan Chin, Monty Freeman,
Charles 'McGyver' McKinney, Max Rudin, James Russell, Amy Schatz

Sunday mornings and Monday nights at NTL,
as was and as will be again

The Saloon at KSWS

Patricia Chao

Jonathan Santlofer